THE CELL BLOCK PRESENTS...

LOST ANGELS

BY

MIKE ENEMIGO AND ALEX VALENTINE

Published by: The Cell Block™

The Cell Block
P.O. Box 1025
Rancho Cordova, CA
Facebook/thecellblock.net

Cover Design: Mike Enemigo

Send comments, reviews, interview and business inquiries to:
thecellblock.net@mail.com

Lost Angels is available in print and e-book

Acknowledgments:

This is for Sandy, for all her years of unwavering love and support, and her unfaltering faith that there was more to come. Also, for Shareen who has been a constant in my life, and whom I would be lost without. For Gerald Davis, who started me writing in the first place, and Lydia Chen, a light in dark places. I would never have gotten to this point without all the support from the Pegel family, Norma Forsyth, Janis Goff, Ned Nassiroghli, Troy and Theresa Rapp, Marty and Jerry Stirtz, Joe Skinner, Andrea Klenakis, and all of the others who have helped me along on the journey; thank you all.

And, of course, to the team at TCB; Janet and Mike you guys are amazing. Together, we're making it happen, one step at a time. Without you guys, this would still be collecting dust on a shelf and so would a lot else.

PROLOGUE

The city wailed in the night. Angry horns and desperate sirens struggled through a smothering summer rain that gave no relief from the day's lingering heat. Then, into this quagmire, a new crying voice was added, as with a final push and a hard slap, David Donovan Rodrigo was born into the cacophony that was Los Angeles.

Three years later, and again amid horns and sirens, Aria Rodrigo, David's mother, let go of her last breath in this life as her young son was lifted free of the twisted metal frame that had once been her used car. That unfortunate vehicle had been all that the young mother could afford after having been disowned and shunned by her very traditional family. For the most part, they had wanted no part of Aria and her nappy-haired child born out of wedlock. Only her younger brother, Tomás, had ever come to visit her and help with the child, though he had only been sixteen at the time of David's birth.

Thomas accepted the role of padrino against his family's wishes, and was already on a path his family did not approve of, so he was encouraged to leave home and find his way in the world. Thus, at the age of nineteen, Tomás found himself changing his life yet again, becoming the tenant and manager of the Starlight Cinema Duplex on Olympic Avenue. He was now the guardian of a curious little boy with bright green eyes and an infectious smile. Little Davy was too young to understand the tragedy of his young life, and remained a fountain of enthusiasm and energy. The boy spent his days watching the crowds of movie-goers from the theater's countless hiding places and sneaking treats from its small concession counter. The counter's teenaged attendant, Monica, most often turned a smirking blind eye to him, and so Davy went about seeking all what manner of wonders there were to be found in the sanctuary of the old theater.

At the age of five, Davy's carefree existence was interrupted by his enrollment in pre-school. He was not used to waking early, and horribly offended by the idea of a bedtime, though the enforcement of the former gradually accustomed him to the latter. As this new phase of his life began, he also encountered the equally sleepy little girl named Luisa, Monica's little sister. Monica and Tomás shared driving duties, and it was not long before Louisa became a regular feature on weekends. Little Lulu tended to follow Davy around wherever he went in his explorations of the new world as little girls are wantingt to do in matters of little boys.

Davy initially tolerated her companionship on the condition that she remains quiet, which she rarely did. Lulu was precocious, loud, and to Davy's despair, quite inescapable. With no other options, he made the best of the situation, even grudgingly holding her hand when they snuck out of the theater and furtively explored the streets within the walking range of five-year-olds. For all her faults, though, Lulu did seem to have one saving grace as far as Davy was concerned: she was not a tattle-tale.

This was the pattern of his existence until Davy reached the age of ten when he first began to take notice of his own life, and that began with a simple delivery.

i

Chapter 1

On a mid-summer Saturday morning, Davy found himself staring at the door to the number two theater, garbage bag in hand. Lulu was nearby, ostensibly helping him pick up the trash left behind by the patrons of the midnight shows, although she had no bag and was nattering on about her new dress. Didn't Davy think it was pretty?

Davy managed a wan nod and smile, wishing he could be almost anywhere else, ideally where the sun was shining and the air was not dank with the stale musk of the late show's patrons. About to despair and plunge ahead into the dark chamber, Davy paused having overheard Tomás on the phone in his office.

"...Sure, Ms. Cohen, uh, I guess I could bring them by today, but..." There was no trace of accent as Tomás spoke.

Davy dropped the half–full bag and quickly made his way around the concessions counter to the door of the manager's office. Lulu followed, continuing on about her dress and growing irritated with being ignored. From his post beside the door, Davy could see Monica leaning against the wall across from Tomás' desk. She was wearing more make-up and a shorter skirt than usual, and she did not look happy.

"...No, I understand. You want to see the quarterlies before Monday, and -" Tomás said into the receiver.

"Bruja," Monica hissed a little too loudly, forcing Tomás to quickly cover the phone.

"Shh!" he snapped.

Monica responded with an angry sniff and a glare.

"What? Oh, no, that was nothing," Tomás said into the phone.

"Nothing?!" Monica barked, craning her neck in a jutting circle. "I'm nothing?!"

"Would you shut up?" Tomás hissed, covering the phone again.

"Shut up?! Oh, I'll give you *shut up*, puto!"

Davy sensed his moment and entered quickly. He shut the door behind him and left Lulu outside where she pouted.

"What's up Moni? Something no bueno?"

Monica bit off her intended tirade and narrowed her eyes at Davy suspiciously. "Aren't you supposed to be getting the trash, eh?"

Davy shrugged. "Well, I heard shouting... and... I wanted to see if everything's bueno?

"If everything's bueno?" she mimicked with an ugly look. "No, eh. He's supposed to be takin' me somewhere nice." She glared at Tomás, who had resumed his phone call. "For once, eh!"

Tomás glanced up at her, but offered no more than a tight sigh. Monica crossed her arms and looked off.

"I'll bring them right over, Ms. Cohen," Tomás finished. "No trouble. Goodbye."

The moment he set the receiver down, Monica was around the desk and peering into Tomás' face before he could stand. "Oh, like that, eh? That old bitch just snaps

1

her fingers and it's all *shut up, Moni*. Whatever you say, Ms. puta-blanca!?"

Tomás backed the chair up and with a quick effort got to his feet. "She owns this place, Moni," he informed her firmly. "It's five minutes out past Whittier and back. You can even come with me"

"I'm not going to Whittier! And it won't be no five minutes! You're gonna be forever, and then say, 'Oh, the bruja made me have tea, but you're goin' to see that White Fence puta again, or that bitch Miranda! You think I'm stupid?!"

"Damnit, Moni, I've been done with Gloria for the longest, and Sleeps was just a little kid with a crush."

Monica smacked him. "Don't even say that bitch's name!"

Tomás only glared back, and so she swung again, but this time he caught her arm. "Ow!" Monica yelped as she twisted free of his fairly light grasp. "Get off me!"

"Are you done, Moni?" Tomás asked.

Her eyes bulged. "Am I done? Pendejo, maybe we're done!"

She brushed Davy aside, and was out of the office with the door slamming behind her. Outside, she collided with Lulu, who had been listening at the door, and a screaming match between the sisters ensued. Tomás only shook his head and began collecting papers from the desk.

"Can I help?" Davy asked.

"You have work to do, mijo."

"I know, but Lulu can do it, and Moni looked pretty mad. Maybe-" Further conversation was cut off with the office door being kicked back open.

"Seriously, asshole? You're not even coming after me? Fuck you!" Monica barked and slammed the door again.

"Shit," Tomás muttered. "Moni, wait!"

A loud foul reply came from outside.

"Would you chill, damnit!?" Tomás yelled back. "Davy' s gonna drop this shit off, but I've got to tell him where the old lady lives!"

From the other side of the door came, "Well, hurry up! I'm hungry!"

Tomás sighed and scribbled an address.

"Just tell him to GoogleEarth it!" Monica complained.

"Alright!" Tomás sighed and stuffed some paperwork into an envelope. "Take this, and don't lose it."

"I won't," Davy insisted.

"Ms. C lives in a real nice place. Ring at the gate and tell her I sent you. If there's a guy named Proctor there... just don't talk to him. Anyway, you gotta talk good English."

"Why? She don't like Mexicans? Or what?"

Tomás sighed, knowing Monica's patience would not last much longer. "Look, mijo, she has me managing this place and lets us live here damn near rent free. She ain't got no problem with our skin, it's just she don't like... I don't know. Not talkin' proper. If you spoke Spanish worth two squirts of piss, I'd tell you to speak Spanish. Shit, hers is better than mine, even. Now don't screw this up, me entíendes? That old lady is a lot more important to our lives than you can understand."

"I got it, I won't," Davy insisted with a ten-year old's whine.

2

"Bueno," Tomás said and, ruffled Davy's hair as they headed to the door.

Just as Tomás touched the knob it swung in wide making them both jump back. "What's taking so long, eh?" Monica demanded, then eyed Tomás up and down. "Is that what you're wearing?"

"What?" Tomás replied.

Monica huffed and left pouting. "I'll be in the car, esé... waiting, "she said over her shoulder.

Tomás trolled his eyes and shook his head. "You know where you're going, right, Davy? If you get into trouble, just call me. And stay out of White Fence."

Davy smiled. "Yeah, tío, but, same goes for you."

Tomás chuckled. "You're a good kid."

"Where are we going?" Lulu asked as she popped up behind them.

Tomás knelt down to look her in the eyes. "Davy's going on an errand, Lulu." She scowled, knowing the tone used for delivering news she was not apt to like. "You're in charge 'til he gets back."

"But there's no one here," Lulu complained. "Why—"

"Because someone could come," Tomás interrupted, Davy had already made his exit, he noticed. Lulu said no more, and found a comfortable chair behind the snack bar in which to sulk as Tomás locked her in the theater and left.

Chapter 2

Davy brought his Huffy to a halt at the stone marker and community walls outside the Glenwood Oaks development on the north side of the Town of Whittier. The trip had been more uphill than down, and had taken considerably longer than five minutes. The air was heavy, and the sun was beginning to bring the temperature past a comfortable California day.

The Oaks though were aptly named, and after a few pumps past the outer walls, Davy was swallowed by shade and cool breeze. No longer caught in the heat rising from baking asphalt, the street felt more like a sun dappled forest path. Davy did have to consult Map Quest on his refurbished iPhone to navigate the development, but he eventually found Ms. Cohen's house, or as he discovered it: the Cohen estate.

Where the other homes in the Oaks were quite upscale, the mansion Davy could see through the wrought iron bars of the front gates was in a class by itself. Even the gate impressed with its stylized 'C' worked in over the top of the arching bar work like something out of an old movie, complete with creeping ivy and faded rust. The polished intercom with its LCD display was the only modern intrusion into this island of Angelino days gone by.

As Davy reached for the intercom button, the speaker came alive, startling him. "Who are you?" an electronic voice demanded.

"Uh," Davy stammered.

"Uh? What sort of a name is Uh? No, no, we'll have none of what you are selling, boy. Be off with you."

"Wait," Davy pled quickly. "My tío sent me with some important papers for you, ma'am."

"Tío? I don't know any Tío. Tío? Your people seem to be cursed with the most unfortunate of names. As well, who would entrust anything important, paper or otherwise, to a boy of... eight, by the look of you."

Davy stiffened and puffed up his chest. "I'm ten."

"Ah, yes, a world of difference," the electronic voice said sarcastically.

Davy took a breath, remembering his tío's instructions about how to treat Ms. Cohen. "Ma'am, I have been sent by Tomás Rodrigo with the important documents you requested."

"Yu? I don't know any Yu. Yu sounds Oriental-"

The voice was cut off, and the gate rattled to life as the sides opened and swung outwards.

"Present yourself at the main house, and leave your bicycle just inside the gate, but out of sight."

The tone of the digital voice had changed and taken on a note of command which Davy felt compelled to obey. Once past the gates, he spotted several outbuildings as he made his way along a swept brick path through an otherwise leaf-strewn front yard. The outbuildings appeared unoccupied, and along with the marginally managed landscaping, gave off the sense of grandeur in slow decline. Still, Davy could not help staring all over as he climbed the pile granite steps to the railed front portico. He came to a stop at the dark-stained and weathered front double doors with their knockers clinched in the jaws of iron lion heads. The doors were nearly twice as tall as Davy, and were quite imposing for the young boy.

Davy managed to shake off their aura after a few seconds, and clacked the head high knockers twice. Then, after a few moments of waiting, he tried again with more force. He still received no answer. After another minute of waiting, he began to feel foolish. Davy pushed ahead and tried one of the great doors. Despite its weight, it swung open easily, but the boy made it only just past the threshold when he stopped slack-jawed.

There *she* stood. With long straight black hair and icy blue eyes, the young girl before him was just coming into the early bloom of adolescence. She turned with the grace of a swan, or perhaps a serpent as she locked her eyes onto Davy. Her poise was perfect, and a wicked smile began from her eyes and spread across her features.

"Oh my. Are you a burglar? You look like you might be," she said as she approached fearlessly. "Or are you simply a ruffian who has barged into my home unannounced?"

Davy had never been so frightened of a girl in his entire life, but at the same time, he was also enraptured, though ten years old, love remained one of the abstract concepts reserved to adults. Here and now, all he knew was that he found himself unable to move, and completely at this wondrous creature's mercy.

"Well? What have you to say for yourself?" she asked as her head tilted far more like a snake than a swan's.

"Uh," Davy managed to stammer.

She drew back, moving as gossamer blown by a puff of wind. "Oh. You're that boy with the unfortunate name. You have business with my aunt. You'll find her down the hallway in the parlor to the left."

She turned away and began to head towards a spiral staircase on the left side of the foyer.

"Wait," Davy said, having regained a fraction of his senses now that he was no longer caught in her eyes. "M... my name's Davy."

He paused to glance back with a mischievous sparkle in her eyes. "Well, I suppose that is a little better than, *Uh,* but not much."

With that, she ascended the stairs. "Wait," Davy pled again. "What's your name?"

She did not pause, only laughed in a golden tone that Davy would never forget.

5

Chapter 3

Davy made his way to the parlor. The room had a red and green paisley carpet, more books on shelves than he could count, and a scattering of old leather furniture near several dolls covered tea tables. An unlit chandelier hung from the ceiling and a lone figure occupied a chair turned to face the wide windows that overlooked the wooded rear grounds. Only one side of the drapes had been drawn back giving a thin light to the room. The seated figure remained in the shadows.

"Come in, boy," Ms. Cohen said; her voice a whisper that sliced through the dust motes caught in the wan light to reach Davy.

"Ms. Cohen, ma'am? I... I have what my uncle told me you wanted. I…"

"Come in, boy," she repeated.

Davy nodded and took several steps, then caught sight of a mirror by the window and Ms. Cohen's shadowy reflection.

"I suppose that will do," Ms. Cohen said as she stood gracefully and stepped smoothly through the shadows, vanishing from the mirror's reflection to stand in the open glare of the windows. She presented as a dagger of shadow amidst the outer light. A woman of indeterminate age, her hair was possibly silver and pulled back into a tight bun. She possessed the same enthralling ice blue eyes as the young girl Davy had met in the foyer. Ms Cohen's gaze, however, was far sharper and more practiced. Davy felt himself moving towards her without even intending to, and then stopping abruptly a few feet from her.

"Sit down, boy," she said, and Davy found himself in a nearly straight-backed chair beside a small table with an empty tea service. Ms. Cohen approached, and Davy held up the envelope Tomás had given him as though it were a talisman to ward off evil.

Ms. Cohen took it from him with a quick flick of her wrist, and then appraised him briefly before discarding the envelope onto another table. She turned back to the window, and after a moment, Davy leaned forward to stand; ideally to get as far away from this room and this woman as quickly as possible. But that was not to be. Before he had moved more than a fraction, she spoke.

"Tell me, boy, what do you know of loss?"

"Um... I don't know." The typical response of a child to an adult question.

Ms. Cohen made a soft noise. "You live with your uncle, do you not?"

"I do," Davy said uncertainly.

"Not your mother or your father. I had thought, perhaps…?" she trailed off, leaving it a question.

"Right. Um, my dad died a little before I was born, and my mom when I was three."

"How did she die?" Ms. Cohen interrupted.

"Um, a car accident," Davy said, beginning to find the stiff chair very uncomfortable.

"Were you in the car with her?"

6

Davy nodded and swallowed. "I was, but I really don't remember. Um, I probably should be–"

"Did you love her?" Ms. Cohen said, ignoring his objection.

Davy choked on a breath. Huh? "Yeah, course I did, I mean, do."

"Do you?" Ms. Cohen said, casting her gaze over her shoulder at Davy. "Do you think it was your fault?"

"What? No...." Davy stammered.

"No?" Ms. Cohen raised a brow, pinning him to the chair as though he were an insect about to be dissected. "Have you never thought that perhaps you were crying, or distracted her in some way, and so caused the accident? Caused her death?"

"No." Davy was breathing hard now. "I don't know."

"I thought you said you loved her?"

"I did!"

And yet you never thought you might have borne some responsibility? So close, and yet you did nothing; had no part in the final moment of her life?"

"I don't know," Davy said miserably, on the verge of tears.

"Maybe that is why you do not really remember. In that final moment, you failed her... Because you did not really love her. "

The boy was beginning to shake, and whimpered. "No. I did. I swear!" A moment more and he was crying in earnest and scrubbing at his eyes. He did not notice the faint smile that crossed Ms. Cohen's lips.

"Perhaps you did. Perhaps it was only that you were so very small and the loss so very great," she offered gently.

Davy nodded, trying somewhat successfully to stop crying.

"And so you do know of loss, but by choosing not to remember the detail, have run from the terrible heartbreak you knew, leaving yourself vulnerable."

Davy continued nodding. "I guess so, but -"

Ms. Cohen turned away. The lioness had suitably wounded the prey for her kitten. The boy would serve her end as she had required of his keeper. "You have met my niece, Selene?"

"Uh-huh," Davy said, feeling as though he could breathe again. "I mean, yes, ma'am. When I came in, I think. She didn't tell me her name, though."

Ms. Cohen said, smiling out the window and into her past. "That will do for today, I think."

Davy rose to leave, eager to return to Moni's yelling and Lulu's prattling, and now understanding why Tomás was so obedient when it came to the scary lady. Ms. Cohen stopped suddenly, as though startled from a dream, and stepped to Davy, taking his hand and putting an arm around his shoulder. She was a tall woman and looked down on Davy. Even her smile was terrifying, and the boy knew he had in no way escaped.

"Come, it was poor of me not to greet a guest in person, and so I shall show you to your leave."

Davy nodded and smiled, not really understanding, or caring about much beyond the fact that she was actually going to let him leave.

As they reached the foyer, they found Selene arranging fresh flowers in a vase on the central display table. She turned with the same smooth grace as before, but Davy was on his guard now. What lurked beneath the wondrous appearance?

"Selene, the roses, at least, are lovely," Ms. Cohen said, casting a critical eye on their arrangement and her niece's dress.

"Thank you, ma'am," Selene said with a curtsey. Her eyes met Davy's for an instant.

And then he had his answer to what manner of creature Selene was. Terrified and trapped, but rather than being envious of his escape, she was relieved to see him go free. In that instant, Davy made a bold decision. Selene was clearly a prisoner, and he would find a way to rescue her. When Ms. Cohen went over to further inspect the roses, Davy picked a small item from a nearby open display case. Selene's eyes widened briefly, and Davy winked at her. Selene seemed to consider briefly, and then chose to remain silent, though she watched Davy more openly now.

"It was a pleasure to meet you both," Davy said, drawing Ms. Cohen's attention to him.

"The pleasure was ours, child," she responded with a hostess' smile. Davy nodded and left through the front doors quickly.

"He seemed nice," Selene offered. "In a simple way."

Ms. Cohen smiled and stroked the side of Selene's face, but caught her chin with a sharp jerk. "Don't they all? But they are not. Never forget that. They all want nothing but to break your heart, and so you must learn to break theirs first. Do you understand?"

Selene nodded, but that was not enough.

"Say it!" Ms. Cohen demanded and tightened her grip.

"I understand. Men will break my heart, so I must break theirs first."

"They are deceivers, all. Ms. Cohen's eyes narrowed and her nails began to dig in behind Selene's jaw where the marks could not be seen. Tears began to well in Selene's eyes as her blood began to seep down her aunt's fingernails. "The little thief. He did not ask to call again where he knew he was so far beneath you, yet had he asked, I would have allowed it. No, instead he stole from me the moment he thought my back was turned, ensuring he would be called back, if only for a punishment. This is the nature of men: to connive and steal what they have no right to. You will not show him mercy in the time to come."

Her nails dug in further, opening old scars, and Selene cried out.

"Say it! Your punishment for remaining silent and allowing him his path back to hurt us. Say it!"

Selene was weeping and trembling. "No mercy! I will show him no mercy! I will break his heart!"

"There," Ms. Cohen said gently as she released the girl and went back to stroking her face. "That was not so hard, was it?"

Chapter 4

Three days had passed since Davy's visit to Ms. Cohen's, but more importantly to him, since he had last seen Selene. Even in the summertime, Tuesday afternoon matinees had a low turnout, and so Davy had retreated from the lobby to the partitioned loft he shared with Tomás. There, he lay sprawled on his bed, idly toying with the pewter figurine of a sparrow on the verge of flight he had pocketed. He sighed, disappointed that it did not seem to have been missed, and that his plan had failed. But then, it had not been a very good plan, he acknowledged. Poor Selene, he thought, trapped like the sparrow -- so close, yet mercilessly bound to the cold earth and forever denied the skies through which she had surely been made to soar. He thought the first part of that, anyway; the rest of the metaphor would develop in his mind in the years to come.

"What's that?" Lulu asked, jarring Davy from his reverie.

Too late to hide it, he had to say something especially since the figurine did look expensive. "It's a gift."

Lulu came right to the edge of the bed. "For who?" she asked, biting her lower lip.

Davy chose the course that would keep him from having to answer questions about its source until he thought up a good lie. "For you," he said, sitting up and presenting it to an immensely pleased Lulu. "It was going to be a surprise."

Lulu began to fidget happily, twisting a foot back and forth. "But, it's not my birthday, or anything, so...?"

"Right, it just looked cool, and I thought you'd like it." Davy eyed her skeptically, not understanding the look that bloomed on her face. "Why are you acting weird?" He tossed her the figurine and got up quickly.

Lulu gasped as she lunged to catch it protectively. "I'm not acting weird. It's... nice," she said with an expectant look. She was certainly now ready to be kissed.

"Okay," Davy said as the conversation seemed to have hit a dead patch. "Um, I've got some stuff to do."

"That's okay," she said and watched him eagerly, holding her breath for what she was sure would be her first kiss. But Davy only brushed past her and left. Her face fell, and her stomach started to hurt in a funny sort of way, so she went to find her big sister. Moni would know what to do. Moni had kissed all sorts of boys.

Chapter 5

Evening had fallen, and Davy was holed up in the projection room maintaining a nominal watch on the DVD system while mentally replaying all too few of his memories of Selene and faintly smiling. Midway through the sure to be cinematic classic about fast moving, pot-smoking zombies, the projection room door swung open.

" maldíto !" Tomás barked, startling Davy. "I knew you'd be hiding somewhere!"

"Huh?" Davy said with genuine surprise.

Tomás snatched him out of his chair by the arm. "Huh, hell, you stupid little bastard! Come here!"

"What? Wha'd I do, eh?" Davy said as Tomás lurched him along out of the projection room and down to his office. As they passed the concessions, Moni gave him a 'WTF stupid?' look, but seemed a little apologetic. Lulu was planted on a stool in the corner and was staring miserably at her shoes.

"What'd you do?" Tomás snorted as he hustled Davy past the few patrons in the lobby. "Get in there." He and shoved Davy into his office, then shut the door behind them.

"Sientaté estupido!" Tomás barked, then snatched the figurine off his desk. "This! This is what the fuck you did, you thieving little shit!"

Davy did his best to remain quiet and contrite. This was not exactly how the plan was supposed to have gone, but maybe it would work out somehow after all.

"What were you thinking?" Tomás growled in disbelief.

"I... I'm sorry!" Davy offered.

"You're sorry?" Tomás blinked. "Do you... You do not know how bad you just fucked up. Goddamnit!" he shouted and pounded the desk.

"I'm sorry," Davy said, and then launched into the speech he had thought up for Ms. Cohen. "I guess I must have been looking at it 'cause it was so nice I got distracted, or sent into see... Ms. Cohen and put it in my pocket. I meant to put it back, I just must have forgot."

Tomás snatched Davy by the shirt and arm, and shook him. "And you're gonna sit there and bullshit me?! You just forgot?! Are you fucking serio?! No one forgets they steal valuable shit from that old lady. No one steals from her, period!"

"I'm sorry." Davy had never seen his typically mild mannered tío so worked up.

"You're sorry?! You made me a liar to her! And... and you're sorry?! She called when I got back. She said that this", he gestured in disgust at the figurine, "- this stupid piece of shit knick-knack was missing after you left, and did I know anything about it? I told her no and you would never do something so stupid as that. That I had raised you better, and for her to accuse you the way she did was an insult not just to me, but to my– " he crossed himself, "-my dead sister, Aria."

Tomás shook the figurine in Davy's face.

"And you made me a liar! Put one more mark to work off, and it's not a small one! You spit on your mother's grave when you do shit like this! Pinche maldíto.

Monica burst in. "Tomás," she said with as soft voice as she closed the door behind her. "They can hear you out there. He doesn't understand. He only–"

"What?" Tomás snapped in a voice thick with anger. "He only stole from the old lady that owns this place and everything in it? Or damn near did, up until today? And now she's got it all."

Monica looked away with a soft sigh.

"And for what? Your stupid little sister wasn't following him around as much as she used to, so he goes and pulls this crap?"

"Hey! Don't talk shit about Lulu, and don't yell at me, fucker. This wasn't her fault, eh. And you know it's not exactly all his either, me entíendes? The hell with that old bitch, you done enough. The hell with this place. You know you ain't homeless... what?" she challenged as Tomás began to shake his head.

"You know I can't go to my parents. You know what they'd say," Tomás said, glancing at Davy.

"I know what they'd say, fucker. And I wasn't talking 'bout them, eh," she said, then her head snapped back defensively, "And you know that."

"Yeah, I know, but it's not that simple," Tomás said as he looked off and ran a hand through his hair, then picked up again before Monica could speak. "And there's reasons for some shit I don' tell you. I am where I am, and there's no getting around some of it."

"Yeah, eh," Monica replied, coming over to put her arms around Tomás' waist. "An I'm right here, stupid. You always got somewhere to go."

Tomás let out a breath and nodded. Monica gave him an extra squeeze and did not let go as his gaze found Davy.

"I'm gonna call her tomorrow," Tomás told him. "And you had better hope she wants to hear you apologize. And if she does, Moni'll help you come up with something better than, *I meant to put it back, but I just forgot.*" He shook his head and snorted, then looked into Monica's eyes. "Cause there's no one better at bullshitting their way out of pedos than her."

"Fucker," she said and playfully slapped at his chest, then nuzzled against him.

Chapter 6

The drive over to Ms. Cohen's in Tomás' old blue Toyota Celica was a tense and largely quiet experience the following morning. Near the gates to the Cohen estate, Tomás pulled up onto the grass beyond the curb and parked behind a large azalea.

"Look, míjo, just say you're sorry, and give her those little kid eyes. If she asks you why you took the statuette, forget what Monica told you to say. You're just a little kid. Your answer is: I don't know. Then fidget, and look like you'd rather be anyplace else in the world," Tomás instructed with a trace of nervousness.

"But Moni said, and you said—"

"I know, all that you're in love with Lulu, but to poor too get her anything, and too proud to show it, and you wanted to get her some big thing to make up for how you ignored her, and just weren't thinking about the consequences? It's too much for ten. A teenager, maybe, but I still think it would be muy mucho. This ain't a novela, míjo, and Ms. C's not as pissed as I thought she'd be... Which is really not a good thing at all."

"I don't—"

"No, just be a dumb kid. She ain't gonna want a dumb kid."

Davy nodded, though he some different feelings.

The two met Ms. Cohen in her foyer. Davy scanned the area quickly, and then felt himself relax when he finally spotted Selene standing in a dark alcove just past the top of the stairs. Even cloaked in the shadows, her ice blue eyes shone like a cat's at night, though she seemed to be hiding more like a frightened mouse. She was at once both predator and prey.

"Ms. Cohen," Tomás began. "I'm sorry we are meeting like this—"

The old woman held up a hand to silence him. "Some of your words when last we spoke were poorly chosen, it would seem." She took a moment while Tomás struggled to hold his poise under her scrutinizing gaze, but then she relented. "Though, you young Latin men are all too well known for your emotional displays. Especially, in matters of family," she said as her gaze found Davy.

The boy wondered briefly at just what had been said over the phone, and why he felt like there was so much else going on that he did not understand.

"I appreciate that, Ms. Cohen," Tomás replied, "and Davy has the figurine to return to you, undamaged."

Davy got a shove to take a few steps forward.

"I... I'm sorry I took the little bird Ms. Cohen. I know it was wrong," he said lamely, looking as pathetic as possible as he held out the figurine.

She retrieved it and set it aside with no more than a cursory glance before she returned her attention to Davy with a stern, but faintly amused expression. "And why did you take it, little boy?"

"I... I dunno," Davy said with a shrug and a huff, looking off as he had been instructed. He almost jumped when Ms. Cohen took his hand gently with both of hers.

"Come now, boy," she said as though it were a spell, her eyes widening and threatening to swallow him whole. "You must try harder, for just as it was the last time we spoke, I suspect you do indeed, know why. Are you thinking more clearly now?"

Davy nodded and felt a tremor in his chest. The monster had him in her clutches.

"Then let us begin again. Why did you take the figurine, boy?"

"I..." Davy swallowed and found his courage. "I was angry."

Ms. Cohen seemed genuinely surprised, though she did not loosen her hold upon Davy. "And why were you angry child? Surely not for being set on such a simple errand by your guardian? Did I give you some cause for offense?"

"You said I didn't–" Davy almost said *love my mother*, but he faltered as the softness left Ms. Cohen entirely. He was no match for her, and he knew it. "I mean, when I was at the gate, I thought it was you that was making fun of me, and so I got angry. That's why when you turned away when I was leaving, I took the little bird. It... it fit in my pocket; that's why I picked it."

Ms. Cohen relented and smiled, releasing his hand and then caressing his cheek briefly as elderly women tended to do to little children, though the performance did not relax Davy in the slightest.

"Well, my poor dear child, I have no wish that there be any misunderstanding between us, ever. And you seem such a clever boy," she said with a dragon's smile. "You acted rashly, and in bad form, but you are young, and... easily provoked. Rest assured, I will speak with your tormentor. She knows better, and will not go blameless."

"No!" Davy burst out. Selene in trouble was the worst possible outcome.

"No, you shout?" Ms. Cohen said, drawing back.

Tomás smacked Davy on the back on the head. "I'm sorry, Ms. Cohen, he really does know better."

"No!" Davy shouted again, and dodged Tomás' lunge to corral him. "It was all my fault, Ms. Cohen. I... I didn't mean to yell. I just – Selene didn't do anything wrong."

Ms. Cohen arched a brow. Her gaze momentarily fell upon the top of the stairs causing Selene to retreat further into the shadows. She turned back to Davy who was moving away from Tomás warily as his tío gnashed his teeth behind a smile.

"Didn't she?" Ms. Cohen asked, and checked Tomás with a quick frown. Tomás lowered his eyes and took a step back.

"No, she didn't!"

"Lower your voice," Ms. Cohen said sternly.

"Yes, ma'am," Davy said, lowering his head as well. "No, she didn't."

"And you've no wish to see her punished, or harmed?"

"No, Ma'am!"

Ms. Cohen turned her attention to Tomás. "The boy is ill-mannered and brash, though both can be remedied."

"You are completely right, Ms. Cohen," Tomás replied quickly. "And they will be. I promise."

Ms. Cohen settled a hand onto Davy's shoulder. "Not that I doubt your ability to properly teach such a young boy, though you are not so far removed from such youth yourself. I do admire your efforts, but I believe the boy would benefit from more mature guidance."

Tomás struggled for words. "I know that none of my older relatives—"

Ms. Cohen smiled gently. "I'm of course aware of your situation, though I think you quite mistake my intention," she interrupted smoothly. "You are of good character, Tomás, I have never doubted. And despite, or rather, because of this... unpleasantness, I can see the boy needs instruction; lessons, one might say. And perhaps something to occupy his idle hands that seem so bent towards finding mischief?"

Tomás wanted to say a thousand things, at least the expressions that warred across his face said so, but he remained silent.

After a few moments, Ms. Cohen smiled with a sound that could have been amusement. "Allow me to be direct. As you can see, this estate is large and full of work for idle hands—" she paused as Tomás lurched, "-manual labor, of course I mean. I do not propose to keep the boy, nor to abuse him, rather he shall be provided with work and training to become a proper gentleman; one fit to advance in society. And of course, I shall provide you with some financial compensation."

Tomás nodded hollowly. "I could bring him over a few days a week for the rest of the summer. But when he goes back to school—"

"Is his school distant?"

"No. He... could probably ride his bike over from where he goes."

"Then it is decided."

"You're not worried?"

"That he will attempt to take what is not his?" She raised a brow; "He says he has learned his lesson. Let us trust him until he proves otherwise, and then let the consequences fall as are due. Our agreement stands."

Tomás nodded, and then caught sight of Davy. "It's a good deal, míjo. Better than most would get."

Davy let out a breath and nodded. Whatever the source of the strange tension was, he did not care. He was getting what he wanted and more. Even if part of that more was falling into whatever plans Ms. Cohen secretly had, that did not matter to him. He was here for Selene; for the sparkling blue eyes that had just now returned to the edge of the upstairs shadows. They held him captive now, and he knew that he would do anything for her, if not quite why, exactly.

"Davy," Tomás prompted impatiently.

"Huh?" The spell broke and he returned to the people in the foyer. "Oh, um, thank you, Ms. Cohen. I look forward to coming here, and for the opportunity."

She made a small chuckle and smiled, and then found Tomás where he was doing his best to stand straightly. "You may bring him tomorrow morning at seven thirty." She turned to Davy. "All things begin with punctuality; all things in their proper time."

The interview continued only a little longer, and as Davy and Tomás got back into their car, both felt a mixture of fear and relief, though each for very different reasons.

Chapter 7

It was not until his third week working at Ms. Cohen's that Selene made her first appearance. Davy was out in the front yard struggling with a push mower under the morning sun. The temperature was rapidly being pressed towards too hot. Ms. Cohen's lessons had thus far consisted of outdoor physical labor that left Davy aching at night. His young muscles' rebellion at this new mistreatment was only just beginning to ebb.

At Selene's arrival, Davy paused in his assault on the weeds near one of the dry fountains to wipe his brow. Even though he was looking at her, he still jumped at the sharp sound of her voice as it knifed through the humid air.

"Boy!" she demanded from the porch.

Davy abandoned the mower and hurried over.

"Hi," he said, a little out of breath.

Selene regarded him blandly, as though he were the equivalent of a rotten turnip. Her dark bangs framed her face, and not that Davy was quite old enough to notice, but her breathing was strained, as if from a bruised or broken rib.

"Hi?" she said. "Is that how you think to properly address me?"

Davy scowled, trying with some success not to notice how pretty she looked in her sun dress with its dotted daisies. "Right. Hi, Miss Snooty-pants," he replied with a smirk.

Selene's reaction was immediate. Her eyes widened with real anger and she up ended a glass of lemonade that had been resting on the porch railing over Davy's head, and then stormed off.

"Thanks!" Davy called after her. "It's hot, and that felt good."

Selene spun back at the door with a wicked grin. "The lemonade had honey in it. Mind the bees and ants. Now get back to work, thief."

And then she was gone. Davy's grin quickly departed, and he began to search for a hose.

Chapter 8

Selene did not reappear for the rest of the week, though Davy was certain he had seen the second story drapes moving back into place when he would look towards the main house. No matter how sly he was with his glances, he could never quite catch sight of his watcher, though he had learned that due to her arthritis, Ms. Cohen rarely left the first floor, and that was enough to convince him. Selene was watching him despite how she acted, he had her interest. It made his additional lessons more bearable as well. Ms. Cohen now demanded he read several passages from various books of poetry that did not rhyme and then trounced him at two games of chess before she sent him out to his chores each day.

It would have been unbearable without the hope of seeing Selene at first, but then he began to notice how his regular chores at the Starlight Theater seemed lighter by half. Monica seemed to frown at him more than usual, but she never yelled, which was just downright strange, but not unwelcome. Lulu flitted around Davy, sometimes disappearing for half the day, and then spending the rest of it underfoot and inescapable, though he did not find her nearly as irritating as he had in the past. As the summer passed, he found the Starlight Theater felt cramped, bare of its former charm, and in a word, dingy. In all, it was a strange time in his life, as though he were caught between two worlds and truly understood neither of them.

One evening, Davy was leaning back in his chair, balanced against the back wall of the projection room near the door, and was somewhat occupied with a shooter-game on his old PSP handheld. Tomás had paid the small fortune of twenty dollars for it at a garage sale a year ago, and new used cartridges for the out-dated unit were easy enough to come by cheaply.

Davy hit pause instinctively as the door opened. Lulu poked her head in, and he nodded, unpausing his game at the same time and returning to killing zombie cowboys.

Lulu frowned as the game beeped back to life. "Hey," she said, shutting the door behind her.

"Oh, hey," he replied, hitting pause again, but not setting the game aside as he looked over.

"You're getting a lot darker," Lulu said, finding another chair.

Davy shrugged. "My dad was Cuban."

"Oh," Lulu said. "What happened to your head?"

"Huh?" Davy touched his brow. "Oh, nothing," he said of the small lump on his forehead.

"So, it doesn't hurt?" Lulu said mischievously and reached to poke at it.

"Hey, quit it," Davy said, stumbling to his feet as he dodged and the chair slide out from under him.

"Nah, I hit it on the stupid shed door. Who cuts a door in half?"

"White people," Lulu said. "How'd you hit your head?"

Davy shrugged. "I was putting that rake away and the wind blew the door shut. And it locked the top half in place."

"The wind?" Lulu said dubiously.

Davy nodded. "Selene," he said. Lulu's features tightened.

"She's so mean to you," Lulu declared. "Always playing tricks and being all stuck-up."

"It's not her fault," Davy said.

"That's what you always say," Lulu sulked, "but has she ever been nice to you? Even once? Does she ever come talk to you?"

"Well, no, but -"

"Would she ever let you kiss her?" Lulu said in a nervous rush, and then began chewing her inside of her lower lip expectantly.

Davy sighed and sat back down. After a moment of staring into his thoughts, he shook his head. "Probably not."

"Well?" Lulu said, scooting her chair closer and batting her eyes the way her big sister had shown her.

"Well what?" Davy said.

Lulu gathered her courage and lunged in to kiss him. Davy nearly jumped out of his chair to avoid her, and she fell, banging her elbow on the empty seat.

"What are you doing?" Davy said. "Why are you acting so weird?"

Lulu's face flushed with humiliation and she began to cry. She stumbled to her feet and gave Davy a hateful look.

"What?" was all he could think to say.

Lulu only jutted out her lower lip as she cried harder, and then ran out calling for her sister, shouting down the hallway that Davy had hurt her arm.

17

Chapter 9

Davy had not had the sense to go after Lulu, and so when Monica burst into the projection room a half hour later, he barely dodged her fist, and then quickly fled as she chased after him. Tomás looked up from his desk as Davy shot into his office and shut the door behind him as he braced against it.

"Moni's gone loca," Davy explained, even as the door handle rattled violently.

Tomás took in the situation. "Muevaté," he commanded, and just in time since the door came flying open from a kick. Monica was many things, but patient was not one of them, and despite her slim figure, she was anything but frail. Also, things she hit tended to stay down, usually because, as she put it, *the puta knew what was good for her.*

"Come here, fucker!" she barked at Davy.

Tomás was quickly around the desk and in between them. "Moni–"

"Really, asshole?" she snapped at Tomás, "Veté-guey!" She motioned him to the side, but he ignored her.

"Moni, calmaté, there are people in the lobby."

"I don't give a damn, eh!" Monica barked, but with less volume. "Little maldíto disrespected Lulu, and he knows what he's got comin', eh."

"Alright," Tomás said with his hands up to ward her off, though the moment he turned towards Davy, she tried to rush past him. "Goddamnit!" he snarled, snatching Monica off her feet and carrying her like a sack of potatoes to the far side of the office despite her best efforts to punch and kick him. "Quitaté!" he ordered and dumped him onto the couch. She glowered, but remained where she had been deposited.

Tomás turned back to Davy. "What the hell did you do, míjo?"

"Nothing–" Davy began.

"Mentiroso!" Monica barked and lept to her feet.

"Sit down, Moni! I got this," Tomás said sternly. After a moment, she relented and sat.

"I'm actually busy, Davy, so let's have it. What did you do? Or do I just let Moni drag you out of here?"

Davy had managed to catch his breath. "I didn't do anything."

"Davy?" Tomás warned.

"No, tío. I was up in the projection room, working–" he paused at Tomás' frown, "-Er, playing my–"

"And then?" Tomás prompted.

"And then Lulu came in, and I was like, okay, hey–"

"Davy," Tomás interrupted, sharply, "why is Moni ready to kill you?"

"I don't know," Davy insisted, and Monica was back on her feet. "Lulu and me were talking, and then she got all weird, and then she got upset and ran off. That's all–"

"'cept the part where you hit her!" Monica barked.

"You did what?!" Tomás roared, and even Monica quieted.

"I did not!" Davy pled.

"So, Lulu's a liar, little thief?" Monica put in from the side. "Why's her arm all fucked up, eh?"

Tomás was boiling. "You hurt Lulu? You should have left this to Monica."

"I didn't!"

"You raisin' your voice to your tío?" Monica piled on. "Eh, them manner lessons is really showin'. It's cool to hit a bitch so long as she's a wetback. That it, eh?"

"Moni, shut up!" Tomás barked, and she looked off with her nose in the air. "Start talking, Davy."

"She hit her arm on the chair when she jumped at me and tried to kiss me, and I got out of the way," Davy blurted. "I didn't mean to–"

Tomás turned his attention to Monica with a sigh. "Moni?"

"Naaah!" she said, waving a finger. "You really fucked up now, Davy." Monica left and then returned several minutes later. She appeared somewhat more contrite. "Yeah, it's all cool," Monica informed Thomas. "Ain't nothing."

She left before anything else could be said.

Tomás closed his eyes, then let out a breath. "Davy?"

"Sí, tío?"

"Always kiss the girl. It's trouble either way, so at least get something good out of it at the start," his uncle sagely advised. "Now, get out of here, and stay away from Lulu for a few days. Me entíendes?"

19

Chapter 10

The summer was nearly over, and after a great deal of yard work, Davy found his last few days at Ms. Cohen's before the school year started were to be spent mostly indoors. Ironically, it was just as the weather had begun to grow cooler. As well, after the incident with Lulu in the projection room and her hot and cold friendship since, he had come to appreciate Selene's icy glares, snappishness, and dirty tricks; at least she was consistent, though she still confused him. For someone who claimed she wanted nothing to do with him, she certainly made a habit of finding him several times a day to let him know it.

On his last summer day at Ms. Cohen's, Selene found him in a study in the main house's east wing. He was alphabetizing and reshelving the room's several hundred books, and it was a very dusty task. Davy was sitting on the forest green carpet end sorting through a stack of P's with his back to the door when Selene made her silent entry.

"Boy? You are to stand in the presence of a lady," Selene said sharply, startling Davy into knocking over the stack of P's along with the R's and S's. She laughed at the display.

Davy sighed, but then stopped. This time, her glare was neither ice nor contempt, but instead, outright hatred. Davy stiffened and set his jaw. "Yeah? Well, you're not a lady. Just a little girl and a spoiled brat. And you're mean!"

"Of course I'm mean. I hate you," she menaced, though the force of her words faded quickly.

"Why?" Davy said with the pout of a ten-year old. "You're the reason I'm here. I..."

Selene jerked as if she had been struck, and then winced at the pains in her sides from having moved too quickly. "Why? Why would you come here for me?"

Davy bit his lip. Here, suddenly, was the frightened girl he had seen that day in the parlor, and not the one who had been making him regret his choice every day since. Still, he did not know what to do. "I came... because you told on me," he said finally, and something in her wilted. "So I got stuck here, and it's all your fault!"

"All for nothing," she said softly.

"Yeah, for nothing," Davy snapped as a light dawned. "You didn't learn nothing. Not how to be nice; nothing. That's why your aunt wanted me here."

Selene regarded him with a snort. "Very well, hate me all you want. Just like I hate you. And after today, we'll never have to see each other again."

Davy frowned. What she had said sounded practiced, but wrong for the moment. "I don't," he shook his head, "I don't hate you, Selene." As he paused again, the frightened girl began to peek out of her beautiful blue eyes, and so he went on. "I just... I just wish you were different."

She came a little closer; "No. No you don't."

"I do," he said and looked down. "I lied before."

Selene came within a few steps. "About what?" she asked hesitantly.

20

"About why I took the little bird." Davy mumbled, "I thought I'd get caught."

"*You did* get caught," Selene prompted.

"Yeah, but not 'cause you told on me–"

"I didn't tell on you," she said sincerely. Davy looked up and found himself gazing into eyes as open as the wide blue sky. "My aunt saw you."

"Well, anyway," Davy said, smiling a little. Selene smiled back. "I got caught when I gave it to Lulu."

Selene's smile vanished. "And why did you give it to her? Is that why you took it?" she demanded.

"No," Davy assured. "I just gave it to her 'cause she caught me looking at it, and I just wanted her to go away. She's a pest, and that way I didn't think she'd tattle on me about it."

The answer seemed to mollify twelve-year old Selene.

"I took it," Davy paused to gather his courage, "I took it so I could see you again. If I got caught, I'd get drug over here, and then... I don't know."

Selene came close, "Why... why would you want to see me again? I was mean to you at the gate."

Davy shrugged. "It was kind a funny. Uh? What a horrible name," he said, and they both laughed a little.

"But you're here with her all the time," Davy went on. "And your aunt's scary. I don't know, I thought that if I came back, then you wouldn't be alone. Or, like, we could play together sometimes, or something, I don't know," Davy brightened. "And I sort of got what I wanted, 'cause she had me come over to teach you to be nice, 'cause you're so mean."

"I'm not mean," Selene said as she turned away and tears began to well in her eyes. "And that's not why she wanted you here. Not at all."

Davy frowned, again confused. "Well then, why did she want me here?"

Selene wiped away the wetness and returned with a smile. "To teach you something. To teach us both something, but it didn't work."

"Well, what was it?" Davy pressed.

"It doesn't matter," Selene said, smiling even more brightly. "And now we'll never see each other again."

Davy made up his mind and took his tío's advice. He leaned in and quickly kissed Selene.

A moment past the kiss, her blissful smile broke.

"Oh no," she gasped, backing away in horror. "No!" She cried, and ran from the room, fleeing as Davy was left to wonder about the consequences of having kissed the girl.

21

Chapter 11

Four summers passed, but Davy did not forget that stolen kiss in the study, though a great deal had changed in his life since. Selene had been bundled off to a boarding school the next day, and Davy's lessons with Ms. Cohen had ended after another school year and following summers. His speech had improved more than his chess, but more than that, there came a new sharpness in his eyes that would continue to grow. Ms. Cohen had assured Davy at their final interview that he was a bright boy with promise, and that she held great expectations for his future. Should he ever need her assistance, he should not hesitate to call on her. She had continued on about her acquaintances on various boards and associations that could help him with recommendations when it came time for him to apply for college, most of which was lost on the twelve-year old boy, especially since Davy only went to school now because his uncle insisted on it. The idea of begging and then paying to go to even more school after what he was already forced to face was ridiculous. No one with any sense would want to go to college.

It was not long after Davy finished with Ms. Cohen that Tomás and Monica's relationship came to a loud and spectacular end. After six years together, Tomás had still not wanted to get married. Moni has shouted in conclusion, "So a hood rat's good enough to fuck, but not for nothing else, eh?!" and then stormed out of his office and kicked over the old popcorn machine. Tomás had neither argued, nor gone after her, only called Davy over to help clean up the popcorn. That was Monica's last appearance inside the Starlight Theater, and her 'I quit' seemed implied.

Oddly, though, Lulu still came around, and by the end of that summer, the now fourteen-year old girl had taken over Monica's old job at the concessions counter. As well, she spent more nights there than not, and was given a partition and a bed in the loft with Davy and Tomás. All Davy knew was that some of Monica's new boyfriends were not very nice to Lulu. At one point, Tomás disappeared for a couple of days without explanation, and when he returned, he had simply told Davy that Lulu would be living with them from then on.

That summer and the next passed, and a tougher crowd began hanging out at the Starlight; mostly East Side Locos and their friends. The alleys and bathrooms at the theater gained a new and distinctly skunky smell, but there was not much in the way of real trouble. At least, not until the end of that last summer.

Lulu looked over from behind the counter and gave Davy a sweetly demure smile, then went back to arranging the snacks. Rico elbowed Davy in the ribs where they were both posted, holding up the wall on the far side of the lobby. Rico was the younger brother of the Locos' shotcaller 'Diablo', and had become a regular feature around the Starlight for the past few months. Rico was dark and gangly, with a mop of wavy hair that never quite saw shampoo often enough, like most other fourteen-year old boys. He was an affable sort.

"Wass up, eh? You gonna get at her, or what, eh?" Rico encouraged.

"Nah, it's cool. Lulu's just…Lulu," Davy said and glanced briefly at the broom and dustpan he was supposed to be cleaning with. The door to Tomás' office was shut, and the broom was within arm's reach if that changed, so he stayed where he was.

"She wants you, fool," Rico persisted, and Davy chuckled a little.

"Nah, we just know each other, that's all."

"So wass up, you aren't trippin' if I get at her?"

Davy shrugged. "Nah. Go ahead."

Rico sifted around, swiped at his hair a few times and cleared his throat, but did not move towards the counter. After a moment, Davy looked over with a smirk.

"Alright, I'm gonna do it. Quit trippin' fool," Rico said in a fluster and sauntered his way over to the counter. Davy shook his head, still smirking.

"Sup, girl?" Rico asked with a smile.

Lulu looked up from where she was crouched, pressing a hand to the top of her shirt to block any view. "Sup?" she said, not rising.

"Um…Um, you got any Raisinettes?" Rico said.

Lulu cocked a brow. "Raisinettes? Yeah, probably. You want to buy them, or something?"

"Um… yeah, yeah, yeah. They're real good. You know like, brown and sweet?" Rico said lamely.

"Okay," Lulu replied dubiously and searched around until she found a box. Meanwhile Rico glanced back with a hopeful nod. Davy snorted a laugh and came over.

Lulu popped up with the box and deposited it in front of Rico absently as she smiled at Davy.

"Sup, my boy? Done cleaning?" she asked, biting her lower lip.

"Huh? Oh yeah, that's what we were doing," Davy said, and then glanced at Rico.

"Yeah," Rico chimed in, and picked up the candies. "Hey, you want–"

"They're a dollar, seventy-nine," Lulu interrupted, then turned her attention back to Davy.

Davy smiled. "Are they good?"

"What?" Lulu asked.

"Those raisin things?"

"Huh? Um, I guess, and–" she paused to frown at Rico, "-are you gonna pay for those?"

"Uh," Rico said with the box open and a few in his hand. "Do you want some?"

"No," Lulu said, still frowning.

"Well then," Rico began, setting the box down, and replacing the candies he had taken out.

"Well, you opened it," she huffed.

"Well, I thought you'd want some," Rico protested.

Lulu looked at him in disbelief, and then to Davy. "Is he retarded, or something?"

"Or something," Davy said. "He's trying to get at you."

Lulu eyed Rico up and down. She shrugged and shook her head. "So, are you going to pay for these?"

23

"Uh, well, I'm kinda broke right now, but when I come up… um," Rico faltered, looking to Davy for help.

Davy put a hand on Rico's shoulder and moved him back from the counter. "Okay, the vato's retarded."

Lulu giggled and smiled sweetly.

"I'll pay for them," Davy said, actually intending to.

"Nah, nah," Lulu said quickly and grabbed the box, then ate a few. "I got it, don't trip."

Davy shrugged. "Are they any good?"

Lulu shrugged back. "I guess. You want some?"

Davy shook his head, then looked around. "Hey, where'd that vato go?"

"I don't care," Lulu told him and leaned over the counter. Adolescence was treating her well, and she did not mind one bit that Davy was not looking her in the eyes.

"So, uh…"

"So, uh… what?" Lulu said. She stood smartly and smiled, deciding that Davy had gotten enough of a peek.

"Nothing," he said, briefly thinking that maybe Lulu wasn't 'just Lulu,' but then Rico reappeared. He and Davy exchanged nods, and Lulu settled back.

"Told you I'd come up," Rico said eagerly.

"Huh?" Lulu said, wishing the moron would go away.

"What's up?" Davy asked.

Rico patted his pants pocket, "Come on, Diablo ain't gonna miss it."

Lulu rolled her eyes. "You swiped your brother's yesca? Oh yeah, you came up."

"Come on, its good shit. Not like that other shit, D," Rico kept on.

Davy shrugged. "Right, fuck it. C'mon, Lulu."

Lulu huffed. "I'm not going to go kick it in the baño and get high," she said even as she was coming around the counter.

"Nah," Davy assured her. "We'll go post up in the projection room. There's couches. It'll be all good."

"Yeah, c'mon, chica. What are you, scared?" Rico prompted.

Lulu looked at him, "Hell no. Let's go."

The office door came open and Diablo came out looking annoyed. Rico promptly slipped the baggie out of his pocket, dropped it, and nudged it under the counter with the toe of his shoe.

Diablo spotted him. "What are you up to, esé?"

"Nothing," Rico protested, trying to sound innocent.

"Yeah, right," Diablo snorted. "Go get in the ride." He turned back to the office. "Hey, Snipes? Come on, fool, you know what's up."

Tomás came out with a tried expression. "I do, and so do you. And if it comes to my door, I'll deal with it. All the rest? That's kids shit, and it's got nothing to do with me. I'm taking care of my responsibilities."

Diablo glanced over at Davy and Lulu and nodded. "Ain't nobody said you don't, Sniper, but shit's getting stupid out there."

"If it does, then you know who to talk to. You know the deal," Tomás replied. The two men had a silent exchange as Diablo gave Davy a glance and Tomás shook his head.

Diablo shrugged and nodded. "Yeah, I guess it ain't that serious, and we don't need that stuffy vato around here anyway. Him and his fucking knife. I'll holler, homie." Diablo paused, seeing Rico had not moved. "Get in the car, esé. What, are you fucked up again?"

"Huh? No–" Rico began, loathed to abandon his stash.

Diablo looked unconvinced. "Lil' bastard. Esé, you better not be dipping in my shit again," he warned as they left.

"Tío?" Davy asked once Diablo and Rico were gone. "He called you Sniper. I thought you never–"

"Forget about it," Tomás said roughly. "You do what you have to do. I made choices, and they have nothing to do with you." He spotted the abandoned broom and dustpan. "You have work to do, so get to it. Me entiendes?"

Tomás returned to his office and shut the door a little harder than usual.

Davy noticed that Lulu was studying the carpet.

"What's up, Lulu? Are you cool?"

"Huh? Yeah, I'm good." She shrugged with a forced smile. "Hey, I thought we were gonna go smoke some yesca?"

"Yeah, huh," Davy said with a smile that widened after he retrieved the sack and took a sniff. "Rico wasn't bullshitting. This is some good shit."

Lulu smiled. "We could just go kick it up on the roof, if you wanted? You know, like when we were little?"

"Huh, back when you made me hold your hand every time we went somewhere?" Davy said.

"Mmm-hmm," she replied, swaying a little.

Chapter 12

The day was warm, and the beat up old couch on the roof was comfortable. Lulu had plopped down right next to Davy as he rolled a less than expert stick – too tight at the ends, bulging in the center. The city sprawled all around them with its blaring noise, but after a few puffs of what really was *good shit*, it all became so much background noise. The whole world seemed slow, soft, and breezy, and Davy was finding Lulu especially soft and breezy.

She lounged against his chest, and his hand found its way to her bottom, which got her smiling attention. They both made noises that were not quite words, but were still easily understood. Lulu was quickly straddling his leg and her shirt was off. After a few seconds of Davy fighting one handed with her bra while kissing her neck, she pulled back and finished the task so that he would have both his hands free to explore her.

Davy's head was swimming. Lulu's lips were soft, and her tongue was all over his face. Every time he opened his eyes, his sight was either filled with her thick curly brown hair, or her big glassy brown eyes. Everything was perfect, and both their hands started exploring further under what clothes they still had on. Lulu was not shy in what she was doing at first, but then as Davy started finding her most intimate places, she started jerking and making unhappy noises.

"Huh?" Davy asked through the haze of a particularly loud whimper.

Lulu tried to look away even as her face squinted. "That's cool, go on and–"
Davy touched her again, but she jerked violently and cried out in what sounded like fear.

"No," she whimpered and started to cry.

Even addled as he was, that word still hit Davy like a bucket of ice water. Real concern began to grow when she squirmed away from him as he tried to hold her around the waist. Lulu huddled at the far end of the couch with her arms wrapped around herself.

"Lulu – I'm sorry." Davy stumbled out as he pulled his boxers back up. "What did I...?"

"No," Lulu said again and snatched at her shirt.

"I don't... understand," Davy said as she quickly dressed and scrambled off the couch.

"No."

It was the only word she seemed to be able to say but this time it sounded apologetic as well as miserable, and then she ran off. Davy shook his head to try to clear it, but that did nothing more than make his vision double. "Fuck," he muttered and found his shirt. He made it to the roof access stairs, but found no sign of Lulu, and he muttered some more. He went back to clean up the mess by the couch, found a spot to stash the weed, and then fortified himself with the roach before grinding out the last bits on the gravel rooftop.

"Damn," he said, wobbling as the weed hit him. He bravely ignored the couch and his extreme desire to just lay down, stumbling instead towards the door in search of Lulu, and – he tried and failed to swallow – definitely water.

Several hours later, Davy discovered a Lulu-shaped lump beneath the blankets of her bed in her cloth partitioned section of the loft. His nearly coherent inquiries were met with noises like, *Nnnngn*, and what looked like vague swatting beneath the blankets indicating that he should go away. Being fourteen and stoned, Davy had not been able to think of what to do, so he went off and found a big bag of animal cookies, ate a dozen, and set the bag on top the covers. "Cookies," he said, feeling dumber than the weed could account for, and then left Lulu alone.

Sometime later, Tomás came out of his office and found Davy standing behind the concessions counter. The floor was as swept as it had been, and now there was some popcorn mess behind the counter where Davy had been munching. Davy saw his tío's eyes were as red and glassy as his own probably were. Tomás shook his head at the situation, checked his watch, and muttered, "Fuck."

He thumbed at the doors. "Do the tickets, míjo. Get them ready – it's almost five." He sighed, "Where's Lulu?"

"Asleep," Davy said.

"Bueno," Tomás muttered, "What's seven plus nine?"

"Uh... eighteen?" Davy responded uncertainly.

"Quit smoking weed, stupid." Tomás shook his head, then tossed Davy a clicker. "Just do the tickets and try not to fuck it up too bad, okay? I got this," he said of the counter.

Davy nodded, and a very long night began.

Chapter 13

Several nights later, Davy wandered out into the darkness with the last of the late show stragglers. The halos of streetlamps guided his way as he peddled to Rohnert Park several miles from the theater where he and Rico had agreed to meet. There were a few girls out by Roberto's, and some cars in the parking lot not far from the park's public restrooms – a fairly normal 2 AM on a Thursday night – but as Davy wheeled to a stop on the pavement leading up to the restrooms, something felt off.

Rico emerged from a shadow with a sheepish smile.

A flicker of movement caught Davy's eyes, and he lept off his bike just as a hand swiped at his collar.

"C'mere, little bastard!" Diablo snarled.

Davy backed up, but spotted two more Locos coming around the corner. He kept circling away and reached in his jacket pocket past the bag of weed for his pocket knife. "I ain't got nothing!"

Diablo rolled his eyes. "Get this little vato!" he ordered, and the other two Locos came at Davy in a rush.

It was not the first time anyone had ever tried to jump Davy, but these two were out of their teens and much bigger than he was. He only barely got his knife out with a slash as they closed.

"Woah, eh!" one shouted as they both held back.

Davy did not hesitate. He bolted for his fallen bike, knife still in hand. On reaching it, he spun and slashed again, backing the two Locos off, though they looked more frustrated than worried. Davy managed a few pumps on his bike before a strong hand clamped down on his wrist, pinning his knife in his grip on the handlebar as he was lifted with his bike by the back of his shirt.

"Hey!" Diablo shouted as he shook Davy loose of the bike and weapon.

Davy bit at Diablo's face as he kicked at the man's crotch. As expected, Diablo leaned back from the bite, and took a hard shot to the groin. Davy was free and dove to retrieve his knife, but the other two Locos were on him, tackling him to the ground and pinning him a few feet from his weapon. "Rico!" Davy barked, and then grunted at the cheap punches they were landing now that there was a knee in his back.

Rico only looked at the ground miserably.

Diablo got up with a grunt and retrieved the knife. "Lil' bastard's got heart," he said, then glared at Rico. "You could learn something, eh." He eyed Davy who was still struggling, and had almost gotten free when one of the older boys had leaned in to run his mouth and gotten an elbow in the nose for his trouble.

"Enough!" Diablo barked and motioned for Davy to be held on his feet. "You're leaking, Payaso. Can't you even handle a little kid? No wonder Green Eyes keeps fucking around on you, eh."

"Fuck you. Little bastard had a fiero, and squirms like a snake."

Diablo snorted. "Then I guess you got lucky the little viper didn't sink a fang in you, fool."

"I told you, I ain't got nothing!" Davy snarled.

"Chill, little homie," Diablo said. "We ain't jacking you, eh. I just want my fucking yesca back, esé. Me entíendes, Vipito?"

"Lemme go!" Davy shouted.

Diablo frowned. "Dem putas as over there ain't gonna help you, or them fools that are paying them to suck their cocks, eh. So quit making a scene."

He waved a hand at the other two Locos and Davy was released, but they stayed posted on either side of him. After a moment of glaring, Diablo snorted. "Damélo esé! I know you got my shit!"

Davy grudgingly took the baggie out and tossed it to Diablo. The man checked it and nodded – there was not too much missing. He folded Davy's knife and tossed it back to the boy. "Don't steal, fucker."

"I didn't steal."

"No? Then how'd you get my shit, eh?"

"You must have dropped it," Davy said, trying to smile and bullshit his way out of this.

Diablo chuckled. "Maybe, maybe not," he said, then shook the baggie. "But it's a little short."

Davy saw Rico was still looking down. This was not going to end well unless he thought of something. Suddenly he found himself thinking about the game of chess he had played at Ms. Cohen's. One way out of a trap was to threaten a piece and trade, mangling the position. "That's cause I took it," Davy said suddenly. "I didn't steal it."

"Oh, yeah, Little Viper? Who'd you take it from?" Diablo said, puffing up and jutting out his chin.

Davy did not miss a beat. "Rico," he said defiantly.

Rico's head came up with a nervous look, and then Diablo laughed. "Fuck yeah, eh. That's right. What's up, esé? He took your shit. What'cha gonna do about it, eh?"

Davy mouthed, 'c'mon,' knowing that now all they had to do was just roll around for a few minutes to avoid actually getting a beating.

Rico nodded. "Yeah, esé, you can't just take my shit!" he shouted and rushed at Davy.

Neither of them were the best of fighters, and so a few scrapes and bumps later, they were pulled apart with a satisfied grunt from Diablo. "Fuckin' little vatos," he pronounced.

Chapter 14

Several days later, the midmorning sun crept in through the front windows of the Center Street Arcade, which was a short bike ride from the Starlight, and it found Davy and Rico battling to the death with greasy joysticks as their X-Men unleashed awesome powers in the two-dimensional world before them; a world Davy and Rico currently ruled for the paltry sum of fifty cents.

A shadow blocked the window's glare on the screen and the boys looked up. Diablo deposited a handful of quarters on the flat part of the console. "Go play something else, Rico, I'm gonna show Lil Viper how this game works."

Rico nodded obediently and left. Davy quickly killed Rico's character, and Diablo laughed.

"Fuckin' Lil Viper," he said.

"Sup, Diablo?" Davy replied warily.

The man laughed again. "That's what I like about you, esé. Bam! Then straight to it. No bullshitting."

Davy shrugged, but half-smiled, recalling something Ms. Cohen had lectured him on. *Little boys are told to keep quiet by their mothers who have so tired of fool men who ruin themselves by talking too much.*

"A'right, esé," Diablo said. "The other night, you did good. Didn't give nothing up, stayed fighting, till it was time to bullshit your way out." He paused for dramatic effect. "And you did."

Davy feigned relief. *Show others the face they expect, and they will hand themselves to you,* the woman had said.

Diablo nodded at the arcade console. "This thing sucks. Oh, it's better than the crap you got at home, but it still ain't shit."

Davy nodded.

"Bet you wish you had an Xbox, or some shit, huh?"

Again, Davy nodded, but more enthusiastically this time.

Diablo looked around to see if anyone was listening. Satisfied his boys posted nearby were the only ears listening, he continued. "I got some work for you, Lil Viper. It pays good, esé, but," he shrugged, "you can't say nothing about it to no one, me entíendes?"

Davy nodded. "You mean, to my tío."

Diablo smiled. "Or my little bro, Rico. But yeah, its better Snipes don't know. You're sharp. You can handle it by yourself."

Davy nodded and Diablo waved one of the Locos over. The older boy gave Davy a hard look and set a saran-wrapped bindle on the console, but kept his hand over it.

Davy paused, but then took the bindle and pocketed it with a nod. Diablo sent the older boy away with a quick gesture. "It's carga?" he asked.

"Yup," Diablo smiled. "You mess with it?"

"Nah," Davy replied seriously. "I just thought–"

"What? It'd be yesca you little vatos could pinch? Nah, I ain't stupid," Diablo interrupted. "Oigáme. This is what I want you to do. Tonight, when you're doing tickets, break that open. There's three bindles, and something for you."

"I told you, I don't."

"It's feria, stupid, now shut up and listen," Diablo said as he lowered his voice and leaned in. "Three homies are gonna come up and ask if they can get tickets for the ten o'clock show next Friday. Tell em, yeah, and give 'em a ticket and one bindle each. That's all you got to do."

"That's it?" Davy asked.

"Sí, Vipito, and there's $50 in there for you," Diablo replied, nodding with a smile. "See, I told you its easy money, homie. But," he raised a warning, "- you can't say nothing to no one. Me entíendes?"

Davy nodded.

"Nah, say it, little homie. You get me?"

"I got it," Davy replied .

"That's right, esé. You're smart. You're gonna be rollin' and doin' big things in no time, eh."

Chapter 15

Davy's first drug deal went off without a hitch, and in short order, he was not just making prearranged drops, but selling to anyone who came around asking for the right ticket, and of course, had money. The cash bumps quickly changed into extra bindles, but Davy had no trouble selling them.

When Diablo would come by to talk to Tomás, one of the other Locos, usually Menace or Chops, would have something for Davy, and pick up whatever cash he had in a sealed envelope for them. It was not the most complicated of systems, and soon, Davy's collection of new things began to pile up. Keeping it hidden from his tío helped in unexpected ways as well. Since he simply could not show off, that squashed the urge to be greedy, dip in, or stretch what he was supposed to be slinging – not that he had much of those urges in the first place. In fact, with that first fifty dollars, he spent none of it on himself, and instead went to address a far more serious concern than new shoes or Xboxes. He bought a gold-plated necklace for Lulu with a pair of doves charm.

In the few days since their tryst on the roof, she had been avoiding him whenever possible, and ignoring him when it was not.

When he had approached her at the counter in between shows, she looked like a frightened doe, ready to bolt. Davy swallowed and set the small box on the counter, realizing that buying the gift had been the easy part. "I, uh… This is for you," he stammered. "I'm sorry… I didn't mean to…uh…" And with that, words failed him.

Lulu eyed the box as though it were a serpent. "It's okay," she replied nervously. "What's that?"

Davy opened the box with a soft smile. "It's for you, I thought you'd like it."

Lulu's eyes widened at seeing the necklace. "For me? But why?"

Davy looked down. "I made you mad," he said shaking his head. "And I didn't mean to. I just wanted to make you happy."

"You didn't make me mad," she said cautiously. "I…I just got scared." She bit her lips and looked away.

"Scared?" Davy said with surprise. "Lulu, I would never hurt you."

"I know," she said and looked up with big eyes as he took her hand. "Do you… do you still like me?"

"Of course," Davy replied, and stroked her hair, making her smile more brightly. "Hey, let me put this on you."

Lulu nodded and Davy hurried around the counter. She held her curly hair up and he fastened the clasp behind her neck, and then she turned suddenly.

"C'mon, we've got a little time til 8:15 gets out."

"Huh?" he said, but let her lead him off to the men's room without another word.

Lulu picked a stall, hustled him in, and was quickly on her knees. Since Davy was fourteen and she seemed to know what she was doing, the rest did not take long. When she stood, Davy reached for her, but she pulled back. "I got to get back to work," she said as she left the stall. "Thanks for this." She fingered the necklace's charm, "It's really pretty."

And with that, she was gone. Davy shook his head. Deep down, he knew he had not made anything better.

Chapter 16

A few weeks later school resumed for the fall, but Davy, now a sophomore at Arcadium High, had little interest in his classes. He was quietly making more than a few hundred dollars a night, and except for more small presents for Lulu, he spent very little. For him, just watching the money stack up was far more interesting than any bullshit High School classes. As well, he had come to firmly believe that seven in the morning was too early for any normal person to be expected to pay attention.

As it came to be, the still ungodly cow milking hour of 9AM found Davy slouched in this seat in the back of his World History class next to Rico. The day's reading assignment was on the board, and the teacher was asleep at his desk near the front of the class.

"C'mon, Vipes, let's spilt, eh?" Rico whispered.

Davy signed. "Quit calling me that. I'm not in the clíqua, your hermano just calls me that sometimes to piss my tío off."

"Chalé, homes, you're in," Rico snorted. "I ain't gonna say nothin'."

Davy signed, "Cause you don't know nothing."

"I know you're slinging out of that ticket window," Rico said with a sly smile.

"Shut up, stupid," Davy hissed, snapping to attention. He quickly scanned the classroom and teacher. Satisfied no one was paying attention to them, he nodded. "Alright, let's bounce."

A minute later, the two were out the door and down the tiled halls as their pace slowed from sneaky to inconspicuous. As they rounded a corner, Rico turned with a bright smile as he held up a small baggie of weed. Davy snatched it quickly as he looked around. The hallway was not empty, but it seemed that none of the other people who were not where they were supposed to be had noticed.

"What's wrong with you, esé?" Davy snapped. "Where'd you get this? I'm gonna whoop your ass for real this time if you stole it form Diablo."

"Chillax," Rico huffed and snatched the baggie back, pocketing it. "Nobody saw and I didn't get it from him," Rico said. "Hey, and anyway, homie, I just let you win that. You can't whoop me."

"Oh yeah?" Davy asked.

"Yeah, eh. I just felt bad, eh. You know," Rico said. It was the first time they had talked about the night.

"Yeah, for giving me up," Davy clarified.

"I didn't give you up," Rico insisted.

Davy frowned with a dubious expression.

"Chalé, holmes. He already knew, or would have, and-"

"Shut up, eh," Davy interrupted. "It's cool. He'd have found out even if you hadn't blabbed. Then it would have been my tío that had my ass for it."

"And you wouldn't be slinging-"

"Shut up!" Davy snapped. "And where'd you get that? I know you didn't buy it."

Rico shrugged. "Don't trip. Let's go find some bitches and get lit, eh?"

And with that, the two continued down the hallways towards the bathrooms.

Chapter 17

"Sup, Bianca? You're looking good," Rico told the curvy junior who was masked by half a pound of makeup.

"Sup." Bianca paused. "What do they call you again?"

"You know my name, chica. Quit playin' the part. Let's go party," he said hopefully.

Bianca only tsked and looked off as a couple of her girls came out of the bathrooms. Davy snickered a little and one of them eyed him; her name was Eva. "And who's this vato?" she asked.

Rico frowned. "Sniper's primo eh. They call him–"

"Davy," he interrupted.

"Sniper from Locos?" Eva asked, ignoring Rico.

"Um, yeah," Davy replied, more than a little surprised.

Eva nodded. "He's cool. He used to fuck with my sister," she told Bianca.

"I didn't know Moni had another sister besides Lulu," Davy said confused.

Eva snapped back. "Oh, hell no. My sister's Gata from Fences, eh. You're talking about that bag whore from East Los. That bitch ain't shit! Her or her little sister. Hey, and tell her I said that, too!" Eva lunged her head at Davy, then snapped her fingers at him. "C'mon, Bianca. Fuck these vatos, they ain't shit!"

With that, the girls turned as one and strutted off.

Rico sulked. "Nice goin' homie."

"Whatever," Davy muttered. "Let's just go find Lulu."

"Oh, the bitch you stole from me?"

"Hey! Don't call her a bitch!" Davy barked with unexpected sincerity.

Rico backed up." Damn, like that? Hey, I didn't know. I was just messin' around."

"Nah," Davy said, and then changed the subject as they headed off down the hallways. "Hey, you knew about my tío?"

"What? That he was a Loco?" Rico shrugged. "Kinda, but I mean, him and Diablo have always been cool, and there was that shit that happened with them and Sleeps a couple years back."

"What shit?"

Rico Shrugged. "I know Diablo did him a paro, and Sleeps went along, or some shit, and then... where you guys kick it on Olympic didn't used to be no one's and now..."

Davy nodded. "Now, it's a spot."

Rico shrugged again as they made their way down to the second floor.

Chapter 18

As it turned out, Lulu was not hard to find. She was actually in class; math, from the look of the numbers and letters on the board. Unfortunately, the teacher was not asleep, and so after Lulu spotted Davy and Rico in the door window, it took a little effort to convince the teacher that she needed to use the bathroom pass that still had not returned with the kid who had left with it twenty minutes earlier.

"Are you sure you can't hold it for a few more minutes, Ms. Sandoval? Class is almost over," Mr. Garcia said, leaving the hall passes on his desk and returning to the dry erase board, hoping that would have embarrassed her enough to wait.

Lulu looked back to glimpse Rico wave a dismissive hand and say something to Davy. That was enough. "Mr. Garcia?" she said urgently.

"Yes, Ms. Sandoval?" he replied through furrowed brows.

"I'm having my period," she blurted, and the class erupted into laughter.

Fully flustered, Mr. Garcia rushed to his desk and quickly wrote her a pass, then dismissed her from class apologetically.

On her reaching Davy and Rico with their puzzled expressions, she asked, "What?"

The classroom behind them was still out of control, and Davy nodded towards it. "What the hell did you say?"

Lulu said, "Mr. Garcia was giving me hassles, so I told him I was on my rag."

Davy and Rico both laughed. "You're loca, chica," Davy said as they all left, and Lulu smiled coyly as she hooked her arm around him.

"You're not, are you?" Rico asked.

Lulu curled her lip at him. "The hell would it matter to you?"

Rico patted the baggie's visible outline in his pants pocket. "This would help," he offered.

Lulu relented and rolled her eyes. "No stupid. I just said that."

She looked up at Davy with a mild pout. "Is that what we're doing? I'm kinda hungry."

"Nah, right now, we're gonna go run around," Davy assured. "Then, like after lunch, or something."

The three quickly made their way to the parking lots, snuck past campus security, and climbed over the cement fence that surrounded the school. They darted off down the sidewalk until they were out of sight of the five-story High School and were mixed in with the light mid-morning foot traffic on the busy streets of East L.A.

"Hey, that isn't the same stuff he had last time, is it?" Lulu asked.

"Nah, he stole it from somebody else," Davy assured.

"I didn't steal it," Rico protested vainly.

"Good, 'cause… that stuff messed me up," Lulu said and waited until Davy nodded before she continued. "So, Rico, who'd you steal it from?"

"I didn't steal it!"

"Quit bullshitting," Lulu replied, unfazed. "You're broke like we are."

"Now who's bullshitting?" Rico snapped, waving his hand at her necklace and earrings.

"They were gifts, " she said snottily. "From a very nice person." She hugged Davy's arm a little more tightly.

Rico frowned. "Well, I'm doin' the same shit this "nice" vato is. This is just extra – so I'm sharing."

"Oh," Lulu said, and then looked away at Davy's questioning look.

"You knew?" he asked. "I mean... what I've been doing?" So much for keeping it quiet.

Lulu huffed. "Yeah, I mean, I'm not stupid. And, I'm like standing right there when Chops gives you stuff. You know behind the counter?"

"Does my tío know?" Davy asked nervously.

"Hell no!" She sounded hurt. "That one time, and I didn't even mean to... Well, you know. I was mad."

It took a moment to register. "Oh, right, no. I know that. I was stupid, and we were just dumb kids back then anyways."

"Yeah, you were real dumb," Lulu huffed, and then eyed the two of them. "I'm hungry."

Chapter 19

Davy, Rico, and Lulu settled on the fine dining establishment of Del Taco. It was cheap, and with enough Del Scorcho sauce, what they passed off as Mexican food became edible. Davy paid with a handful of crumpled ones and fives, and they found a booth in the corner. There were not many people in the restaurant, so Lulu and Davy kept a lookout between bites as Rico sat between them and rolled the weed. They need not have been so concerned since even the management had come to accept that Del Taco food only tasted good when the eater was stoned. Davy and Rico made the first trip to the bathroom and left Lulu watching the food. The moment they were gone she promptly began stealing jalapeño poppers.

From the smell when they entered, Davy and Rico found that they were not the first ones to have this idea today, and the cloud coming from the stall told them everything was currently cool. After a few hits each, the world started to become *groovy*.

"This shit ain't bad," Davy coughed as he leaned back against the stall wall and closed his eyes. "Where'd you get it?"

"I told you-"

"Bullshit," Davy said and laughed at how funny the word sounded. "If your hermano won't give me this shit 'cause he thinks I'll pinch it, he sure as hell didn't give you any." Davy had a serious thought. "Hey, are you doin' shit at the spot?"

Rico reclined on the toilet, wedging sideways in the stall with, one arm draped over the toilet paper holder, and his feet angled up against the other stall wall. "Nah. He's just got me runnin' shit around. Sealed up. It sucks, but it's better than jackin'."

Davy nodded and let the haze settle in for a little bit until the stall door swung open.

"The hell?" Lulu huffed, craning her neck around in that way only pissed off women can manage. "The rest of us would like to get right too."

"Calmaté," Rico pled and held up a pristine joint all for her.

Mollified and a few puffs later, Lulu was giggling. "It tastes like bubble gum. How they do that, eh?"

Davy shrugged. His mind was in no condition for such complex thoughts.

"They should make shit that tastes like a taco," Lulu opined.

Rico laughed. "Yeah, like a fish taco, eh."

Lulu scowled and swatted at Rico. "You're fucking gross, eh!"

Rico laughed some more. "Listen to her, eh. Get her stoned, and all the hood rat comes up out of her!"

"Fuck you!" Lulu pouted. "I ain't no hood rat, you... you shit weasel!"

She stormed off shouting, "I'ma eat your cheese-breads, asshole!"

A somewhat chastened Rico turned to Davy. "Hey, homie?"

"Yeah?"

"Hey, what's a shit-weasel, eh?"

Davy laughed. "I don't know, but it sounds pretty fuckin' bad."

39

"Yeah, but," Rico started laughing, "It's pretty funny; Shit-weasel," he said, and the two fell into hysterics.

After cracking themselves up by repeating the word a few more times, Davy paused for breath. "Hey, where did you get this shit? It's damn good... I don't even feel all stupid... shit weasel."

They both laughed again, and Rico nearly fell off the toilet. "I swiped it."

"Ah, hell no," Davy complained. "I told you—"

"Not from him. From that stupid vato, Lurch. In homeroom this morning. Dumbass just left his bag open and went to sleep. It was just sitting there. He's lucky it was me, eh, and not Miss. Dillhole," Rico went on. "She'd a got his dumbass kicked out, or some shit."

Davy shrugged. "It'd a been one less of them Maravilla cats around if she had. Them dudes suck."

Rico nodded, "Yeah, fuck them Mama Vergas!" he shouted.

A stoned moment later; the stall door was kicked in. "What the fuck did you say, esé?!" demanded a fat man with MV tattooed on his left cheek.

Davy swore and dove under the divider to the next stall. Rico jumped off the back of the toilet to flop over the divider as the big man lunged at him.

"We gonna stomp your punk ass out, bitch!" the man said.

What saved Davy and Rico from ending up dead in the bathroom of a Del Taco was that their pursuers were more stoned than they were. The mad scramble in, out and over stalls was a desperate, but comical affair.

Outside, Lulu had just gotten up to investigate the growing clatter from the restroom that now had the attention of the half-dozen other people in the restaurant as well, when Davy and Rico burst through the doors and bounced off the wall as they got their feet under them.

"Run!" Davy shouted as two large bald men burst out of the bathroom behind them like a pair of angry bulls.

Lulu's eyes widened and she grabbed her drink, flinging it at the man who had almost caught Rico. The hard plastic cup bounced off his head and splashed the other man. He stopped long enough to set hateful eyes on Lulu. "Puta !" he shouted and pulled out a .38 snub-nosed pistol.

Lulu shrieked, and Davy jumped over the back of the booth to tackle her to the ground as the man fired. The shot exploded in the small space and blew a hole in a pane of safety glass on the far side of the restaurant.

Both men were a little dazed and their ears were ringing from the shot fired in the small hallway. "Blast them fuckers!" the wet one shouted as he shook his head to clear it.

Davy and Rico wasted no time in bolting for different exits. Davy was nearly carrying Lulu, and as Rico reached the front exit, he turned back to shout, "East Side Locos! You bitches!"

Another wild shot in his direction cut off anything else he had to say. It blew a ketchup dispenser apart and took a chunk out of the wall behind the doors. Rico was gone before there was time for another shot. During the distraction, Davy had gotten Lulu safely out the back and away down the street.

Sirens blared in the distance, but another pair of shots rang out from the far side of the building. Davy spotted a clothing store across the street and pulled Lulu along, dodging cars, and into its relative safety. They stopped, panting, but jumped as Lulu bumped into a mannequin and it crashed to the ground. A short Korean lady came out shouting from the back for them to get out of her store, but stopped at the sound of another distant gunshot. As she stared at Lulu and Davy, distaste spread across her face, though she seemed undecided.

"No gang! No trouble! You go!" she barked at Davy, but nodded at Lulu.

Adrenaline and THC made for a bizarre mix that left Davy feeling not too far from invincible. He nodded at the angry woman. "Just stay here," he told Lulu, and then was back out on the streets. He needed to find Rico, though he felt as if he were being watched. Rico suddenly appeared, leaping over a chain link fence in the alley to cross the street with the two Maravillas in hot pursuit.

"Fuck!" Davy spat as Rico spotted him. He jerked his arm to point up the street, and Rico nodded as he turned out of the alley and darted in between the traffic to join Davy as they ran for their lives. The two made it another block to where they ran into four Korean men in their late teens.

"Where fuck you go?" one barked, but before more could be said, a shot blasted a hole in the brick wall by Davy's head.

Davy and Rico were pushed aside as several of the Koreans shouted, "Asian Boys!" and then all drew automatic weapons. They started shooting at the two Mexicans without hesitation. One went down in a spray of red. Contrary to the movies, aluminum car door panels do not stop bullets, and so the other one was also quickly sent off to the next life.

Davy and Rico were huddled behind a car as well when one of the Asian Boys came over with his gun barrel lowered towards them. "Where you from?" he demanded.

"N... nowhere," Davy stammered and Rico nodded.

The Asian Boy remained unconvinced, but stopped to look off in the direction of the approaching sirens. "Get fuck out of here! No come back, fuck wetback."

Davy and Rico had nothing to say and quickly left to collect Lulu from the clothing store.

As they found their way to a MetroLink stop, Rico looked over. "I didn't even know there were gooks in East L.A."

Davy nodded, still stunned from seeing his first murder. "Yeah, fuckin gooks," he said and they boarded the bus and mixed in with L.A.'s typical hodge-podge, that rode the MetroLink. Rico rolled another joint, but Davy shook his head at the offer as Lulu nestled her head against him and stared off into nothing. He put a protective arm around her, and she mumbled something.

Chapter 20

A few days later, Diablo came by the theater while Davy was at the ticket window.

"Sup, Lil Viper?" Diablo said with an unreadable expression.

Davy shook his head and shrugged. "Tío's in the office."

"Not here to see Snipes," Diablo said. "You sure you're straight?"

Davy nodded. "Shit's moving good. Did you need–"

"Nah," Diablo smiled and nodded back towards Lulu where she was working the concessions. "I heard about you trying to be all SuperVato, and divin' over shit to save your girl."

Davy grudgingly nodded. "Stupid Rico," he muttered. "That's not what-"

Diablo laughed. "He's your boy, but don't trip. He ain't gonna tell nobody else. But he did have to tell me."

"He's not in trouble is he?" Davy said quickly. "I don't know what would have gone down if he hadn't broke for the door and then started shouting."

"Nah, he did good, sort of," Diablo assured. "That's your boy. Dumb as shit, but he's got your back." He shook his head and sighed. "On a serious tip though, that little bastard coulda yelled out any *fucking* thing else."

Davy frowned. "I didn't even really hear. My ears were ringing."

"He yelled East Side Locos after disrespecting them two Mama Verga putos." Diablo lowered his voice and pointed a finger at Davy. "And that coulda got you both in some shit, q-vó?"

Davy paused uncertainly.

"Ain't neither one of you two vatos Locos, is you?" Diablo said. "Maravilla ain't no small clíqua, and you two almost go and kick shit off with them cause you're smoked out and sayin' stupid shit? You gotta be smarter than that; que no?"

Davy blinked, not having thought of any of that.

"Hey, look at me, fool," Diablo said with a stern expression, "This shit ain't for dummies. That's why I put you here slingin' this shit. You can't be doing stupid shit, or out lettin your boy do stupid shit either. Es serío, homie. Hey, come outta there, we gotta talk."

Davy swallowed and nodded.

"Hey, don't act all scary," Diablo assured, putting an arm around Davy and walking him over to the nearby bus stop. "You ain't in trouble."

Diablo stepped back and Davy suddenly found himself surrounded. The Loco in front of him lunged, but as Davy went to dodge and block, something hit him in the back and he went stumbling. After that, he was left swinging wildly and getting hit much more than he was hitting in a failing effort to stay on his feet. When he finally got taken to the ground, he clung onto one of his attackers, head-butting him and holding him close as a shield that kept him taking most of the force of the others' kicks.

Then, as suddenly as it had begun, the attack stopped and Diablo was roaring with laughter.

"Let go, fucker!" his shield barked, dripping blood from his nose. It turned out to be Chops.

Davy scrambled to his feet, still angry and swinging, though the others had joined in the laughter, and did no more than stay out of the way. "What the fuck?!" Davy barked.

"I don't know," Diablo said jovially. "What the fuck, Loco!"

That stopped Davy.

"Alright, the rest of you get the fuck out of here. I gotta holler at the new little homie," Diablo said grandly, and the two quickly found themselves alone. "Now listen, Little Viper, I like you, and I know ol' Snipes has been in your ear about this, but it's not like it was back then. Our old jefé was a fucked up vato, and we answer up to a whole different set now. Back then, ain't nobody cared about the difference between a smart vato, and one only smart enough to pull the trigger. But that's not me – not us, q-vó?"

Davy nodded, though Tomás had never said anything more than to heavily warn him to stay out of the gang life.

"Now see, I love my hermanito, but he's a little dummy," Diablo confided. "That's why I always brought him with me to come kick it when I had business to talk with your tío."

Davy frowned, having a number of questions, foremost, who did Diablo answer up to? But Diablo went on.

"You got Snipes' smarts. He did good with you, and that's no bullshit," Diablo said as they walked back towards the theater. "You gotta be the brains to keep Rico outta dumb shit, q-vó?"

Davy nodded.

"And you're doin' good with this spot right here. I been checkin up. You ain't stretchin shit, or bein all flashy," Diablo encouraged. "See? You're smart, and you're comin up. Startin' a little crew *and* got yourself that loca-ass hina? Little bitch flingin' sodas at vatos with guns? That's a down-ass little hina. Her apple fell far from that tree, so you be grateful, q-vó?"

All Davy could do was nod along. He had doubts and questions, but they were all pushed aside by a growing sense of pride and belonging.

"Alright, last thing," Diablo pulled him into a shadow and grew serious. "This is for you." He put a pistol into Davy's hand.

It startled Davy, but he kept his grip and quickly had the weapon out of sight. "I thought you said–"

Diablo smiled in the darkness. "Any dumb vato can pull a trigger. It takes a smart one to know *when* to pull it, or *when* to give it to a dumb vato to pull, q-vó?"

Davy was still breathing quickly.

"And now that you are doin' real shit, it's a good thing to have. Even in that little box, you're gonna get dope fiends that don't think they gotta pay, or'll just wait on you to come out." Diablo nodded to Davy's jacket pocket. "That little fiero you got ain't gonna do it, and neither is Lois Lane pitchin' soda from that counter, SuperVato. Now don't trip. There's always gonna be some Loco around, and he'll be strapped, too, so it ain't like it's all on you or some punk's gonna try and jack you every night. But this is serio and I'm lookin' out for you, q-vó?" he finished with a smile.

"Símon," Davy said, smiling back; his questions and doubts forgotten. He had a gun, a sack, a wad of cash, good homies, and a crazy-ass hina—it was the stuff of dreams for a fifteen-year old boy on the East Side.

Chapter 21

What Davy would count as 'real trouble' did not rear its read for him until Christmas break that year. Later in life, he would look back to that December evening and see it very differently. It was not the start of 'real trouble', but one of several missed opportunities where much of what was to come could have been prevented, and so many lives lived differently, or simply lived.

Winter in Los Angeles was more figurative than literal. Some places never freeze over. That night, the 8:30 show had just let out and had interrupted Davy and Lulu's latest round of grab-ass. The two grinning combants retired to their corners; the ticket window and behind the counter. Davy sighed as he shut the door behind him. He glanced down at the small box by the stacks of blank spools of tickets, not much more for him to push tonight, and then he could text Menace to come pick up the take. That meant he could put his thermos away, too; it was not full of coffee, just a loaded .38. Seeing the Dodger emblazoned container drained the warmth from him and deflated his ego. Later on, he would understand that the reason he did not get the same dick-hardening excitement from holding guns that most other people did was because when he picked one up, it was because he absolutely planned to kill someone with it. As it was, the thermos calmed him down, but not in a way he much liked.

It was a weeknight, so only a few dozen people showed up over the next half-hour; most already had tickets. With the advent of NetFlix and the like, small theaters had become no more than a cheap place to get high, have sex, or do whatever else dark, semiprivate rooms lent themselves towards. And there were bathrooms and snacks nearby. Of the five people standing in line, only one specified which of the two shows he wanted to see.

None of them had had any special ticket requests, and Davy idly considered texting Menace and pushing the next three bindles tomorrow, but then a knock came on the plexi-glass. Davy looked over, a little startled to see the emaciated woman with scraggly dark hair, sunken eyes, and a pallor to her skin which the halogen lights only made so much worse. Her eyes did not seem to be able to settle on any one thing, and she could not hold still. She was continually licking her lips and grimacing. It looked like he would move some more tonight after all.

"Hey, Davy," she panted. "Been awhile, eh?"

He stared for a moment, and then his eyes went wide, "Moni?"

"Yeah. Hey kid," she smiled, though pained. "I need a little somethin'."

"Wha...?"

"C'mon, kid, I got the malas; you know, sicky-sicky? It's bad," Monica kept on.

"Uh... I thought you moved?" he said, his mind still having trouble matching up the Monica he remembered to... this.

"Yeah, sorta. Look, I need it, me entíendes?" she pled, spitting a little on the glass, then scrambling to wipe it off with a ragged and dirty shirt sleeve. "Sorry, eh."

"Uh, I don't..." Davy stammered, still horrified.

45

"Ugh! I can't remember the pinchi password crap, eh! I gots feria– well some, eh," Monica pled. "You gots to ayudame, míjo. Soy maldita. Tía Moni la necesita!"

"I... I don't have any more. I got rid of the last of it like two hours ago," Davy said. He was sure that if he sold Monica anything, Lulu would never forgive him.

"Mentiroso!" she wailed. "You got somethin' left. Look, here's this feria. She stuffed a few ragged ones through the slot. "Hey, come on out, and I got somethin' else for you for the rest, eh. Whatever you want. You're almost as big as your tío. Spensa, bigger where it matters, I bet, eh?"

Davy could hardly believe what he was hearing. "Shut up, Moni! I'm comin' out, but I ain't got no more." Lulu looked with interest as he hurried past, but he waved her back behind her counter, then rushed outside. Monica was waiting for him with the most disgusting 'come-hither' smile he had ever seen and he hustled her away from the plexi-glass paned double doors towards the alley. By the time he got her there, she already had her top open and her skirt hiked up enough to reveal that she had no panties on.

"Just get me better, Davy," Monica begged. "I'll be real good to you, I promise."

Davy pulled back and shook her. "What the fuck is wrong with you?! Cover up, Tía! It's been years, and you... where have you been? Lulu's been living here and... and she don't never talk about why... And what the hell happened to you?!'

Monica jerked free with a miserable expression, then tripped and fell into a pile of trash. Davy reached to help her up, but she swatted him away. "Get off me, eh! You shove me around and talk shit?! Fuck you, eh! Life's hard! Now, you gonna help me, or not?!

"Yeah, Moní," Davy said, running a hand through his hair and pacing.

"So... you got something?" Monica said, instantly calmed.

"Yeah, Moni, I'll take you to get something to eat." He shook his head, trying to think, "Then we'll get... Solo's got a pad you can crash at."

"Davy," she whined. "I don't need no food. I need to get well! Me entiendes?" Davy could not look her in the eyes as she crawled over.

"I got no dope, Moni!" he barked, on the verge of tears. "And I wouldn't give you none if I did. You need help, Moni."

"Mentiroso!" She was suddenly fierce and flying at him; her ragged nails like talons. "You got it on you!"

Davy caught her, but despite her appearances, she nearly overpowered him, tumbling them both back in a heap as she kicked, clawed and tried to search him all at once. Then her gun came out. Where she had it stashed, he could not have guessed.

Monica had it trained on Davy in an instant. "Gimme the fuckin dope, Davy. I ain't playin' with you. Gimme the fuckin dope, or I'll kill you." Her eyes were wide and wild, but her tone was calm and measured.

"Okay, o... okay," Davy stammered. "Calmaté, Tía."

"I didn't want to do this to you, fool, but you're not giving me any fucking choice."

"I know, I know. Spensa. I'm sorry–"

Monica swallowed and shook off a wave of nausea, then regripped the gun. "Quit bullshitting! Just gimme the shit... and your fuckin' money, too, eh. For pissin' me off and making me do this!"

46

"Okay, Moni, okay," Davy said with his hands raised. "I got nothing on me, but-"

"Fuck you, eh!" she lunged and pushed the barrel into his temple.

"No, no, I got it, but it's inside! I never keep shit on me!"

Monica ground her teeth, but relented and stood, motioning him up with the barrel. "You better not be lying esé!"

"I'm not." Davy stood warily with his hands still raised.

"Well then go get it! I ain't trying to stand here all dammed night!"

Davy nodded, and they headed around the corner where she waited until Davy reappeared. She let out a sigh of relief at seeing the bindle in his hand, and snatched it. "And the feria, too! I ain't goin' through this shit again!"

"Moni, we can help, -"

She cocked the gun. "Go get the money, or I'll go in and start blastin'!"

Davy could only blink at first. "Moni, that's Lulu in there. Your little—"

"You think I give a damn?" Monica snarled. "Little bitch fucked off the best thing I had goin'. Her and your fuckin' tío, and that bitch Sleeps! Now éit playin' the part and go get the goddamned money!"

"Okay," Davy said. "Calm down. It's all good. I got the money right here."

He took out a roll of bills, and Monica nodded. "About time you quit bullshitting."

Davy nodded and handed over the roll. She snatched it and let out a sigh of relief as she lowered her gun. At the same time though, Davy whipped out his. "Drop it, Moni!"

A more useless or ignored warning was never uttered. Davy fired as her arm began to come right back up. Though nearly point blank range, the shot missed, but the concussion was so loud that Monica's whole body flinched.

She dropped the money and the gun, then plastered herself against the wall as Davy steadied his aim with his other hand.

"Davy, please don't," she begged as urine began to trickle down her leg. "I wouldn't have. I swear. It's this shit – it's got me."

"Get the fuck out of here, Moni," Davy said raggedly. "Lulu – you were gonna–"

"No, I wouldn'ta. I'm sorry! I just,–"

"Yes, Monica, you would have," Davy blinked as he thought about what she had said before, and then at how Lulu would make every part of herself available to him, except for the most natural one. He regripped the gun. "What did you do to her? Before she came here for good?"

"Nothing!" Monica pled, beginning to cry.

Davy pressed the tip of the gun into the shallow flesh beneath her chin. "What did you do?!"

"No, fuck you. It was Hector! He... he was taking care of us, and... he liked her. Liked her more than me... I just worked for him."

"Shut the fuck up!" Davy burst out, wishing to God he had never asked, so he would never have known for certain. Monica took his moment of emotion to attack, kicking for his groin and trying to wrestle the gun away from him. Davy was not so surprised by her ferocity this time, or maybe he just did not care about hurting her anymore. They grappled briefly, until he hit her hard in the stomach and she collapsed to the ground. She still clawed, everything in her eyes telling Davy that

47

she wanted to kill him, and it was not until he jammed the barrel into the center of her chest she froze.

Where or why Davy found restraint, he did not know, but instead of pulling the trigger, he pushed her back with the barrel, and then shoved her flat. His hand was shaking, but not from fear. It was the tension of restraint where almost every part of him was screaming for him to pull the trigger. He took several ragged breaths before he found words.

"I'm giving you your life, Monica," he said and swallowed hard. "You... you meant something to me once. My tía, my família, but you're dead now. Dead to me. To all of us here. Don't ever come back." He shook his head as she began to crawl backwards. "Don't ever come back, or I'll kill you."

Monica crawled back out onto the street, her eyes never leaving Davy's or the gun, and then she sprang up bolting off into the night. After a few moments, Davy looked around. Apparently, a single gunshot at night in East L.A. was not enough to warrant notice. Or, not much notice.

"Davy?" Lulu called softly from the partly open front entrance.

He spun. "Get inside!"

Lulu shrieked and ran, and Davy silently cursed. He picked up Monica's dropped gun and the roll of money, then went inside. He found Lulu hiding behind the counter.

"I'm sorry I yelled at you."

"I heard the shot, and ...and then nothing. I was worried."

Davy shook his head. "You should have gone and gotten tío."

Lulu looked away. "He's asleep."

"Asleep? " Davy said in confusion.

"You know?" Lulu made drinking motions. "Asleep?"

Davy nodded with his eyes closed. "Right. Has he been... sleeping a lot, lately?'

Lulu nodded.

"I guess I've just been, I don't know, trying to avoid him you know?"

"Yeah, I think that's why he's so tired."

The boy let out a breath and knelt beside her. "Lulu, when you got to the door, what did you see?"

Lulu shook her head. "Just... just some woman running away."

"You didn't hear anyone say anything?"

"No, why? Who was it?" Lulu said a little too calmly. "Did someone we know try to jack us?"

"Nah," Davy replied, wanting to believe she was not lying. "It was nobody." He knew he was not good at lying to her any more than she to him, and her expression said as much.

"Do you think she'll be back?"

"No," Davy assured.

Lulu stood up and looked down at him with a hard expression. "You should have shot her. Then, we'd be sure."

Davy stood as well. "Yeah, but then there would have been the placas to deal with."

Lulu shrugged, but nodded. "I guess–"

"When shit like this starts, –"

"Oh, yeah, the spot's hot. Better to stay low," Lulu replied.

"Don't trip, though. I'll still get you nice stuff."

Lulu pushed away from him as if slapped. "You think I care about that shit? That I'm some kind of hood rat whore? Do I ever call you fucking Viper?!"

"No, uh–"

"That's right," she said, swiveling her neck. "And do I ever let you call me Bashful?"

"No, and I wouldn't. I don't even get why you–"

"Oh, you don't?" Lulu snarled. "You don't get why I had to join your little clíqua?"

"No, Lulu, and I wish you hadn't," Davy snapped.

"Oh yeah? Well the hell with you then, eh." She ground her teeth, "Go to hell, I don't talk like no hood rat! You make me loca!" she barked and stormed off.

Chapter 22

Lulu and Davy's spat was a short-lived thing, and by the next morning, it looked to be forgotten. Diablo was not happy over Davy insisting that the Starlight needed to cool off, but in the end, he saw reason and set Davy to be on call to run errands and learn how to boost g-rides with Solo and Chops. School became an optional thing, but somehow Davy was passed along from the tenth grade, though as summer began, he had no real plans to see the eleventh in the fall. Ten years of school along with the fading speech habits he still had from his time with Ms. Cohen made him enough of a nerd as far as the rest of the Locos were concerned.

"Quit bein' a scared little vato," Solo complained.

"Yeah, Vipes," Rico joined in. "It'll be badass! The homie just did a county lid, so we gotta pick him up in a g-ride."

Davy could only shake his head and sigh. "You vatos want to head down to county in a stolen car to pick up the homie who just did a year for possession and jacking–"

"They dropped it to joyride," Solo interrupted.

"Whatever! It's still a stolen car!"

Solo tsked. "Them placas don't give a fuck. They're retarded."

"No, homie, they're not. That's how dumbass Menace got cracked" Davy snarled. "We'll go get my tío's coche."

Rico showed his disappointment. "That thing's a buster-ass ride."

"And it's what three broke esés should be rollin' in when they pick up their homie from county," Davy said, getting tired of arguing. "The placas may be lazy, but they run the plates of what drives right up to their door!"

"Chalé, homíes," Solo said, waving a dismissive hand. "They're too lazy-"

"They got computers that do that shit for them. Now quit bullshitting, and let's roll," Davy said, getting up from the ratty couch in Solo's crash pad. He headed out the screen door to the front porch and kicked a couple of empty beer cans out of his way.

"That's cool," Solo said, getting up from a recliner that did not recline. "Eh, we can pick up Bashful there. A cool present for the homie."

"No," Davy said without turning.

Rico and Solo shared a grin. "Wassup? She's the homegirl, ain't she?"

Davy turned with a dangerous look in his eyes. The first 'errand' Diablo had given him to run, was to put a bullet in the head of a rat. That look was a new feature that had come after he had almost killed Monica, and actually killed whoever Beto had really been. His stomach rolled now as his thoughts went back to what he had been steadily realizing about Lulu. Her odd quirks were not just Lulu being Lulu, they were the result of what Monica had let be done to her little sister. Lulu had been right. He should have killed that bitch.

Rico and Solo were not privy to his thoughts, only that it was time for them to shut the fuck up.

50

"We're rolling through Fences on the way out," Davy said coldly. "So when we come back – rolling through White Fence in the same buster-ass ride, shit's probably gonna jump! We're rolling hot, that's why no bitches. Now strap up and get in the fucking ride."

Davy turned and headed out as Rico and Solo's eyes grew, then they hurried to get their pieces out of their stash spots. In the moments before they reappeared, Davy brushed his fingers against the little .32 through his jacket in his armpit holster. He still heard Ms. Cohen's voice from years ago. 'See to your ends, and let fools prattle as they will.' The rest of the Locos said that his .32 was a pussypistol, opting for louder, bigger Mac11s, Desert Eagles, and .38 snubnoses. Only, ammo for a .32 was cheaper, and the kick was almost nothing. When Davy had asked Diablo for something lighter than the .38, the man had nodded and given him the target pistol, along with lessons in how to hold it, and proper stances. The difference then, between Davy and most of the other Locos was that he hit and killed what he shot at.

As Davy sat behind the wheel of their latest G-ride waiting for the other two, his lip curled when he noticed the open 40oz of Mickey's planted in the center console. He smacked the wheel, snatched up the bottle and jumped back out. He flung it to shatter on the stoop's cement steps.

"Hurry the fuck up, you putos!"

He did not know what had started his anger boiling, but it was going now. White Fence? By tonight, they'll be calling it Red Fence, he thought. He took a breath, then got into the passenger's seat and began to roll a joint. Unsurprisingly, Rico and Solo took their time and only came out once they saw smoke in the ride.

Chapter 23

"Hey, tío," Davy said, poking his head into the office. "I need a ride."

Tomás looked over from the monitor and past the half full glass of vodka and water. The bottle was not far away. "What for? You got work to do, and you've screwed around with your friends enough for today."

Davy sighed, regretting having even bothered to ask. "Tío, its Wednesday. No one comes to the matinee on Wednesday. I just gotta swing downtown for something. I'll be back by two. Gas in the tank and everything."

"You didn't answer me," Tomás said with a slur as he turned in his swivel chair. "Qué estas haciendo?"

Davy sighed again. "I'm just going to pick up the homie."

"The homie?" Now the slur was angry. "Damnit, Davy! How many times have I told you not to get involved."

Davy looked off and rolled his eyes. "Really? You're lecturing me, Sniper?"

Tomás slammed his hand down on the desk. "Yes, goddamnit! I don't want you making the same stupid mistakes I did! It's bad enough–"

"Bad enough, what?"

"Bad enough you tried to push dope right under my fucking nose! You could have ruined your life in way you can't even imagine, and dragged stupid little Lulu right along with you! She wouldn't have even blinked. But I told Diablo–"

Davy scoffed. "Told Diablo? Told him what? That you weren't going to wash his money through this crapass theater anymore?"

That stopped Tomás in his tracks. "You don't know what you're talking about – who you're talking about..."

"Yeah, whatever. It's not a big secret. Fuck, it's obvious to anyone with half a brain. There's no way this theater should still be in business," Davy scoffed. "But you had nothing to do with why I stopped. I shut it down because it was getting too hot. Because... because something happened."

Tomás stood warily. "What happened? You should have come and gotten me."

Davy looked off in disgust. "Lulu tried to that night, except you were passed out." He looked back to the bottle on the desk, and this time it was Tomás' turn to look away. "And it was your shit that came up to call. And I had to deal with it."

"What? What are you talking about?"

"Who the hell is Hector? And what did he do to Lulu?"

Tomás grew even more hesitant, "What did Diablo tell you?"

"Diablo didn't tell me shit, but that's only because I didn't ask him. I'm here, now, asking you."

Tomás shook his head heavily. "He's dead. That's all that matters, and all you need to know."

"Yeah? And what about Monica?" He could barely say the name without being sick.

"She's... she's gone. Moved out of the neighborhood."

Davy shook his head. "Now she's gone. And that's all you need to know," he said sarcastically.

"Davy—"

"Nah," Davy replied, waving a hand and starting to leave. "It's Viper. You aren't shit to me. Remember that."

"You're sixteen, You don't talk to me that way!" Tomás shouted, coming around the desk.

"Sit the fuck down," Davy snapped as he touched his jacket back to reveal the holstered pistol.

Tomás looked as if he had been shot. "Where did you get that? His eyes flicked to a Casablanca poster and the wall safe behind it.

"I'm not stupid, tío. It's not yours," Davy said, not quite able to keep up his bravado after doing something as shameful as threatening his own family; his only real family.

They both stood silently, not knowing what to say now that it had all gone a step too far. Finally Tomás looked down.

"Get out," he said softly.

Davy did not move, but not knowing what to do, either. "Tío."

"No," Tomás said facing Davy sternly. "Get out, Viper. This isn't your home anymore. Go and do what you do. Be whoever the hell you think you are."

Davy shrugged defiantly. "Don't trip. I'm gone."

Chapter 24

Davy was quickly up to the loft to retrieve his stashes, or as many of them as he could quickly; some cash, ammo, and a few clothes. He stuffed it all in a jump bag, then took a quick look around. He paused at the car keys hanging on a peg, then he dismissed the idea. He decided he did not want any of it. Just as he was about to leave, Lulu appeared in the doorway. She eyed the bag and bit her lip.

"I... um, I'm going to be at Solo's for a little while, so..."

Lulu shrugged. "I'll come."

"Nah," he said, and she flinched as if he had hit her. Davy had to run to catch her before she got away. "It's not like that," he assured as she tried to struggle free.

"What the hell do you mean, *it's not like that*?" she demanded as tears began to form. "I heard you and tío fighting. He told me you're gone for good. You're bouncing and you ain't coming back. You ain't leaving me! Not like this, I–"

"Goddammit, Lulu, you're gonna stay the fuck here," Davy shouted, and she tried to slap him as she started crying harder.

"Don't you fucking yell at me, eh! I love you, stupid!"

Davy shook her. "That's why you're staying here. Here, you're Lulu. You come with me, and you're just the home girl: Bashful. I'm gonna be all over, so when I'm not around..."

"I know," she said miserably. "But–"

"But nothing. Is that what you want?" Davy demanded. "You cried for two damn days after the night you got... brought in. And I know–"

"You know what?" Lulu cried, finally shaking loose and wrapping her arms protectively around herself. There was real fear in her.

Davy could not look her in the eye. "I...I know," he had to think of something that was not a lie, and then it came to him, "I know I want you to be happy. To have a good life. To be safe. Runnin' around with me, you won't have any of that." Then he swallowed, making a decision. There was only the one way. "I...I fucked up, but you stay here with tío...Tomás. He'll watch out for you."

"Davy, no" she pled. "You don't have to go for good. Maybe just a few days, and then...It was just words."

Davy shook his head. She did not understand what he was saying, but eventually, she would. "It was, more than just words. It's ...it's a lot of shit that has to end. I gotta bounce," he said in a rush as he pushed past Lulu and fled the theater.

Chapter 25

"Get in the ride," Davy said as he came out of the theater, bag in hand and a dark expression on his face.

"Wassup?" Rico asked. "I thought we were gonna–"

"Nah," Davy said in a clipped tone. "It's goin down, and using Sniper's ride would just bring the placas down on this spot. Between here and county, we'll spot another Toyota whatever-the-fuck and switch its plates, onto this one."

Solo shrugged and nodded. "That's cool. Sup with the bag?"

Davy barely acknowledged the question, then finally said, "We'll be hot, so I got shit to lay low. Get in."

Rico was content with that answer and planted himself in the back seat, but Solo paused at the driver's side door. Solo grudgingly followed.

"Alright, so wassup?" Solo asked more insistently as he turned the ignition over.

Davy shrugged with a hard expression. "We're up."

Rico cheered. "Fuck yeah!"

"Up for what, fool?" Solo kept on.

Davy turned with contempt. "What, you bitchin' up, esé?" The look hid the workings of his mind while he invented the details of where he would be directing his anger.

"Whatcha homie!" Solo snapped. "You may be Diablo's boy, and got a couple notches, but you don't tell me-"

"I don't motherfucker?" Davy snarled, and Rico was immediately quiet in the back seat. "I told you twice already we're goin' through White Fence, and shit was gonna pop. How much do I gotta spell shit out, homie?"

"A little more than that, *homie*," Solo said impatiently, but kept on driving towards Whittier. "Wassup? You don't trust me, or something?"

"Nah," Davy assured. "Shit's just gonna go down, and I'm trippin' a little."

"Well?" Solo demanded. "It's obvious we're in, fool, so? Wassup, Vipes? Hey, and it's nice you finally stopped soundin' like some rico gava, and learned to talk like a fuckin' homie. Makes your shit a lot easier to take, eh."

Davy snorted. "Mob Deep Pirus tried to roll two of our spots last week."

"Yeah, no shit. They got handled–"

"See, this is why I don't try to tell you shit. You don't listen, you babble," Davy said.

"Oh, spensa, homie," Solo said, rolling his eyes.

"Them niggers weren't east side nothin'. Mob Deep's north; way north in Pacoima," Davy said, and then came the invention. "So, how'd they get here? Why'd they come to the east side in the first place?"

"They're stupid niggers, who the hell knows? Probably got lost, or some shit," Solo said.

Davy shook his head. "Two crews come all the way down from Pacoima to roll two spots they shouldn't even know about? And they rolled hot through White Fence goin' and comin'? And none of them vatos out there busted a grape?"

"Huh?" Rico put in, wanting to be part of the conversation.

Solo leaned back and flexed his hands on the wheel. "No shit," he said, almost to himself.

Davy nodded. "That's right. Now we're gonna let them vatos know what time it is. We'll show them bitches how Locos roll a spot."

Solo was nodding slowly. "Yeah."

Rico began cheering and waving his Mac-11 around. "Fuck yeah, we're gonna come up big, homies!"

Solo swerved, and Davy snatched the flailing gun, aiming it and Rico towards the rear window. "Put that up, stupid! Don't wave a gun around in the fucking car!" Davy barked, then shoved Rico back into his seat. "You better have the safety on, dumbass!"

"It is, eh!" Rico protested, calming down to sulk, and then flicking the safety switch to *on*.

Chapter 26

By the time they had gotten to a liquor store a few blocks from County, Davy had realized that he was probably sticking his nuts in a vise with this stunt, but it was also a little late to back out. He had to tell Diablo something before he kicked off a war really for no better reason than he was having a bad day. More than that, Solo was acting sketchy again. How long did it take to pick up a fifth and some smokes? Davy got out while Rico was sitting in the back and rolling weed. On impulse, he tapped on his phone and then tapped the autodial icon of a cartoon devil that was Diablo's cell.

After a half dozen rings, it went to voice mail. At that, Davy pulled back and blinked. At this time of day, even if the vato was on Green Eyes, or Tiny, or Sleepy, he would have either answered, or the phone would have been off and it would not have taken six rings to go to voice mail. Paranoia set in; and it was not helped when Solo came out of the store ten seconds later looking even more sketchy as he carried a small paper sack.

"What took so long?" Davy asked, turning his phone off and stuffing it in his pocket. His .32 was in easy reach, and he knew he was a lot faster on the draw than Solo, especially if the fool was going to try and pull something out of a paper sack.

"Huh? Nothin' eh. Stupid gringo hassled me over my ID. I told him Lincoln don't need no fuckin ID," he said with a nervous laugh.

It sounded like bullshit, but Davy nodded anyway. "Let's bounce, then, Menace is waiting."

It was a tense forty-five second drive to the pickup area of County, and they had barely parked on the sidewalk when Solo was up and out of the car.

"I'll go get him, don't trip. Get your puff on, fool, and crack that thing, Rico. Get this party started," he said.

Rico cheered, and Davy tossed him a lighter. While Rico was occupied, Davy slid the Glock and Mac-11 out from under the driver's seat and popped out the clips.

"Want some?" Rico asked.

"Nah."

"Whatcha doin', eh?"

"Just checkin' them. Don't trip. Get your puff on. You know Menace is gonna blow whatever's left, and we still got shit to do," Davy said as he emptied the clips and cleared the chambers of the weapons.

"Uh, don't look like you're checkin' them," Rico said in puzzlement even as he took another look.

"Homie," Davy said, thinking quickly as he emptied the brown bag and dumped the bullets in it, then locked it in the glove box, "We are right outside County. If we get hassled 'cause there's a gang of placas everywhere, there's a big difference between a loaded gun, and one that ain't got no bullets. Me entiendes?"

"Oh, damn, hell yeah?" Rico said, quickly stubbing out the joint, then ejecting the clip from his personal .45 H&K pistol. "I didn't even think that. Here, homie."

A few seconds later, Davy handed back the empty clip with a tight smile.

"And the chamber?"

"Uh, I don't think I had one"

"Check, eh," Davy said, keeping a watchful eye on the release area.

There was an empty clack. "Nah, eh. I'm careful," he said with a smile, and Davy rolled his eyes. His stomach unknotted only slightly. He and Rico were tight, but Diablo was still Rico's brother. Davy touched the phone in his pocket, but then decided against it. *See to your ends.* Ms. Cohen's voice echoed in his mind. Every instinct he had told him that he was dangerously close to his own.

"Solo's takin' his time," Davy casually observed.

Rico shrugged. "Hey, what's up with the drink?" He said about to crack it.

"Open container?" Davy said off handedly as scenarios flashed through his mind. Then an idea struck him – he could turn Rico here and now. "Funny thing for a vato have suggested with all those placas around."

"Huh?"

"Almost like the homie's scared and wants us all to got popped so he ain't gotta do shit."

Rico scrunched his face at the thought, but then he swatted his hand and laid out across the back seat. "Nah, you're trippin'."

"Am I? That vato's been acting funny," Davy said, glancing back to make sure Rico was still relaxed.

"Bump some tunes, Vipes, and chilax. This is some good shit."

Davy turned on the radio and scanned until he heard a satisfactory grunt from Rico. It could have been Kenny G for all Davy could care. The scenarios started playing out again, and then Davy snapped alert; Solo had appeared by the release gate, but he was alone.

Davy said nothing as Solo approached, his mind was racing, and his mouth was dry, but he did everything he could to at least appear calm outwardly.

"What's up?" he asked as Solo got in.

"Oh eh, it is gonna be a couple more hours. Some paperwork shit," Solo assured. "Let's go kick it up at the wash, eh. Bein' round all these placas ain't cool."

"Man, the hell with Ontario. It sucks out there," Davy said, leaning back in his seat and gauging every word Solo said.

"Who gives a shit? It's like fifteen minutes away, eh! I ain't really tryin' to be runnin' around out here. There's all kinds a stupid vatos," Solo complained.

Was there tension in his voice, or was Davy imagining it? Davy did some quick calculations. If Solo had called from the liquor store, and gotten a green light from Diablo that fast, the wash was a set up, but it would still take a half hour for anyone to get from their hood all the way to Ontario. Either that, or Solo was going to try to live up to his name – it would be a better story than the truth, since he had gotten *Solo* for getting caught masturbating at a party when he was twelve. Davy laughed a little. The stupid fuck might actually try it, but too bad for him that Davy would have the only loaded gun at this party. Either way, Davy would only have a small window of advantage when they got to the wash, and he could not afford to hesitate: wrong meant dead.

58

Chapter 27

As it turned out, Solo had a lead foot and barely ten minutes later, they were at the wash. Hyper-vigilant, the two had both been sneaking glances at each other the whole way, and hoping the other did not notice.

After they skidded to a halt on the gravel at the base of an isolated ravine, Davy was out of the car a little too quickly, scanning for any signs of other cars or people. Seeing none, he tucked his jacket back with his ears straining to catch the sound of the glove box's latch.

"Grab the bottle!" Davy said sharply, and Solo banged his head on the roof as he was getting out.

"Yeah, yeah, yeah," Solo replied, reaching under his own seat "Got it!"

Davy nodded and let out a tiny breath of relief as he walked around the rear of the car. He was far from surprised when he reached the other side and found Solo holding the Glock.

"Don't try no shit, eh," Solo said, and flexed his fingers on the grip, "with that little bitch-gun you got. Toss that shit, eh."

Davy began to reach for it.

"Slow. Slower. Slower!" Solo shouted and pulled the trigger of his weapon. It dry fired, and Davy squared into a three point stance. Solo dropped the Glock. "No, homie, no! What the fuck, eh? I was just fuckin' around," he begged.

Davy did not hesitate. Both shots were for the center of mass, and at close range, his .32 target pistol was just as lethal as any of its bigger cousins. Solo went down in a heap; the look of shock and terror etched upon his face. Davy stared calmly and shook his head. So simple, and now the world was forever changed. Had it really just happened?

The gentle ponging of the car's far side rear door brought Davy back to reality. Whatever else, this was far from over. He knelt quickly and retrieved Solo's phone.

"What was that, eh? Are you vatos shootin' shit? I wanna shoot shit," Rico said in a happy stupor as he came around the car. "Oh fuck, eh!"

"Kick back, fool," Davy warned. There was no overt menace, only deadly certainty.

"Woah, eh!" Rico cried, backing up and raising his hands as though they could deflect a bullet.

"Just kick back," Davy said in a now almost curious tone. Would this work? "This punkass vato tried some stupid shit." He watched Rico closely. "What's up?"

"Wassup?!" Rico blurted in utter confusion. "I thought we were gettin' Menace, then goin' on a sick one. What the fuck is this, eh?"

Davy shrugged. "A change of plans. Get in the ride. In the front," he amended quickly. "We gotta go."

Rico nodded and was in quickly. Moments later they were spinning on the gravel and going down West Foothill bound for… Davy did not really know where. After fifteen minutes of Rico looking like he was going to wet himself if he did not get some kind of explanation, Davy nodded and pulled into a shopping center's parking lot. "I'm going to call Diablo, and let him know everything's been taken care of. You just kick back. Get out of the car, take a few breaths, just chilax," he said with a smile, using one of Rico's favorite nonwords.

Rico was only too happy to obey, and Davy got out the other side. Davy took a few steps so that he could both keep an eye on Rico and talk privately.

He tapped Solo's phone and called Diablo. It picked up on the first ring.

There was a dead moment, and then, "Sup?"

"Sup?" Davy said gruffly, trying to sound like the older boy, Solo.

There was another pause. "Who's this?"

"Who the fuck do you think it is?" Davy snarled in a whisper as he flattened the phone against his face.

"Alright," Diablo replied, and then said nothing.

"That's all you got?!"

There was another pause. "Yeah, motherfucker, I'm still trying to wrap my head around this shit, eh?"

"What, that I'm not dead?"

"No, eh. That does not entirely shock me. But, that you would pick this fucking day. The worst possible day, to go off the fuckin' rails! You couldn't have waited one..." someone was shouting in the background. "Hey shut up, eh! Now listen, you, I gave you every trust!"

Davy eyed the phone suspiciously. "You're pingin' me right now, aren't you? Check it out."

"Pingin?! I wanna ping your brains all over the fuckin' street!"

"Don't bother."

"Don't bother?! You know what? I'm on my way to that rattrap theater you live in. Old bitch can send me the cleaning bill if she can find me–"

"Then let me save you some gas, esé," Davy interrupted, not really hearing, having already considered this threat. "I got Rico with me right here. Anything happens to my tío, or to Lulu, and I'll mail you a piece of him on your birthday every year. You'll be fifty by the time you've got enough to bury open casket!"

Davy winced. It had sounded a little less bat-shit crazy in his head.

The line was silent for a good ten seconds.

"That's it, I'm gone," Davy began, knowing that he only had a few more minutes before whoever had been sent after him could be redirected to this new location that his phone's GPS would reveal.

"No, no, no," Diablo said shakily. "What the fuck are you on, eh?"

"I see anyone roll up, I'm putting two in his head and then I'm gone," Davy warned.

"Viper," Diablo said in a calm and steady tone. "What are you doing, eh? And quit fucking channeling your inner Hannibal Lecter!" There was a pause. "Hey, real serio, is there some gava with a fancy fiero there with you? If...if you can't talk, just say, 'yeah, yeah' "

"Huh? No."

"Oh my fucking god, so this is all you? Whatever," Diablo said with what sounded to Davy like relief. "Look, eh, I'm on my way to pick up Snipes 'cause it's all hands on deck. We're rollin' hot and deep on those Mob Deep niggers. You were just supposed to go take my dumbass little brother and go get Menace so you little fuckers would be outta the way. Solo was getting' scary, so I let him bounce with you. Then, you could deal with him, later."

Again there was a long silence. Neither side really knew where to go from where they were.

"Well... he's dealt with," Davy replied lamely.

"Are you serio? Did you seriously just say that to me?!"

Davy sighed. "Right. No. So, what do we do now?"

"I don't know, Davy, you tell me. Are you going to kill my little brother?"

Davy looked over at Rico, who was lighting up another joint. The idiocy of the moment was beginning to set in. Everything was twenty miles out of hands for no reason, and now it was too late to do anything about it except to not make it considerably worse. "No," he replied.

Diablo's end was muffled, but Davy could still make out "...shut up, eh. This did not still sorta work out..." Then Diablo came back on. "Look, I got heavy shit to deal with tonight. This is not a good day."

"Yeah," was all Davy could think to say.

There was another long pause before Diablo spoke again. "Here's your deal. You keep Rico wherever the fuck you are, and out of the varrio for the next twelve hours, then you got twelve hours after that to get someplace we ain't gonna find you."

"Alright. What about my tío and Lulu?"

"You mean Sniper and Bashful?"

"No! I mean Tomás Rodrigo and Luisa Sandoval!"

"Calmaté, motherfucker!" Diablo roared. "Sniper can take care of himself. This is your shit, not his. And as for Lulu? Well, Lulu can do whatever in the fuck Lulu wants. You want to call her? Get her to come meet you somewhere that ain't the east fuckin' side of L.A.? I don't give two shits!"

Davy drew back, puzzled. "Serio?"

Diablo sighed. "Do you not think this is gonna be a bad night, esé? Them niggers rolled three more spots last night. It's on. It don't matter that they got more guns and numbers. Do you not think if I could think of any way I could give you a pass so your psychotic little ass could be out here tonight, I would?! Just keep my fucking brother safe, esé! And don't ever show your face on the east side again!"

61

Chapter 28

Davy shut off the phone, and then tilled his head up to gaze into the pale grey skies of heaven. He laughed softly, at the coming storm – God, it seemed, lacked any sort of subtlety. Rico turned quickly at Davy's approach. His expression was a mix of confusion, fear, and a plea for hope all muddled in his bloodshot eyes and THC slackened features.

"D...Davy? What's going on, homie?" he said miserably.

Why complicate things? Davy thought. He just needs to be told what to do. "Shit's changed," Davy said firmly. "Solo tried to pull a move, fucked everything up, and got what he had comin'."

Rico nodded, hanging on every word. "So, so what now? What did Diablo say?"

"He said to kick back. Shit's going down tonight, but we're on hold," Davy replied.

"On hold?" Rico frowned. "Wassup with Menace? Ain't we–"

"No," Davy broke in. "He's on hold, too. Everything's all fucked up. Get your shit, we're ditching this ride."

"Here? But–"

Davy shook his head. "No," He looked off a street sign, trying to think of what was out there. Some low-rent clíquas and bullshit, but then he had an idea. It had sort of worked for them once before, so why not again? "Get in, we gotta bounce."

Rico nodded. "Where are we goin', eh?" he asked as he piled in to the back seat and began rolling another joint.

"Chinatown," Davy replied.

$$$$$

"Uh, are we lost, homie?" Rico asked a half hour after they had left Ontario. "Them vatos is strain'. And this don't look like no Chinatown."

"No shit," Davy snapped, wishing that he had a much better plan. "Past the freeway, Olveras Street turns into Chinatown. And quit starin' back at those vatos! The light's going to change in a second."

"Viper?" Rico said with a nervous edge and a hand on his Mac-11. The boys on the corner were throwing up signs.

"I see them," Davy said with mounting frustration.

"Fuck this light," Rico whined.

"Traffic cam," Davy snapped. "I run it, and it takes a picture of us in this ride that we have to ditch clean." Davy tightened his grip on the wheel. Olveras Street was not that big of a hood, and it was about to rain. *What the fuck are all these assholes doing out here?!* he thought as he tried to remain steady in a rapidly deteriorating situation.

Just as Davy was about to commit to a more drastic course, the light changed, and he peeled out. A half dozen boys gave chase, but they soon gave up, throwing up more signs and insults at a car now too distant to hear them.

"We shoulda blasted them putos!" Rico complained, and then began stroking his Mac11.

Davy had a quick thought, smiled, and hit the brakes. "Yes, we should have," he said with pleasant certainty. It really did not matter who jacked the car so long as someone did before the placas got it. "Lock and load, esé."

Davy flipped a bitch and then headed back up Olveras as Rico whooped and flipped off the safety. They parked a good fifty feet on the far side of the light and spotted the group that was just starting to break up now that the clouds had begun to drizzle. Rico was almost out the door when Davy caught his arm. "Don't throw anything out. Just talk shit and shoot. Mentiendés?"

Rico nodded, his enthusiasm only slightly dampened. A moment later, and he was on the pavement shouting every disrespectful thing he could think of. The pack rushed them; some were pulling guns. Rico stepped away from the car door and opened up hitting no one. Their new enemies scattered, firing back wildly as Davy settled into a three point stance. He aimed, breathed out, and fired three times. Three of their enemies dropped never to rise again.

"Get in!" Davy shouted as he jumped back behind the wheel and spun the tires on the asphalt. The force of the U-turn slammed Rico's door shut for him, and he rolled into Davy who had to elbow him back into his seat.

"Go faster!" Rico shouted, not seeing the needle pass 35mph.

"Traffic cams! Now watch," Davy said calmly as they hit one green light after another for the next ten blocks. Just past an old church and under the overpass, Davy parked the car. Rico was still speechless.

"Get your shit, and let's bounce," Davy said as he wiped his .32 down, cocked the slide back, and bent the firing pin with the car key. He tossed the ruined weapon in the back seat. "Move it, esé!"

Rico finally made it out of the car just as Davy finished adjusting his holster to accommodate the larger Glock. "You want to stash that, stupid?" Davy said of the machine pistol in Rico's hand as they headed on foot towards Chinatown.

"Yeah," Rico said breathlessly, tucking it into his waistband and pulling his shirt over it. "Hey, that was like some shit out of a movie, fool! Eh, you killed them vatos! Blam! Blam! Blam! And the rest of this shit? Homie, the little vatos are gonna be tellin' this story forever, eh!"

Davy nodded quietly as Rico continued on like a happy puppy and the rain began to fall.

Chapter 29

An hour later, the dark skies had shed their last hints of daylight, and the rain was coming down in full. Davy and Rico ducked into an alley, sheltered by laundry lines and a rat's nest of who knew what, several stories up. As their eyes adjusted to the gloom, Davy spotted a couple of girls with high heels, short elastic skirts, and a lot of makeup, standing in a doorway halfway down the alley. One looked his way, and Davy shrugged. He elbowed Rico. *Why the hell not?* That seemed to be the order of the day.

"Wassup, homie?" Rico said excitedly.

"I mean, we're here," Davy said with a shrug, and they headed over.

The girls had purple lipstick that nearly glowed, and satin black hair with red highlights. That probably meant something, but Davy could not even tell what type of Asian they were, though he knew what kind they were. The only thing legal about them was their age, if that. Scanning the area, Davy spotted a shadow two floors up on a fire escape. He nodded to the shadow while Rico stared at the girls, their hard nipples dented the flimsy shirts they wore which were straining to hold their large breasts.

After a moment, the shadow moved off and the door behind the girls buzzed. The one with the choppier dyed hair turned an acne scarred face to Davy. "You want fuck? Then come in."

"Hell yeah!" Rico blurted and grabbed a handful of her ass.

"I say inside," she snapped, and shoved him back.

"Settle down," Davy cautioned. The other girl who was maybe the older of the two smiled at Davy and lead the way inside.

They were barely past the threshold when the door shut behind them. The girls disappeared behind side curtains and a large Asian man with a pair of gleaming pistols in a shoulder harness stood with his arms crossed in front of another large black door. There were dragons and flowers tattooed on his arms, and he did not look happy.

"You know where is you?" He asked.

"Chinatown?" Rico offered, and the man snorted at the stupid answer.

"I look like Buddha-head to you?"

"No," Davy said, hoping that was the right answer.

The man looked at Davy and frowned. "What you do here?"

Davy shrugged. "It's raining. We saw the girls, and I figured, why not? Better than standing in the rain."

The man snorted. "You no sound like... esé. Where you from?"

"East Side Locos, eh!" Rico burst out, very frustrated with the delays.

"Am I talk to you, maddafucka?"

Davy put a quick hand on Rico to keep him from reachin'. "Chill, homie."

He glanced meaningfully at the curtains on either side, and the guns certainly aimed from behind them.

The man snorted. "You two far from home, but you not as stupid as he look: You got money?"

"Some," Davy said hesitantly.

"You want fuck girl?" he asked, and Davy nodded, glad this was getting back on track. "Leave gun," he said as the door behind him unlocked.

Davy nodded to Rico. "You go first. I'll wait here."

At that, the man laughed. "Okay, Joe. You come this way. Bring you shit," he said to Davy, beckoning towards the right side curtain. Rico grudgingly gave Davy his pack and weapons, but then perked up as he was tugged into a bright red perfumed room by four sets of soft female hands. Davy flicked the weapon's safety on and stowed it with a sigh. The man laughed again, and beckoned him through the curtain and side door into a smoky room beyond.

The light within was a dim yellow-green. There were a few tables where men clustered playing some game that used dice, cards, and a roulette wheel.

Whatever it was, Davy doubted it was Mah Jonng since he did not see any tiles, but he could not be sure. On the far side of the room was a small bar. A few scantily dressed woman were lounging away from the men, though no one much seemed to notice them.

"Sit," the man said, indicating a table by the wall opposite the bar, and they both did. "Give me money," he said with patient expectance.

"Uh-"

He gave Davy and unreadable look. "For girl?"

" Oh, right," Davy replied, opting for his sock stash and came out with a hundred and forty dollars.

The man stared at the bunch of bills, then shrugged and pocketed it without counting it or asking Davy how much it was.

"Is... is that enough for both of us?" Davy asked.

The man shrugged again. "Is it?"

Davy had no idea what to do, so he took out his wallet and handed over a couple more twenties and a ten. The man simply accepted them with the same good humor, then waved at the bartender. A moment later, one of the girls was tasked to deliver drinks.

"So," the man said as he sipped the cloudy liquid. "Why you here?"

"It's... been a day," Davy said, then chose his words. "We ended up in a tight spot and have to lay low 'til we can get back to East Los tomorrow.

"We saw girls and... better than spending the night in a fleabag motel or an alley."

The man nodded, considering carefully. "Why you ditch car?"

Davy nearly choked on a sip of his drink. "What?"

The man's eyes narrowed. "Hear on scanner three suspects flee scene of shooting. All catch was stolen car and gun. But, here is you and friend who no belong and need lay low, but no scare," he paused, "and now you smile? You definite not as dumb as look. Why come here?"

Davy shrugged. "You're Asian."

The man gave him a puzzled look. "And you is esé, so?"

"You might kill us, but you're not going to turn us in... to anyone."

65

The man burst out with sudden laughter. "What they call you?"

Davy paused, he was not Viper anymore, and the man's humor began to ebb. "Davy," he said finally. "My name's Davy."

The man blinked and nodded, having made the instant decision. "I Bao. You good. Come, we eat."

Bao led Davy to another room with a more normal lighting arrangement. There were two bare hanging bulbs above an unusually large table. Several other men were seated at the far end with several bowls in front of them.

A girl appeared with a smile and a flimsy dress, though she was more willowy than curved. Bao said something to her in Vietnamese, and she hurried off towards a kitchen.

"You like cat?" Bao asked.

"Uh–" Davy's eyes widened.

"No worry, taste like chicken," Bao said, laughing and slapping Davy on the back. "You sit here."

Davy sat with a nervous smile, though he relaxed when the girl came back with several bowls of rice, and what was clearly seasoned chicken. She smiled at Davy, and then knelt on all fours and crawled under the table.

"What the...? Oh," Davy grunted, lurching, but certainly not getting out of his chair. Soft lips and a wet, flicking tongue quickly swallowed the length of him, and Davy was soon breathing hard as the woman's mouth did its magic up and down his shaft. With all the control of a typical teenager, Davy was gasping and shuddering less than a minute after she had begun.

"Uh-"

"You no like food? Eat," Bao said with a grin.

"Yeah, the food is... damn good, and–" Davy jerked again. Apparently she was not finished, and she set to all sorts of strange maneuvers with her tongue and lips to get him hard again. Davy lasted longer the second time, and even managed a few bites of chicken. Then, just as he was beginning to catch his breath, she began again with her lips, hot breath, and fearless tongue.

"Uh..." he stammered. "How many times is she gonna–"

Bao shrugged. "Till you get bore. Then tell her go. Oh, you no speak, so just give little kick. She go."

After his third time, Davy was glancing around and started to feel a little embarrassed. He reached down and tapped the girl on the head. She paused and made a questioning noise with her mouth still full. He gently pushed back on her forehead, and she took the hint. Then he felt a soft cloth swath his genitals before she tugged his boxers and pants back into place and zipped him up. A moment later, she crawled out from under the table and discretely headed off to the kitchens.

Davy let out a sigh. Also, the chicken and rice were very good. Spicy, but very good. "Damn. You fools know how to live."

Bao half smiled, and was about to say something when every cell phone in the room vibrate at once. Bao cursed and leapt from the table, as did the other men. "No, you stay," he told Davy as he rushed out.

Davy pushed his chair back and put on Rico's pack, pulling his jacket back to expose the Glock, then picked up his own bag. It was time to go. He turned to see a couple of the girls poke their heads out of the kitchen. On seeing him, they darted back in like frightened mice. Just as he reached the door to the other room, an explosion rattled the building, and the sounds of automatic weapons grew louder.

Davy swore loudly. If the fight was out front, he would have to go through it to get to wherever Rico was, but then he looked back at the kitchens.

Whores eat, too, he reasoned, and rushed through the swinging door. Inside, four older or otherwise unattractive girls shrank back, and a shriveled old man in an apron snouted in surprise before grabbing a meat cleaver.

"No! Hey, my friend? Where is he?" They only stared uncomprehendingly, and Davy cursed again. The girls huddled away under tables, and the man started shouting in Vietnamese. Davy rolled his eyes and spotted two other doors.

"Where's the ho's?" he shouted, pointing at the girls, and then the two doors. "Ho's?"

Repeating it had no effect, but Davy's question was answered as one of the doors burst open seconds later with a dozen barely clad or naked shrieking woman pouring through with a couple of half-dressed men and Rico stumbling after. Rico had blood on him.

"Homie!" Rico shouted.

Davy had the Mac11 out, and his eyes were wide. "Are you hit?!"

"Nah, eh!" Rico shouted, "Gimme!"

Davy tossed him the gun, and Rico started shooting. Two men in body armor burst through the door as Rico uselessly sprayed the wall.

Davy swore, praying they weren't S.M.A.S.H. or any other semisecret placa unit. He breathed out and fired his Glock. Heads were small targets, and the weapon had much more of a kick than he was used to, but it only took three rounds to put the two men down for good. They had only managed to kill the cook. Rico's Mac was clicking empty.

"Get theirs!" Davy shouted, covering the door.

"Fuckin' gooks are everywhere!" Rico shouted, ditching the machine pistol for a pair of AK's and extra clips.

"This way!" Davy shouted over the shrieking women, as he kicked open the remaining door. Beyond, Davy quickly swept an empty room. The haze of hash pipes and opium still hung in the air around vacant cushions and couches, but there was another door, and somewhere nearby there was more gunfire. It was impossible to tell which direction it was coming from so Davy charged ahead. Someone else had thought they could get out this way, it appeared.

Through the door was a stairwell. *Up or down?* Davy opted for up, and shouted for Rico to move his ass! The windows were boarded up, but through the silts, Davy could see a gunfight raging outside. There were no flashing lights, or ghetto bird spotlights, so Davy kept going up. The second floor door was open a crack, and Davy burst through, rolling and aiming down the hallway with Rico right behind him aiming the other way. Both were breathing hard and their adrenaline was spiking.

There was a lot of noise behind them, and they both spun, flattening against the far wall, ready to shoot as soon as a target appeared. At the last instant, they checked up as several of the girls peeked out around the doorframe for an instant each, and then returned to whispering and occasionally yelping in fear. Most were somewhat clothed.

Rico and Davy shrugged and laughed before they got up and headed away from the street side of the building. At the end of the hall, they came to a busted window and a fire escape. Davy was through and out onto some scaffolding since the ladders down were gone. Rico followed at a run, and as slight and fluttery as the nine women seemed, they kept up easily. Davy led the way on and up, then down around and through more scaffolding into the adjacent abandoned building; a flop house that had been recently vacated.

Though Davy had no idea where he was going, somehow he found the street a block away from the shifting firefight. Unfortunately, it seemed to be shifting in his direction. There was another explosion, and he had let out a breath. *These gooks do not play*, he thought.

"Vipito?" Rico hissed. "What the fuck are we waiting for, homie?"

Davy's eyes narrowed. The rain was pouring down, but he was fairly sure the bastards that had their backs to him were wearing body armor. "Rico, a bajo," Davy ordered as he settled into a shooting stance. Something in him had given way. These bastards were going to die in the rain.

Rico did not hesitate much either, only long enough for the women to get behind him and Davy, and then they opened up. Two men were down before the other three could turn around, and they did not last much longer.

Two very long minutes later the shooting everywhere had stopped. Davy had retreated to Rico's side to get the other AK after the Glock had run out of shells. Then came the sound of tires pealing out, and more sporadic gunfire in the distance. Then nothing, only the rain beating down on the wreckage.

The girls apparently felt the situation was safe enough to start crying and wailing; Davy and Rico nearly jumped out of their skins at the sudden noise. "Shut the fuck up, eh!" Rico shouted.

There was some barely audible Vietnamese, and then, "Hey! Is, Davy? Is you?"

"You told those fools your name?" Rico said incredulously.

Davy nodded. "Bao?!"

"Hey!" Bao shouted back.

"Hey!" Davy shouted with some relief.

"Okay, I come! Stay!"

A moment later, the big man appeared as a shadow in the rain. Bao stared at them and the girls, and then laughed. "Okay, we go get van."

Chapter 30

Twenty minutes later, they were all heading down the Pasadena Freeway in a van packed with nine gabby, wet girls. Davy and Rico were in the front row, and Bao was riding shotgun with a squat Vietnamese called Risky driving. Bao was drinking, but had politely refused Rico's offer of a joint. Davy had taken a few swallows when Bao had offered, but then had just leaned back against the window pane and watched the city speed by. He tapped on his cell phone, but then shook his head. There was no one to call, and Lulu was probably trying to run the 10 o'clock show all by herself. He cursed and wished he had not thought of her. He noticed that Rico looked ready to pass out, and Bao had started to sing with Risky drinking along and joining in. One of the girls reached out to pet Davy from the back seats, but he batted her hand away.

There were some unhappy noises and pouting to follow, but the girls' incessant chatter soon returned to its former lulling patter.

As Davy stared at his phone, he knew he should call Lulu, but he still had no idea what to say. He hit the autodial anyway. Like everything else today, he would just think of something. One ring and it went straight to voicemail. That surprised him. Why was her phone off?

He called the theater's landline, thinking that maybe she just wanted to be left alone by everyone else since nearly no one had that number. Four rings, and he got the answering machine. Davy nodded. Maybe she had just turned everything off and gone to sleep. No one would be calling tonight with any good news anyway. Just to be sure though, he tapped the app's icon to 'ping em', and put in her number. Unless she had pulled the SIM chip out, that would find her within a few blocks, and a moment later, it did.

Davy dug in his bag for a pen, then scrawled the GPS location on his hand and hit Google Earth to enter the numbers. After a minute of connecting, a dark image came back with a superimposed street map. Davy frowned – none of the street names were familiar, and then he pulled the display back and nearly dropped the phone at what he saw. What the hell was she doing in Pacoima?!

Davy pinged Tomás' phone and got a Google Earth location a few blocks from Lulu's phone. Davy swore and dialed his tío. It rang several times, but the call was refused. Davy swore loudly enough to briefly interrupt Bao's singin', but not for long. Davy's head was throbbing from the adrenaline rush, stress, and chaos of what looked to be a night that was only just beginning to get out of control.

The boy scrubbed a hand over his face, then remembered Solo's phone. He pinged Diablo first, but the location was identical to Tomás', so he hit autodial.

Two rings, then a third. Then it was picked up.

"I swear to fuckin' God, Davy," Diablo began.

"Tell my tío to pick up."

The sound of gunfire erupted in the background. "He's busy motherfucker, and I ain't got time for no more of your shit!"

The disconnect tone rang in Davy's ear. With a frustrated bark that again interrupted Bao's singing, he called Tomás from Solo's phone.

It picked up after one ring, but there was only loud background noise.

Davy forged ahead into the dead space. "Lulu is three blocks east of you!" he shouted.

There was a tired sigh on the other end and then a whisper of, "I'm sorry, míjo." The call disconnected.

Davy could only stare at the small screen. The girls and their gabbling noise started to split through his brain. "Shut the fuck up, you stupid fucking putas," Davy raged at them.

The women were immediately silent and huddled together. Rico shook his head and somewhat came back to consciousness. Bao had stopped singing again and now eyed Davy seriously.

"Mí família," Davy said miserably, completely at a loss.

Bao grunted and said something to Risky. Risky's glare of protest only lasted until Bao moved to speak again.

"Davy?" Rico asked.

"I lied to you," Davy said, shaking his head and shutting his eyes as me tried to block out the thoughts, and visions of everyone he cared about brutally dead.

"Huh? About what, homie?"

"There wasn't..." Davy could not seem to find the words. Apparently it took more courage to tell his friend that he had lied to him than it did to kill someone. Diablo had been right. Any idiot could pull a trigger.

"There wasn't any mission. Not to White Fence, or anywhere."

Rico scrunched his face and struggled to focus his eyes; "I don't comprendo, eh? You said... and then Solo... Why'd..."

Davy shook away the maudlin self-pity. "Because I had to. That's it. My job today was to get you as far away from East Los as I could, and to keep you busy while Diablo and everyone else rallied and mopped up those Mob Deep Pirus that hit three more of our spots last night. Solo bitched up, but...it wasn't supposed to go down like it did."

"What the fuck did you just say, esé?" Rico slurred as he started to grow more agitated than the weed and alcohol could suppress. "You did not just tell me that my fucking carnal is rolling on a hood full of niggers and you're babysitting me like I'm a little bitch on the other side of town?"

Bao studied the exchange that followed, but not quite not understanding either as the yelling became a mix of wrestling and fighting, which dissolved into more yelling with the stupid one pinned and Davy speaking into his ear until the stupid one began to cry and was let up. For his part, Bao was getting a little sick of waiting on them, and his bottle was almost empty. He sure as hell did not speak Spanish, but família seemed close enough to 'family', and he knew that word of English. Family – what else needed to be said?

"You stupid friend done cry like little bitch?" Bao said. "Where we go?"

Davy couldn't meet Bao's gaze. "It's too late."

Bao made an irritated snort, "Too late for revenge?"

Davy looked up and shook his head. "You don't understand. There's too many, and it's too far away. It's not your fight."

"Fuck you, stupid wetback!" Bao exploded; then loudly explained everything to Risky in Vietnamese, pausing to spit after repeating the words, *It not you fight*, Bao spun back to Davy. "You no one, maddafucka! You no tell me when war, or no! I say is my fight! Me! Now tell me where we go, maddafucka!"

Davy looked around the van and saw that Rico had picked up Bao's glare; the back seat passengers were wide-eyed and silent. He sighed: "His brother and my uncle took everyone we know to go roll up the Mob Deep Pirus. They're losing."

"And?" Bao pressed.

Davy looked off. "And nothing. It's too late."

Bao nodded to himself, then whipped out one of his Desert Eagles and pointed it at the center of Davy's head." I give one more chance! Tell whole truth right now, maddafucka! Or I blow head all over dumb bitches!"

Davy swallowed. "Somehow... my... home girl, Lulu, she went with them, or after them, I don't know, but she's three blocks from where they're getting killed and she doesn't even know how to shoot a gun."

Bao held the gun out a little longer, then snorted and laughed. "Should have know. Of course is over bitch. Back there, twenty maddafucka with AK and RPG, and what you two stupid wetback do? Save nine dumb bitch instead of just run. And.... How a homegirl not know how to shoot gun? How she home girl? Sound more like dumb bitch." Bao turned and holstered his gun. "Where is Mob deep Piru?"

"Pacoima," Davy said as he let out a breath. "But there's just the three of us."

"Four, bitch," Risky interrupted.

Davy let out a tight breath. In his entire life, he had not been called 'bitch' and 'wetback' as many times as he had in this van ride. "Horalé," he said through clinched teeth. "Mob Deep is a big set. The four of us with mostly empty guns won't make any difference. We won't even get close."

Bao waved a dismissive hand. "We got gun, and homie. It slow night anyway."

Davy nodded solemnly. The path back to East L.A. was inescapable. He would face the consequences of his actions, add to the suffering of those around him, and only if he was lucky, end up dead before he witnessed the tragic end of everything he had ever cared about, he was certain.

Chapter 31

Half an hour later, Davy and Rico were rearmed wearing flack jackets and speeding towards Pacoima in a slammed Acura sedan. Risky was drunk and hitting corners at speeds that had Davy holding onto the door for dear life. Also in the backseat with them was a young girl named Je-hua, introduced as Risky's little sister and who had proclaimed herself as 'Violence', but everyone else called her Jeanie. With raven black hair, a few small scars on her face and arms, and a psychotic gleam in her eyes, the thirteen-year old had been waiting in front of the crash pad in light body armor with several guns hanging off of her when they had pulled up in the van.

Though she made a lot of noise, most of which Bao advised Davy and Rico that they did not want translated, it was also clear that she would not be doing any actual shooting that night. Her armor and guns were quickly taken away, much to her annoyance, and replaced with a headset and a pair of iPads on her lap as she coordinated the eight other dots on her screens which were all moving towards Pacoima at top speed. Ten miles out, she started barking in Vietnamese about something.

Bao winced and took out his earpiece briefly as he glared at her. She thumbed her chin at him, and he sighed. To answer Davy's confused look, he said, "Three ghetto-bird, SWAT and SMASH on way, big wreck on 210 and 15. Maddafucka not know how drive in rain. No patrol, all tie up," then he added with wide-eyed glee, "It go be live!"

Davy couldn't help but smile. Something about how Bao just lived in the moment was infectious, and all the other craziness that had happened up to this point did not seem to weigh so heavily anymore. Davy was at the spearhead of a small army about to descend in to a war for a reason not much better than, *Why the fuck not?* He doubted that he would live through the night, but at least he would make a decent showing in the end, and that buoyed him more than he would have ever believed possible.

Davy shook away the moment of euphoria, but Risky's driving did not seem quite so out of control to him anymore.

"What the fuck you smilin' 'bout, eh?" Rico said, looking like he was going to throw up.

"No idea, homie! No idea!" Davy replied, then tapped on his phone and called Diablo.

It picked up on the first ring. "What, esé?"

"Don't get killed in the next ten minutes," Davy told him.

The call was terminated and Davy laughed. He pinged Diablo, Tomás, and Lulu. Their phones had moved a half mile south, and they were more spread out.

On relaying the information to Bao he nodded and said something that quickly had Jeanie squawking angrily at both Davy and Bao.

"What did she—" Davy began, but Bao shook his head while he tried not to laugh.

Jeanie covered her mouthpiece. "I say, I know they moved stupid. What is you anyway? Look like some nigga eat taco, then take shit." She finished with a bark that rivaled most gunshots, and then ignored everyone as she went back to work, chattering to other vehicles and tapping her pads. Traffic cams and LAPD communications were not that hard of the thing to hack.

"You ask," Bao said to Davy with a shrug. Ricky grunted something, and the widows all lowered as the car spun to a stop. "We here!" Bao announced.

Chapter 32

Two primer-coat Caddies were parked end to end across from a shot up liquor store. The cars were shielding five Pirus as they unloaded auto and semi-auto fire through the no longer existent store windows. The return fire was sporadic and somewhere inside was Diablo's cell phone. A fair distance down the street, an SUV lay tilted sideways from where it had crashed through a Goodwill store.

There were random people running and hiding, along with more shooting from down the block. Tomás' cell was somewhere near that Goodwill, but he was not answering.

Bao barked and stuck his AK out the window as Davy did the same with his Mini-Uzi, and they began dumping on the Caddies. The shots were wild, but had the effect of causing the Pirus to flee down an alley to escape the sudden crossfire. A moment later; Bao, Davy and Rico were out of the Acura, and Risky was speeding off with their Command-and-Control in the other direction. Somewhere in the clouds above was the sound of a ghetto-bird's rotor. A police loudspeaker echoed down orders that were unintelligible and angry. A spotlight swung its beam wildly, doing no more than adding to the night's surreal chaos.

The three made their way in a crouched run to a shot up parked car a half-block away when the nearby sidewalk and store windows were peppered with small arms fire coming from an ally several buildings down from the liquor store. Bao wedged himself between the curb and a wheel well, and then fumbled with something while Davy and Rico shot back from behind the engine block.

Davy glanced over, and his eyes widened. "That's a grenade!"

"No shit," Bao replied calmly; then pitched it at the new gunfire with another soon to follow at the alleyway behind where the Caddies were parked now that a few spray were being directed at them as well as at the liquor store.

One booming concussion followed the other, and all the gunfire stopped.

"Di di mao! Up! MOVE!" Bao barked as he led them over and to the north of the Liquor store.

"But the homies is in the store!" Rico protested as they ran and ducked into an alley. "We should–"

"No!" Bao shouted. "We move, draw rest out. You homie get out," he turned to Davy, "Call. Tell, say go south. Hurry, hurry."

Davy nodded as he tapped his phone on. Diablo's phone picked up on the first ring.

"Fuckin' Viper?!" Diablo shouted.

"Yeah, esé, that was us," Davy replied, "Get south. Far and fast."

"Yeah! We got these dumb niggers handled!" Rico shouted as Davy covered the phone and scowled at him in the darkness.

"Us, esé?! Who's us? That sounded like–"

"Just get going. There's like thirty of us out here strapped to the teeth. You heard the grenades? Yeah? So don't trip!"

"Vaya con Dios, little homie. I'm gonna miss your stupid ass. You watch out for my little brother, good? eh?" Diablo said.

"Yeah, you got, -"

"Swear it, homie" Diablo said with a cough.

"I… I swear," Davy replied, hearing something in Diablo's voice that told him it was the end for the old devil.

The call disconnected.

Davy nodded to Bao and they were up and moving again, Bao paused at the corner. There was gunfire and squealing tires in the distance. "When say… you run," he whispered, and then lit up several parked cars across the street.

"Run!"

As Davy and Rico bolted down the street, there were muzzle flashes from a dozen different locations across the street that seemed to chase Bao's bursts as he headed in the other direction. After ducking behind a mailbox while Rico scrunched in a doorway, Davy took careful aim with his Glock at the shadows in the rain that were pursuing Bao. "Shoot the flashes in the windows," he told Rico before he fired at the moving targets. He was certain that a few of the shadows went down for good, and the others sought cover as the fire from the windows was now spraying in random directions. He held up a hand for Rico to stop.

"No!" He shouted as Rico took aim again after reloading, then he spun and almost fired at the figure coming up from behind him.

"What fuck you wait for? I say run; not run, stop!" Bao hissed. "We go. Dumb nigga shoot at each other now." In the distance, there were several more explosions. "Girl this way." Bao urged, and the three were up and moving again,

"How the hell do you know how to do all this?" Davy said as they ran and ducked down another alley.

"Army," Bao replied. "Father was General."

"Here?" Davy asked with real surprise.

"Nngh," Bao grunted, "Back home. I come to here when I you age."

"No shit?" Rico whispered. "Hey, how long were you in the army, eh?"

Bao shrugged. "Since could hold gun. Pick rice suck."

"I thought you said your dad was a General?" Davy asked.

Bao shrugged again. "He run camp, so, he General. Government find, so all who not get shot, come to here. Enough talk. Come we go."

"Fuck, eh, China sounds like it sucks, eh," Rico whispered as they set off again. Bao muttered something, and Davy chuckled quietly.

Chapter 33

Several short-lived gun fights later, Davy, Rico, and Bao reached the shot-up Astera Records where Lulu and Lulu's cell phone were hiding. A street full of broken glass and bleeping car alarms, along with two bullet-riddled corpses attested to the violence that had swept past. Most of Bao's homies, an Oriental Boys click, had stayed in their cars and were playing hit and run with any pockets of Pirus they ran across while avoiding the very heavily armed and armored SWAT and S.M.A.S.H LAPD tactical units. S.M.A.S.H. troopers had rappelled in from their air support, and were coordinating with the aid of aerial drones to begin controlling the area.

Fortunately for Davy, S.M.A.S.H. had begun its assault several miles away where most of the Oriental Boys and Pirus were squaring off. What Locos that could were in full retreat. If Davy had felt the need to check, he would have found that Diablo's cell was not moving with the others, and was still inside the liquor store, slowly losing power. It would be out of service long before it was ever discovered.

"Shh," Davy hissed as Rico stumbled over a box as they made their way through the remains of a door and a window. The security bars had done little to stop the shot up Camry that had careened into the front of the store. Bao took a post just inside and behind a CD bin that left him with a clear view of the street. He muttered occasionally into his Bluetooth.

Davy almost stumbled when he ran into Rico. The boy had stopped to stare at the wreck, and was mumbling prayers. Davy shoved him out of the way, and then a wave of panic seized him, this was what he had most not wanted to see.

Neither the driver, nor the passenger had made it out of the car. Bullets had spider-webbed the windows. Green Eyes was pinned by the steering wheel, but she was staring at nothing. There were two small holes in the front of her head. The holes in the back, though, were not small. Nor was the one in her little sister Sticker's forehead. She hung halfway out of the passenger's window where someone had plainly run up and shot her in the back of the head as she had tried to climb out of the wreck. As Davy watched, a Strawberry Shortcake sticker detached from the strap of her overalls. It fluttered to the ground. Rico stopped his prayers to watch, and was caught for a moment by the smiling face on it. Then he threw up. Stickers had been barely thirteen, and certainly not a home girl, just a little girl who loved pretty stickers.

Davy contained himself, but not without effort. *What the fuck had they been doing in the car?* Was all he could think, and then he heard a noise in the back of the store. Davy and Rico both dropped low. Davy put a hand on Rico's shoulder, and then moved past him with both hands on his Glock. After a few steps, he heard the noise again; a shuffling sound from an overturned tee-shirt carousel. He stayed low, inching forward in the near total darkness as sweat dripped into his eyes; his pulse pounding in his ears.

Then, from his left, a shot rang out; a flash in the blackness. He spun and fired without hesitation. Rico jumped up and fired with his AK, and a few more shots sunk into that darkness from Bao's direction as well.

A gun clattered to the floor, and the pile of tee-shirts shrieked, nearly getting shot for its trouble.

"Lulu!" Davy called in a desperate hushed voice as he strained his eyes trying to pierce the darkness where the first shot had come from.

The tee-shirts emitted a terrified high-pitched whine, but did not move. "Fuck," Davy spat. "Light it up!" he shouted and dove on top the tee-shirts firing blindly into the darkness as Rico and Bao did the same with their automatics. There were flashes from the far left that briefly illuminated a hallway and two fleeing figures. Neither of them made it to the back door. As Davy landed, the tee-shirts erupted with a shrieking, kicking, scratching girl.

The struggle was furious, but brief as Davy dropped his pistol and pinned the thrashing Lulu down. "Hey! It's us, stupid! Quitaté! Ow!"

Lulu paused for only a moment before she latched onto Davy and burst into hysterical caterwauling.

"Hey, shut her up, eh!" Rico barked nervously and Davy got a hand over her mouth and managed to contain most of her noise.

From the front of the store, Bao grunted. "Je-hua is home girl. That is dumb-bitch," he concluded, and then opened up on someone across the street. "Is time get out of here!"

"Right," Davy said as he scuttled by Bao with Lulu still clinging to him and sobbing. Bao had not gotten up. "Hey, you're hit!"

Bao only grunted as he pressed a wet hand in a failing effort to staunch the bleeding from an unlucky shot that had ricocheted off of the floor to hit up under his vest and into his abdomen "Risky come. I okay. Keep shoot."

"Homie," Rico said, seeking his head. "You ain't okay."

"Stupid wetback, what you know?" Bao grunted, and then glared at Davy until the boy started shooting. "Better hope I no die."

"You're not going to die," Davy insisted. "Risky's on his way. You just said."

Bao tugged at him. "You get me kill over dumb bitch? I see you in next life. Kick you ass."

They were interrupted by a sustained burst of gunfire that came in through the window and had them pressed flat against the floor. A moment later, there was the screech of tires, and then a loud explosion, followed by two more. Apparently, Risky's Acura had an RPG mount, and Davy let out a sigh of relief as the black sedan ground to a halt again in front of the store.

"Quit laying around, you lazy Mexicans!" Jeanie shouted as the back and side doors kicked open. Something heavier than an AK opened up from where Risky was standing to clear the street ahead the squat man was not one for small weapons, especially not with his stupid sister in the car.

Davy and Rico drug Bao out of the store and into the backseat. They all piled in: Rico half-climbed and was half-pushed into the front seat. Lulu was unceremoniously dumped in the floor space as Risky got in and hit the gas.

"Hold him still!" Jeanie shouted at Davy with a horribly pained expression etched on to her face.

First aid at high speed and in the rain was not a pretty affair, and soon there was blood everywhere. By the time they had gotten out of Pacoima, Bao was only shouting one word over and over. Davy did not need to speak Vietnamese to understand he was saying 'stop'. Finally, Jeanie listened, and she leaned back as her eyes started to water.

"Stop cry... dumb-bitch," Bao choked out.

She jerked away. "Fuck you. I no cry. I no dumb-bitch. I am homegirl."

"Good," Bao whispered, then looked up at Davy. "You wrong before. We not know how live. Just know how die. How die, that what matter. You learn... then maybe," his glance flicked to the whimpering Lulu, and he shook his head, "Maybe was worth this life. Next life, you owe me."

He said something in Vietnamese to Risky.

Risky only grunted in response and pressed down harder on the accelerator.

Chapter 34

Davy had not expected to see the dawn, much less all what had come by the morning's light. He was sitting on Diablo's couch wearing the clothes from his jump bag, while Tiny and Gata were busy washing the blood out of his and the other two dozen Locos who had survived the night and not been arrested. Rico was bounding about, retelling their adventures in Chinatown for the third time to a rapt audience. More than thirty of the Locos clíqua were absent; most dead, but a few arrested. Tomás had been one of the few arrested.

As for the Mob Deep Pirus, S.M.A.S.H. had taken care of what the Locos and Oriental Boys had started. As the saying went, the darker the skin, the better pigs aimed. S.M.A.S.H. was an off the books unit – they did not make arrests, only corpses.

Lulu was still attached to Davy, but finally he disentangled himself and made an excuse to go out back. He had managed to get most of his cash out of his bag, but that was all he had been able to take as he snuck off towards the back gate.

"Sup, Vipito?" Sleepy said from the back door, just as he reached the gate. "Where you bouncing off to, eh? Party's this way." Her large brown eyes held him in place. "Or could be right here if you want?"

She had lush curves, a tight body, and a perfect ass. Her shirt was already loose and halfway unbuttoned. From where Davy was standing, he could see the twenty-four year old woman did not have a bra on, or much need one. She was unable to have children, and so her body was easily winning its battle with gravity no matter how much she used it.

"Nah, Lulu's in there, Sleeps," Davy said, not seeing a gun on her, though that did not mean she did not have some sort of weapon within easy reach. "I… was just stretching."

"Uh-huh," she said dubiously, swinging her hips as she walked towards him. "Don't be running, Davy."

"What's up?" Davy said, glancing around, but seeing no one.

She made a throaty chuckle. "Diablo told you."

"Nah, he said–"

"Shut the fuck up, eh," Sleepy snarled, and then resumed her sexy demeanor, though the jaguar clearly still lurked behind her kittenish eyes. "He told you to watch out for his little brother, eh. I know what's up. I was there, eh." She had closed to within a foot. Her breath was hot; a jaguar panting over the hole of a frightened bit of prey. "The last thing he said was, *watch over my little brother*."

"The last?" Davy said as the situation began to dawn on him.

"See, Davy? You can be smart when you try," she said, biting her lip and running a finger down his chest. Her expression turned cold as stone, and Davy jerked as he felt the tip of a knife poke against his abdomen. "And you can be really fucking stupid, eh. And… Don't fucking talk, eh. This ain't the part where you talk. Just fucking nod when I tell you to, eh?"

Davy nodded.

"See, Davy? I told you you were smart," Sleepy said with a kiss-me smile. "If I wanted you dead, you'd be dead. Obviously, I don't. Now see, I loved Diablo... Nah," she laughed, "You don't believe me do you?"

Davy froze, doubting that the right answer was to nod.

"Ah! Trick question, eh. I'm just fucking with you," Sleepy laughed, but the knife still did not move. "I didn't love him, but I had love for him, and those were his last words. Tú sabes?"

Davy nodded, and the knife point vanished.

"So, all your dumb shit's swept under the rug. I told Menace how Solo was bullshitting about you. And he does what I tell him anyway. After last night, eh?" she gave him a happy shrug. "Everyone in that mother thinks you can walk on water, eh." Her mood shifted again. "But we know different, don't we, eh? We both know you do stupid shit, and right now, we can't afford no stupid shit."

Davy nodded.

"Good. Now, I hope you can snap your fingers and make that army of chinos pop outta nowhere again, eh."

"Maybe, I don't... I'm not sure."

"Well, you had better be sure, eh. Cause if White Fence starts thinking we're out here by our lonesome, weak and licking our wounds, it's gonna be some bad shit."

"Yeah, yeah, I get it."

Sleepy nodded. "Yeah, maybe you do, but not all of it. There's a lot of shit you don't know, and some of it's gotta get cleaned up. You really don't know just how much you fucked up with your little stunt," she waved the thoughts away. "Anyways, what about product. How much you think they'd front, eh?"

"I... I have no idea," Davy said warily.

"Don't trip, we'll get shit sorted out," Sleepy said. "For now, go enjoy your party. We'll talk more later. 'Sides, I still ain't made up my mind about Bashful. She might have to go."

"What?" Davy blurted.

"I said, *might*, esé. Calmaté, míjo, and it ain't like I'm gonna... Well, you know. I just don't want you having any more bad influences so you don't do no more stupid shit," Sleepy said sweetly, leading him back into the house. "I got love for you, míjo. I'm just trying to look out for you, and everyone. Tú sabes? I ain't like Lulu. I'm a real homegirl. You'll see. And you'll learn what that means. But, first thing's first. You gotta get in touch with those Chinos. Then we can see about getting Sniper out of County."

"Right. I almost–"

"Forgot? See, that's what you got me for," Sleepy assured, taking his arm and rubbing up against him as they went through the doorway.

She paused him with an expectant look. Davy nodded, and she gave him a big smile. "See, míjo, you're learning. And I'm gonna teach you good. I may just be a homegirl, but I'm still the *older* homegirl. Tú sabes?"

Davy nodded.

"Oh, you're so smart, I could just eat you up," she said, and rubbed her breasts against him, then spun away. "Kick back for now. I'll come get you in a minute."

A moment later, she turned back, breaking Davy from his thoughts of how she very likely could eat him, and do it in one bite. "This is the part where you step up, Viper. You do get that you're having this conversation with *me*, yeah?" She took a step towards him. "Hey, and don't just nod if you don't cause this is serío pedo."

Davy did begin to shake his head, and Sleepy drew him back outside.

"If not you, then who?" she said seriously.

Davy blinked. If he had not known better, he would have said that there was a little fear in her voice. "We're all that's left. You know what's up, and there ain't no one gonna listen to a hína 'cept a stupid vato that fucked up and then got real lucky... like me," Davy summed up.

Sleepy nodded. "See? See what I did there? That was the part where I shut the fuck up and nodded. And didn't I? We'll make it, eh."

"Tú sabes," Davy replied with a smile.

"Fucker," Sleepy said and slapped his chest playfully. Then she paused, eyeing him up and down, and then gave him a shrug that said, *why not?* At that moment, Davy did not even pause to consider as he let Sleepy take him by the hand and lead him off.

Chapter 35

Unlike his somewhat practiced fumbling with Lulu, Sleepy was a woman who knew what she wanted, and not one who was hesitant about making such things clear. The door to Diablo's bedroom was barely shut when she ordered, "Get'em off."

Once in the room, Davy had to shake off a little nervousness. This had always been the area of the house that had been 'off limits'. Still, he managed to get his shirt off. In the same time, Sleepy was out of her shirt, pants, and the nothing else she had been wearing in two unhesitant steps. Davy's shirt was tossed aside as she shook her head to loosen her wavy light brown hair. Then, the rapacious force of feminine nature shoved Davy onto the bed none too gently.

She did not give Davy the chance to get his pants off, seeing to the task herself in such a manner that it left Davy with no doubt as to who was in charge. Clothes on or off, she seemed equally comfortable, and now crawled over his body with a predatory gaze locked onto his eyes. All he could think was, *Why in the hell do they call her Sleepy?* As he lost all sense, hypnotized by the sway of her ripe, hanging breasts as they swung back and forth.

As her tawny arms wrapped around him, and her hot kiss burst across his mouth, her entire body slid against his. His whole body swelled and stiffened to match his manhood. His hands swept up her soft tan skin as the tight muscles of her back rippled beneath, and then his fingers found their way into her hair.

Clenching fistfuls, he tugged her back as he rose, and she gasped with excited pleasure. She arched her stomach into his, and ground her pelvis against him as Davy strained to sit up; to at least face this creature that sought to overwhelm him. She ground against him again, and then struck like a cobra, sinking her teeth onto the muscle of his neck as her nails dug into his back. Her hot breath was in his ear as her teeth scraped one lobe. "C'mon, míjo, get some," she panted, shifting her hips back and forth, then grinding her wet sex on his stomach.

Davy freed a hand as she lifted a little to let him position and then she met his thrust, grinding down to envelope him. Davy lost his breath. It was so hot inside her, like plunging into a wet inferno that just kept squeezing tighter and tighter. Her thighs squeezed against his hips as she slid her lower legs under him hooking her feet against his knees and locking onto him with every bit of her strength.

A feral look of lust filled her features as she started to grind again. Davy's hands found her shoulders and pulled down and back, squeezing her harder and arching her body against his. A moment later, she flung her head back, rattling out a sound of pleasure that more fittly belonged in some lost, dark jungle, and she began to thrash with abandon. Whiping her hips up and down, and undulating like a wild serpent, Davy lost all control of her. He gave up trying to set the pace, and just clung on for dear life as her sweat and musk sent him into near delerium. And then she did something else with her hips, not grinding up and down, but swirling in a circle or something that felt unbelievable.

Davy lasted mere seconds after that, and exploded inside of her. He was gasping and shuddering as she laughed crazily and clamped down harder, still twitching and swiveling her hips against his. Whatever she was doing, it was drawing every last drop out of him until he sputtered and collapsed.

She let him drop to the bed, still astride him, still clinching him inside her even as he briefly softened, and gazed with a wicked smile. She ran her tongue across her upper lip and teeth. "Holà, míjo. Now it's my turn, eh," she said, and descended upon him again. Neither of them noticed that the bedroom door was ajar, or that they were being watched.

At first, Lulu had watched in shock, and then with horror and jealous anger. Davy was being taken away from her, led away willingly by this puta that Lulu was now watching take her pleasure. Oh, how the hatred came. This whore could so enjoy giving herself to Davy in ways that Lulu never could. What Hector had done to her had not been her fault – everyone but Monica had told her as much – but that did not make it any better. And now, the one person who had understood; the one person who had just saved her, was tossing her aside like so much old trash. Davy had used her, Lulu saw, and now he was abandoning her, leaving her broken and alone to the untended mercies of any who would find her. Lulu continued to silently watch Sleepy position and direct Davy though all manner of carnal exploits. Lulu's hatred continued to swell, buoyed on by her own body's betrayal. Watching as she was, parts of her were growing excited, and so she hated those parts all the more. Just as she had begun to so long ago when Hector had been on top of her, pumping away, raping her over and over again. Her foul body had refused to flee to safety with her mind – especially, that dirty thing between her legs… It had enjoyed it.

Lulu kept watching for nearly an hour until Davy and Sleepy had finally finished, and then had slunk away into the shadows of the house. She did not know how, or when, but she vowed she would make them all sorry for hurting her. She would make them all hurt like she did.

Chapter 36

The phone picked up after three rings. Davy heard Risky's grunt of response to 'Hello?'

"Hey, Risky? Hey, I, uh-"

Risky interrupted with a grunt. There was highpitched protesting in the background, and then Jeanie took over the call. "What do you want?" she demanded.

Sleepy was watching anxiously from the far side of the bed. She had put a short shirt on but nothing else. Davy glanced at her as she unconsciously began to chew her lips, and then he turned his stare into nowhere before his eyes locked onto the open area between her legs. He thought of all the ways they had discussed as to how to open this door; these people would not tolerate bullshit.

"Bao," Davy said. "I owe him a lot and I'd rather start paying sooner rather than later."

There was silence on the other end, then some muffled highpitched yelling, a pause, more yelling, and then the microphone was uncovered. "Funeral tomorrow. 5PM. Meet at Willow and Market. No be late... and bring dumb-bitch, I want his father to see."

The phone was jerked away. Risky grunted a goodbye, and the call was terminated.

Sleepy's look of expectation was turning to irritation. Davy stayed looking elsewhere. "His funeral's tomorrow. I don't know if I should-"

"Of course you should, eh?! Esé, that was the-"

"No, I'm going," Davy said, and Sleepy settled back with an angry sigh, then scratched and started searching for her discarded shorts.

"Jeanie just said something about bringing Lulu."

Sleepy paused, hopping on one foot as she threaded the other through her shorts. She thought for a moment, then shook her head and pulled them all the way up. "His homeboy told you that? Wait, who's Jeanie?"

"Risky's little sister, sort of. She's adopted, I think. He jerked the phone away from her, but he didn't say not to bring Lulu."

Sleepy sighed, then shook her head. "Fuckin' Chinos," she finally concluded. "They're weird, eh. I've fucked with 'em before, eh. Diablo got some straps off different ones, once. It was weird how they did shit, though. They tripped at first that he left me in the ride and went in with Menace. Something about they'd heard me talking in the background when they were settin' up the meet, but not Menace. Then they changed the price, and we had to call people, and that fucker, Proctor, showed up, and the price changed, and shit just kept goin' sideways. We just ended up gettin' the fuck outta there."

"Who?" Davy asked.

"Nah, don't trip. No one you ever want to fuck with. Him, or his old bitch boss."

Davy frowned. "So, because Jeanie said it, you think it might be disrespectful if I didn't bring her? Even though they don't want her there?"

Sleepy shrugged. "Maybe, eh. Here, esé," she said, and tossed him a bottle of pills.

Davy dumped a couple of tablets out. They were half-brown, and half-white. He looked up with a question.

"Just take half the blanco part, eh. When you wanna crash, take the other half," Sleepy explained. "Some old military shit."

"I never fucked with agua, I don't think that now-"

"Naw, it ain't speed, eh. It's like glass, but not all fucked up. I get these from a homie that fucks around with cats out at 29 Palms in the desert. Pilots take that shit, eh. Air Force, so it's way cool," she assured, then broke one in half and took the white part. "It's like super-coffee, but not all wiry and fucked up."

Davy nodded and took it, washing it down with the last half of a stale beer that was still sitting on the nightstand from who knew how many days ago.

"It takes a minute, eh. Go get Bashful and clean her up. I'll see wassup with the homies in County. They gotta be somewhere some vato's got a phone. Even if I gotta fuck with them *big homies*," she rolled her eyes. "Someone's got a number. Don't trip, I got this. Now, go míjo," she said with a wink as she climbed back onto the bed, then started scrolling through her iPhone's contact listing.

Chapter 37

Weariness departed like a fog burning off in the midmorning sun as Davy stepped over a sleeping homie who had passed out in the hallway between the living room and the kitchen. There were empty bottles and remnants of quickly made and eaten meals. Gata was parked at a small table on the far side of the kitchen, slouched in a chair with her legs splayed as she stared at an open pack of cold cuts and a bottle of ketchup.

She looked up tiredly, her eyes taking a moment to focus on Davy. "Ain't no more tortillas, eh. Or queso, but there's–" she waved a hand around, "-shit if you're hungry. It's all fucked up, eh."

"It'll be alright," Davy assured. The amphetamines had him feeling inappropriately optimistic. "It's all good."

"All good?! Are you fucking loco, Viper?" Gata began to cry. "They said Green Eyes and Stickers is dead, eh. They ain't never gonna be *all good*, you stupid little vato! Stupid fucking Green Eyes, she knew better." Gata shook her head angrily. "But then that stupid bitch, Bashful! It's her fault they went! She was saying all sorts a stupid shit!"

Gata descended into sobs, and Davy blinked, then went over and put an arm around her, but she shook him off.

"Get off, eh! Sleepy took care a you already, esé," Gata sputtered a snort. "In Diablo's bed. What's that loca puta thinkin'? You're his boy, and you did some real hero shit last night, but she still fucked up, eh. That wasn't right, eh."

Gata paused and gave Davy an apologetic look.

"Spensa, eh," she went on. "It's not your fault. You're still just a little homie, eh. Don't know no better." There were still tears in her eyes as she looked up at him. "I heard what Rico was saying, eh. We all did. And you did real good. Don't trip. When Diablo gets back, it'll be all good again," she said, trying to convince herself as well.

"Gata," Davy began.

"Nah, eh. It's cool," she said, wiping her eyes. "Sleepy is fucking stupid, eh. She don't know her place, or how to really watch out for little homies, just how to spread her ass and shoot shit up. You gotta be hungry, eh." She got up, occupying her mind with taking care of the clutter around the kitchen sink, and a trace of a smile wisped across her face. "What you want, eh? I think we still got some eggs?"

Davy did not really know what to say. Gata was sweet, and an empty part of him really wanted to feel a women taking care of him, but then he shook his head. Sleepy had been right, before. This was the part where he had to step up.

"Nah, Gata. I'm good. We gotta go get the homies out of County, or at least see what's up."

She gave him a dubious smile. "All by your lonesome, eh?"

"Nah. Me and Rico'll go. Sleeps is making the calls right now."

"She is?" Gata frowned. "But, shouldn't she wait until Diablo gets back? I mean, we should wait, shouldn't we? Before we do anything, eh?"

"Gata," Davy said softly.

"What, eh? What's that look?" She drew her arms against her chest protectively. "Where's Diablo? When's he coming back, eh? The placas? They got him in County?"

"He's dead, Gata." There was no other way to say it. "Everything's up in the air, so for right now, we just have to keep everything cool."

"No, eh!" She jumped up hysterically.

Davy rushed over and took hold of her by the shoulders, and though she tried to struggle free, Gata was a small woman; more a mouse than a cat. "Mira, everything is bad right now, but before it goes sideways worse, we're gonna get it in hand."

"Lemme go!"

"No. I can't have you running around and waking all the homies up screaming and making a fuss," Davy said firmly. "I may just be a little vato, but someone's got to start getting shit back in hand me entíendes?"

Gata began to calm down, but she was still skittish.

"You're the homegirl, Gata. What's a good homegirl do?"

Her breathing became more steady. "She takes care of the homies."

"That's right," he said, and she began nodding along with him. "Now, a couple of us have stuff we still gotta deal with, but everybody else just needs to stay calm and chill. Can you be a good homegirl, and help do that?"

Gata bit her lip and nodded as she stared into Davy's eyes. Davy relaxed and released her, but then she turned and narrowed her eyes at something over his shoulder. "What you want, Bashful?"

Davy turned and saw Lulu standing with her arms crossed in the doorway. Something about her seemed off, but he could not tell what it was. For some reason, she did not look tired.

"I was looking for Viper. Guess I found him," Lulu challenged.

"Yeah, bitch, lucky you," Gata snarled.

Whatever this was, Davy did not need it, but he did need Lulu. "Gata," he said sharply. "You're all good, right? You're gonna go keep the little homies calm and cool, yeah?"

Gata let out a hot breath through her nose, but nodded.

"Yeah, Gata," Lulu mimicked. "Why don't you make the little homies some tortas? It's all you're good for, bitch."

Gata reared back, and Lulu had her fists clinched, but Davy stayed between them. "Enough! Both of you! Lu -" he winced. "Bashful, we have to talk, now."

Lulu paled with anger as she faced Davy. "Oh, we do? I don't-"

"I said, now." Davy snatched her by the arm and drug her outside through the sliding glass door and shut it behind them as she shook loose.

"There's no time for this shit right now, Lulu!"

"Oh yeah, Viper? Whadda you got time for, eh?" she mocked. "A quick one before you bounce for good?"

Davy stopped. "You know about-"

"Why do you think I was out there last night, puto?! I got that retarded bitch Green Eyes to get all jealous of Sleepy, her not being with her man when it mattered, but

Sleepy was. That Sleepy was taking her spot," Lulu spat. Every emotion she had was swirling within her.

"If you knew, then why in the fuck??! The only reason I came back was you were in all that!"

Lulu twitched as if in pain, and grew far less fierce. "I needed a ride. A way to find him." Her glare was love twisted into hate and back. "Cause I thought you were dead. And... and I was gonna kill him. I was gonna do that for you!" she accused.

Davy shut his eyes and smiled as he shook his head.

"This is funny to you?!" Lulu shrieked. "I'll fucking kill you right now!"

She attacked with claws aimed at his eyes and throat, but Davy grabbed her wrists and forced her up against the fence. When she hit it though, her whole body shuddered and for a moment, the life seemed to go out of her. As she stared at Davy, a terrible whimper began to build in her throat.

"I just told you, Lulu! The only reason I came back was for you!" Davy shouted at Lulu. "I had a deal with Diablo. I keep Rico out of harm's way for twelve hours, and don't kill him myself, and then I get twelve hours to get somewhere he wouldn't find me. He said that if I could talk you into coming with me, then, *Lulu can do whatever the fuck Lulu wants.* His words. I only waited until everyone else should have been gone before I called so maybe I could have come back and picked you up. Then, I saw where your phone was. He paused to give her a shake and make sure he had her attention.

"I didn't do all that shit last night for Diablo, or Rico, or even my tío. I did it for stupidass you!"

Lulu was frozen with undreamed of hope. She had forgotten so many other terrible things, she could forget the last hour, she was sure. "So... so all this," her smile brightened. "You're doing all this? Sticking around when you could get blasted at any second? All for me? All so we can run away together?"

Davy smiled. "Well, not quite. I mean, Diablo's dead, Solo's dead, Sleepy convinced Menace that Solo way bullshitting, so except for us three, no one else knows shit. And the way Sleeps is rolling with it, she can't really ever turn it around. So, I mean, everything's fucked up right now, but it's actually all good for us."

"Yeah," Lulu said as her face became a tight mask that sealed away everything. "Everything's good. So, what did you need to holler at me about?"

Davy smiled, not noticing the change in Lulu, and he went on to explain how he needed her to come with him to Bao's funeral, and why it was so important.

At the end, she nodded. "So, that one time from when you left the couch to when I found you in the kitchen, you and Sleepy were just figuring stuff out? Just talking?"

"Yeah, of course," Davy assured, not at all guessing that this was only her way of giving him one last chance to be truthful, and possibly unseal his fate as far as she was concerned. Lulu smiled and gave him a quick kiss as though she believed every word.

Chapter 38

"Miranda Amendola?" LAPD Homicide Detective Brian Sanderson asked.

Sleepy's head came up as she rose from the plastic seats outside the swinging double doors that lead to the County morgue. This should have been a bad day getting slowly better, but with her every step, it seemed to keep getting worse.

"Yes, Detective?" she said with barely a trace of varrio accent.

"Ma'am, if you'll come this way?" He opened the doors for her as he eyed her. She moved with grace in her black and white floral print blouse and black slacks. Her flats made no sound as she passed. *Not your average hood rat*, he thought.

"Thank you, detective," Sleepy said as she stared down the hallway to the shuttered Plexiglas window of the actual morgue. Her steps did not falter.

It all should have been so simple. Come down with Rico and bail out Tomás like she had promised Davy, along with any of the other Locos she could manage with what should have been plentiful resources. However, for some as yet unknown reason, Tomás Rodrigo was being held on the high-power floor, and had an unspecified hold to go with a petty possession of a firearm charge. No bail. Her next unpleasant surprise had come when her two 'emergency' credit cards had been declined at the bondsmen's office the accounts were frozen. Rico's small roll of cash had been enough to cover three of the nine Locos currently detained, and Menace had gotten himself released. He was elsewhere. So much for any great addition to the number of boots on the ground in East L.A.; the end of things was not going smoothly.

As she and Rico had waited by Central Processing and Release, and he had teased her about how she looked like a white-girl, there had come this latest round of unpleasantness. She had been prepared for Gang Task Force, or some nameless representative of S.M.A.S.H. –those placas were obnoxious, but where there were cameras, they tended to be more bark than bite. LAPD Homicide was a different animal. More delays, she did not need since she had no intention of letting that little moron, Davy, just wing it with that idiot girl on his arm. How much trouble was that little puta already the cause of? Bashful had to go, Sleepy had been deciding when a uniformed officer had taken her aside.

She had been told that the Detective was only interested in her, which was even more worrisome, but at the time, she had been sure as she was separated from Rico, that there was nothing for it but to get it over with as quickly as possible. No matter how much it made her skin crawl.

"I know this may be difficult, Ms. Amendola. Especially given the condition of the body," Det. Sanderson said as he drew back the sheet.

Sleepy swallowed and nodded. "That's him, Detective."

Sanderson raised a brow. "You're sure?"

Sleepy took a long look at the corpse whose face and jaw had been mangled by gunshots at close range, and whose arms had been scorched by fire. "I'm certain that's Armando Fagin. That rosary tattoo around his neck –I'd know it anywhere."

"So, this is Diablo of the East Side Locos?"

"He made some mistakes when he was younger. I had thought… I had thought we had gotten past all of them."

Sanderson watched her reactions carefully. "Tell me, Sleepy-"

"Excuse me?" she said with a trace of quick indignation.

"They do call you 'Sleepy', don't they?"

"Not since I was little. I was a dropsy baby. And as I said, mistakes when we were younger."

"Alright, Ms. Amendola, or may I call you Miranda?"

"Of course, Detective," she said with a smile. "Excuse me, but… would you mind? The sheet?"

The Detective smiled tightly and nodded. His was just as fake as hers. "It's Brain, please." After a moment more, he recalled to pull the sheet over the ruined body.

"Of course, Brian. Is there something else?"

Inwardly, he sighed. As calm as she was, he had no doubt that she was up to her eyebrows in that unbelievable flare up two nights past in the ghettos of Pacoima, but that was not his problem. His problem was the dead end currently laying on the slab, and a lack of any other evidence in his case beyond a drugged-out prostitute's babbling about a four-year old murder the Feds were still pissed about. If he did not turn up something soon, the hold on his prime suspect was going to expire.

He had been about to give Vice another call when a 'Person of Interest' alert had flashed on his desk monitor. The 'registered domestic partner' of his dead lead had just walked into Central Processing after having tried unsuccessfully to bail out his suspect with a credit card from an account that had only been found and frozen a few hours before. Forensic Accounting had almost missed it – who had both a spouse and a 'domestic partner'? His guess was someone concerned with qualified immunity from providing testimony. Though, what this, Miranda 'Sleepy' Amendola, had to do with the murder of Hector Ortiz was still a very vague notion for the Detective. The Feds breathing down his neck certainly thought she was involved though. Too bad they would not say how.

"Well, Miranda, I do have a few other questions, if you have the time?"

Sleepy kept her smile even as her stomach clinched. "Maybe you could just give me your card, and we could find a better time? After all, I just lost my–"

"Registered domestic partner? That's an odd arrangement, especially considering– "

"That he had a wife?" Sleepy said, hoping this would be her way out. "Armando wanted children, and I'm what I suppose you would call, broken. Celia wasn't, and children should have their mother around."

"I'm sorry." Det. Sanderson was indeed shaken from his thoughts. "You're a… very understanding woman."

"I leaned to be," Sleepy said bitterly, fully in character. "Now Detective, really, this is all becoming very upsetting."

"Yes, and again, I'm sorry for your loss," he said, leading her out of the morgue. "But there are a few questions I still need to ask you, and you will have to answer."

Sleepy pouted miserably, seeming on the verge of a breakdown. "If it has to be right now – alright. Ask."

Sanderson cleared his throat, the interview rooms were not far, but the woman looked rooted. Part of him told him to just drag her in there and smack the truth out of her before he turned the cameras on, but there was too much he did not know. "How well are you acquainted with Tomás Rodrigo?"

"Who?" Sleepy said with a sigh and uncomprehending look.

"Sniper, when he was younger," he pressed. If this was an act, then she was good.

"I… I don't know. Maybe? I think I remember a 'Sniper'. Is he kind of tall?"

"No, he's the man who worked at the theater on Olympic with his nephew. Little Viper, I think GTF has the kid down as."

"You mean the Starlight? I… I can't even remember the last time I was there," Sleepy said as she let the pitch in her voice rise. This needed to end, and soon. "What is this about? I don't know any Sniper that works at the Starlight, or his nephew. Now, please."

"How about Hector Ortiz?" he demanded. In another life, this bitch could have won an Oscar, and he was getting sick of this little drama.

"Who?" Sleepy demanded loudly to get attention. She needed to get out of there now.

"A man who was beaten, and then shot to death."

"I don't know anyone who has been beaten and shot!" she shrieked.

"Except for your 'registered domestic partner'," Sanderson snarled. "And I wonder, Ms. Amendola, just how many other bodies in there could you identify? This isn't Burbank, or West Wood, so we can dispense with your bullshit theatrics."

Sleepy froze in a caught expression, then her limbs began to tremble and she completed the scene by collapsing with a wailing shriek. Sanderson almost caught her, but she dodged well and the commotion was enough to get the attention of several morgue attendants who had poked their heads out just in time to witness the large Detective appearing to bully a grieving widow. One of the medical examiners rushed over to intervene on behalf of the sobbing, well dressed, and attractive young woman whose top two blouse buttons had come open during her fall. In the ensuing fiasco, Det. Sanderson had not even been able to foist his card upon Sleepy before several of the doctors from the Medical Examiner's Office had sent him on his way.

Chapter 39

Sleepy allowed herself to be consoled for a half hour until she had been assured that the Detective was not still lurking nearby, and she had been offered an escort to her car, or a ride somewhere if she felt she was too distraught to drive. She left that possibility open to the intern who made a point of being the one to escort her. He stopped smiling though when they arrived at the clean, but old Chrysler LeBaron parked across the street from County with four obvious gang members inside. He did not know what to say. In fact, he was still staring after she thanked him, kissed his cheek, and got in. When Rico brought the engine to life, it startled him enough to at least get out of the way as their LeBaron pulled out and shot away.

"Hey, Sleeps? Who was that nerdy vato?" Snaps asked from the backseat. Unconcerned with an answer, he continued. "Hey, so wassup? Can a homie get some play now that he's out, eh?"

Sleepy spun in her seat and centered the nose of her .38 on Snaps' chest. "Who the fuck you think you're talking to, esé?" she demanded as the homies on either side of Snaps flattened themselves against the side doors.

"Hey, be chill," Snaps pled. "I was just fucking around."

"What? Like you was just fucking around the other night? Fucking around while our homies were dying, eh? Is that what the fuck you were doing, puto?! Diablo's dead because of bitchass little putos like you that ran off to the placas to get arrested when the shit started goin' down. Tú sabes?!"

"Sleeps, clam down, eh," Rico said to her ass where she was halfway into the back seat. It was a nice ass, and at that moment, he really envied Viper.

"Hold that fucking vato!" she barked at Tríste and Sapo, then shoved herself back into her seat. "Calm down? Because of weak little vatos like that, your brother is dead. I just saw him in the morgue, and we are all in a world or shit! Now put the pedal down, esé. Viper's by himself, eh."

"But-" Rico began.

"Vipes got their homie killed, eh! It don't worry you a little that the Chinos want him to come to the funeral. And to bring the puta that the shit was all over?" Sleepy snapped. After that Detective, this little performance would be just too easy as far as she was concerned. Vatos were stupid.

Rico swore. "I didn't think."

"No, no one is ever thinking until it's too late. Tú sabes? Why the fuck you think I always say that?!" Sleepy shouted, shaking the gun for emphasis. "So maybe one of you stupid vatos will listen and try it!" Sleepy sighed and slumped back into her seat, and then looked in the rearview mirror. You vatos can let that dumb little fucker go, eh."

Snaps scowled briefly at his homies as they did. "Hey, hey Sleeps? I...I didn't-"

"Híjo de! Shut up, eh! My pussy's got bigger balls than you, puto," she said and sighed, then turned, gun in hand, but not pointed as anyone specific. "You all think I'm a fucked up vata, huh? Disrespecting you and shit?"

There was a long silence.

"It's okay to say, 'yeah', eh," Sleepy said, and Snaps nodded slightly. "Nah, see, I got love for you little vatos, and I'm tryin' to wake you the fuck up. I'm not trying to see you vatos go out there and get disrespected, tú sabes? Míra, bad as I am, I still got a little love for you, eh. But a bullet? It got no respect for nobody.

"The other night shoulda taught you that, but it don't look to me like it did 'cause you're all, 'just fuckin around', eh? From now on, when I tell you to do something, or especially when Vipes tells you to do something, you do it and don't bullshit.

"Cause it's for your own good. Tú sabes?"

The three nodded and sat back quietly, eventually starting a soft chatter. Sleepy had noticed that Rico had glanced over at her several times.

"What?" she asked gently. "He's your boy, ain't he? And he always been your boy, yeah?"

Rico nodded, not entirely happily.

"You wanna be the out there in the middle of all them Chinos, trying to bullshit them into promising to come save our asses? You know, like if Fences jumps, or them Pirus got homies that are pissed, or just wanna push up on a wounded neighbor? And do it without letting them gooks decide to up and move their village to East Los? And… help us with other shit?" Sleepy said quietly. "Viper's the only one who can be that vato right now. You think he likes it? You think he don't wanna just run off and play house with Bashful?"

Rico grudgingly nodded. "I guess, eh."

"Disrespectful vato… you guess."

"Wha?"

"Your brother, your carnal – he picked a quick death over a slow one for us that night," Sleepy said in a harsh whisper. "Them niggers were taking us bit by bit. Grinding us into the ground with White Fence's help, just 'cause they could. Diablo made Viper turn his back on his whole familía, just to see you safe."

Rico began to glower with shame.

"But what did Viper do, huh? He found a way to save the whole fucking varrio, and keep you safe. How do you not owe him everything? When has he ever done you wrong? Tú sabes?" Sleepy saw that she almost had him. "Now, ask yourself, eh, who's he got to trust now that shit's all on him? My crazy ass? Fuck, I don't even trust me. His tío's slammed, but we'll get to that later. So who?"

Rico looked over, about to speak.

"Oooo, no," she warned. "Don't you even say that dumb slut, Bashful. Let me tell you, that worthless puta is why Green Eyes and Stickers is dead. We are all in a gang a shit, all over that bitch, and it ain't got nothing to do with the other night, eh. I'ma tell you, but for now, you gotta keep it hush, tú sabes?"

Sleepy glanced in the rearview mirror to make certain that the three in the back seat were only pretending not to be listening before she started in on what could sort of be called a 'version' of the truth. It was all mostly the facts, sort of, from a certain point of view.

Chapter 40

Davy parked his tío's old Toyota Celica a block away from where Willow crossed Market. It was nearly 5:30 in the evening, and Sleepy should have gotten there long before he did, but there was no sign of the LeBaron. Outside, the sky was still a darkening grey; despite KTLA's assurances; the heavens were not yet finished with their deluge of L.A.

The trip had been a quiet one except for some low music on the radio to which neither he nor Lulu had paid much attention. The whole way, and for the past day and a half, she had seemed on the verge of saying something: He had come close to asking her what it was, but neither of them had come far enough out of their own thoughts to speak. Now as they sat parked and wearing the nicest dark clothes they owned, it seemed there might be one last moment, but then Jeanie appeared on the distant corner. Davy let out a breath, and opened the door. The moment was gone, and he stepped out into damp air that was not quite a mist.

Davy looked around one more time and cursed. Still no sign of Sleepy. He went around the rear and opened Lulu's door, though she seemed faintly surprised that he had. Her eyes quickly found Jeanie; smaller than she remembered, though the girl's scowl was still in place just as it had been before.

"Davy?" Lulu asked as she stepped out. "Are you sure?"

"No," he said flatly, and swallowed. "But she's seen us, so now it's too late even if this was a mistake."

"Yeah, she has."

Davy's eyes were fixed on the dimunative whiteclad figure in the distance, and so missed the irony that flashed across Lulu's features.

Jeanie eyed Davy and Lulu as they reached her, then gave a soft snort of decision. "At least you're not late. Get in." The girl's English was markedly better when she was calm. Jeanie jerked her head at a dark blue Infinity sedan parked around the corner. Risky was behind the wheel and gave Davy a slight nod of recognition.

"Hey, I thought-" Lulu began.

"You thought? That a shock. No, we not have funeral on street corner. No pour beer for dead homie. We go to temple. Get in," Jeanie snapped not waiting for them to follow.

Davy put a hand on Lulu. "She's just a little kid."

Lulu's lip curled as she looked at him. "Aren't you just Mr. Simpatico, Viper?"

"Davy or David. It… it might help with them, and if Sleepy manages to show up in the next five minutes, call her, 'Miranda', but -"

Lulu jerked away. "Sleepy?" she hissed. "What's that puta doing-"

"Shh!" Davy said, taking her by the arm and leading her over to the waiting sedan. "You gotta be quiet and play along. You aren't really supposed to be here, but… It's complicated."

Lulu wore a mask of composure. "Don't trip," she said, and then got into the backseat without another word.

Davy got into the front, and Risky looked over, then back at Jeanie. He made a vague grunt, and she threw up her hands in response.

"Didn't think I had to tell them wear white to funeral. At least they not late," she declared in full pout.

Risky grunted, then shook his head to dismiss Davy's look of concern.

Chapter 41

They were somewhere in Westminster, but that was all that Davy could be sure of. There were not many signs in English, and none in Spanish. Risky parked in front of a curio shop on a street whose curbs were lined with cars. He got out with a grunt and a nod that indicated the others were to follow. Ten blocks away, they came to a small park filled with several hundred people, all mostly dressed in white. Behind a couple of trees, there was a small shrine with a ceremony going on inside. Davy could faintly hear repetitive chanting over the crowd's soft chatter. Some in the crowd had separated themselves as well, and were repeating quiet prayers, counting them off on strands of beads. Davy had never seen anything like it before, and neither had Lulu.

The two could not have felt more out of place. "I thought you said we weren't late?" Davy asked Jeanie.

"You not," she replied. There was a trace of confusion along with her typical annoyance.

"Okay, but it looks like the funeral is over," Davy pointed out.

Jeanie snorted. "Of course funeral is over. Funeral is only for family. It was this morning. This is memorial," she clarified, and then added, "to show respect. Is what you said. You owe Bao, and want to show respect. Yes?"

Davy nodded.

"So, you here. Duh."

Davy sighed. "Right. Do I speak, or something? Or offer–"

Jeanie stared at him in disbelief. "What you mean, speak? You mean make speech? No."

"Right. Then what do I do? I want–"

"Maybe be quiet? Let other people share grief," Jeanie looked off, but then Risky grunted and nudged her. She huffed, though quietly. In the presence of her elders, her attitude had limits. "Maybe wait for father. If he come out of the temple. Maybe you go say sorry you get his son kill over dumb-bitch. Ask him forgive you. That what you are doing here."

Davy closed his eyes and nodded. "Right."

"Other people have more important thing to say to General. You will probably have a long wait," Jeanie snapped and turned away.

Chapter 42

Three long hours later, Davy, Lulu, Risky, and Jeanie were nearly the last of the remaining mourners in the park, though they had taken shelter under a cypress tree once it had begun to drizzle just after sunset. Lulu's teeth were chattering, and Jeanie had taken a silent post near Risky as she kept her entire body clenched in an effort to stay warm. Davy sensed that putting an arm around Lulu would somehow be inappropriate, though he also could have used the shared bodily warmth. Risky, however, seemed immune to the elements. As though whatever world his mind resided in lacked the concepts of wet, cold, or bored.

Then, for no apparent reason, his head lifted, and he indicated with a grunt that it was time to approach the small shrine. Bao's father did not come out. Davy suspected he was one of the older men that were kneeling rigidly to face an ornate jade box and a large photograph of Bao. Davy had seen few mountains that were more expressionless and solemn than these men.

After a moment, a dour man of middling years with only faint specks of grey at his temples stepped from inside the doorway and into the drizzle. His gaze was fixed on Risky, then it moved over to Davy and Lulu, at last setting briefly on little Jeanie. She shivered away the cold and lifted her chin.

"He with Bao when he died," Jeanie said, indicating Davy. Her breath caught briefly. "Bao not sorry. Go to next life at peace."

There was a moment of silence, and then Davy's voice seemed to startle everyone. "I didn't know him long. He saved my family and friends. He lived without fear and hesitation and he died the same way. I've never met anyone like him, and I probably never will again. I couldn't not come here…"

The man nodded as Davy's speech trailed off. "Then you understand the depth of our loss." His attention turned to Risky. "Did my nephew count this boy as a friend?"

Risky grunted and nodded fractionally.

"Then it is good that he has come. A time of grief is best shared among friends," the man said, and then returned to his station inside the small temple. The rain began to fall more heavily.

After a few more silent moments, a very wet Jeanie complained, "No one else is coming out. We can go now." She looked back and forth between Risky and Davy impatiently. "I hate the rain."

Risky gazed directly at her and said something in Vietnamese.

Jeanie barked profanely at him in Vietnamese. Risky shrugged and turned back towards the park's entrance.

"What'd he say?" Lulu asked as they began to leave.

"He say is tacky to bring dumb-bitch to service," Jeanie began, but Risky smacked her on the back of the head. She scowled, then angled her glare at Davy. "He say: *rain is the handmaiden of the nameless*."

Davy blinked, and took a new measure of Risky.

"Huh?" Lulu said.

Jeanie simply snorted and smiled a look of derision in response.

Chapter 43

Davy and Lulu made it all the way from Market to the eastbound 10 freeway before she broke the silence. They had not even bothered to turn the radio on this time.

"My new name ain't gonna be, 'dumb-bitch'," Lulu said crossly.

"What?" Davy said, lost in his own thoughts.

"That little brat. Ever since that night."

Davy sighed. "Right. No, I know, míja. You did good."

Lulu twitched. "Míja? Oh, now I'm your hína again? Just like that, and you're done with that bitch, Sleepy?"

"Hijo de, I forgot," Davy said to himself, not noticing Lulu's wide-eyed outrage. He turned his phone back on. He sighed at seeing that he had thirty-four new messages, and twice that many waiting texts.

"You forgot?! What'd you forget, eh?" Lulu snapped, and then ground her teeth for having added, 'eh'.

"Not now," Davy growled and hit Sleepy on autodial.

It picked up on one ring.

"Where were you?" Davy said without waiting for her to answer.

"Still tied up with shit at County. It's all fucked up, eh," Sleepy replied. "Where the hell are you? How'd it go? Will they work with us?"

"Davy," Lulu demanded.

"A minute, Lulu, damn!" Davy barked. "Yeah, I'm still here. I'm on the way, and it," he sighed, "it went."

"The fuck does that mean, eh?" Sleepy demanded as a nervous edge crept into her voice.

"It means Bao was the head motherfucker's kid. And I'm officially a friend now – whatever that means," Davy replied with growing frustration. "So, will they do business with us? Probably. Will they come if we snap our fingers? No. If we're really fucked, will they help? Maybe. Three fucking hours standing in the fucking rain, and I got thirty seconds with, I think, someone important."

"So…?"

"So, I don't fucking know!"

"Hey, don't shout at me, esé!" Sleepy barked back. "I been pulling shit together for you all fucking day, then you leave me hanging, looking stupid and go disappear for three fucking hours! It's been about all I could do to keep Rico from leading a search for your dumb ass!"

"What? You all knew where I was," Davy began.

"Yeah, well, he thought maybe the Chino's had it in for you and Bashful. A setup, tú sabes?"

"Why would you tell him some shit like that?" Davy snapped, and then let out a breath as he looked over to Lulu for some commiseration. All he got from her was an angry glare.

"Me? I didn't, -"

"He's too dumb to come up with it on his own," Davy interrupted. "What have you been dong, exactly? And... and what shit at County? Where's my tío?"

"What I told you, eh? Getting shit organized. You did your part, sounds like, and I did mine."

"What shit at County?" Davy repeated through clinched teeth, then took a breath to slow down. "You got my tío out, right?" He glanced over at Lulu and saw that there was at least some concern in her angry glare now.

"I got a few homies out, but the rest are gonna have to chill for a few days, I told you, shit's, -"

"What about my tío?" Davy pressed.

Sleepy sighed. "No, eh."

Davy blinked. "Why not?"

"Tío Tomás isn't home?" Lulu asked, and Davy shook his head.

"We gotta talk about it," Sleepy said.

"We're talking right now."

"Later, eh. In person."

"What's the difference?"

"When Bashful ain't around."

"Bullshit, Sleepy! He's her tío, too. Anything you know, she can hear."

"It's complicated, eh!" Sleepy burst in. "Maybe you trust your dumb little hína with your life, but I don't, or with Sniper's."

"What?! Make sense, Sleeps!"

"It involves her."

Davy missed the rest of what she said, having to drop the phone and swerve as Lulu lunged for it, colliding with him and she shouting, "Fuck that puta!"

"Quitaté!" Davy barked, shoving Lulu back into her seat. "What are you trying to do? Kill us?"

Lulu slouched back in a huff with her arms and legs crossed.

"Sleeps?" Davy said after he retrieved the phone. "Right. Meet me at the Starlight."

"No, eh. Homicide jammed me about that spot," she said quickly. "Serío, it's watched, eh. They were asking about your tío... and – do not say this name out loud right now – Hector Ortiz."

Davy paused. It was familiar but he could not place the name. "Who?"

"That puta Monica's pimp after Snipes kicked her out for fucking around on him," Sleepy replied. "What he gets for trying to play Captain Save-a-Ho. Not even a homegirl, just a puta. Pinchí burro vato." Sleepy paused to laugh. "And I thought he couldn't do no worse than when he was messing with that bitch from Fences, eh. But that's Snipes. He don't never want the good thing that's staring him right in the face. Stupid vato."

"Sleeps?"

"Huh? Oh, shut up, eh. Just dump Bashful off and hoof it over to Solo's spot. I'll be there and don't trip. We'll get this all sorted out," Sleepy said tiredly. "Then we can crash for a minute."

"So this ride's hot? What about-"

"Nah, it's cool if Bashful or you drive it, just not to meet anyone, eh," Sleepy said. "Tú sabes."

"Símon," Davy replied with a grunt of agreement before disconnecting. He looked over, but it was clear that Lulu was ignoring him. He sighed again. Whatever Sleepy had given him two days ago had worn off, and he no longer had the energy to deal with Lulu's moods. He knew that if they could just get through the next few days, everything would be better. He vowed to find a way to make Lulu smile again. He wanted to tell her that they were going to be leaving together like she had wanted, and that everything would be all right and just like it used to be. Soon, he promised himself. He would tell her soon.

Chapter 44

The walk had helped, but Davy's eyes still burned with weariness. It was nearly midnight, and he sagged further as he sighted Sleepy standing rigidly on the stoop of the crash pad with her arms folded. She was bathed in a harsh glow of a streetlamp, and there was only one light on inside the house. It appeared that again, he alone would continue to be denied while the rest of the world was cradled in the gentle embrace of sleep.

She peered down at him with an arched brow as he reached the front of the stoop. "Sup? Wasso funny, eh?"

Davy did not let go of his half-smile, but shook his head. "I just figured out why they called you Sleepy. You don't."

"That's not why," she said sharply, growing colder and more imperious than a marble stature of Athena. She led the way inside without another word.

Davy cursed silently as he followed on into the lighted room, wondering as well just what fresh hell awaited him. On the table was a mostly full bottle of Jack Daniels. There were no glasses or mixers present. A single bare bulb hung off-center from the spackled ceiling, casting a sharp glow over the room's smattering of third-hand furniture.

"Sit," Sleepy instructed, nodding at the ratty couch against the wall by the door, and then she took a pull from the bottle. "Better."

"Right," Davy said, sitting back and kicking a foot up on the empty industrial sized wooden wire-spool that served as a coffee table.

Sleepy took a moment, then pushed off from leaning against a card table that looked to be on the verge of collapse. "They got your tío down for a hot one. There's other shit, but it doesn't immediately concern you."

"What do you-" Davy began, starting to get up.

"Sientaté! Fuck!" Sleepy snapped, rubbing uselessly at her headache. "We'll get to the rest later... If it still matters."

"I don't understand-"

"Cause I ain't told you nothing yet, eh," Sleepy interrupted with a huff. "Por ejemplo, if you took Bashful and ran off to play house someplace that ain't never heard of David Rodrigo and Louisa Sandoval, that would solve a lot of shit, and none of the rest would matter to you no more."

Davy stood all the way up with an expression of disbelief. "You do remember that was exactly what you stopped me from doing two days ago, right? If all you needed was–"

"Caiyaté! I said it would solve a lot, not that it was what we needed to do. Now look, eh, some Homicide placa jammed me up at County over Hector Ortiz."

"That's the one that fucked with Lulu?" Davy said, now fairly certain how the pieces were arranged on the board.

"What do you know about that?" Sleepy asked warily.

Davy closed his eyes and shook his head. "Nothing. Just that my tío was gone for a couple of a days, then Lulu came to stay with us for good." He snorted and shook his head. "And Diablo and everyone started showing up right after. So, my tío must of popped that punk; his old homie Diablo helped him clean up or something, and now he's slammed... And that's because I didn't pop that bitch when I had the chance. Fuck."

Sleep reared her head back with a puzzled smile. "Close, míjo. He didn't call Diablo." She winked at Davy. "But you didn't pop what bitch? You were just a little vato."

"Monica," Davy said, seeing the woman before him a little more clearly. Diablo would have never thought to turn the Starlight into a money laundering operation, but the huntress in the dark before him would have, and she certainly would have no problem cutting down whatever stood in her way to sinking her claws in whatever she wanted.

Sleepy paused to think, and then shook her head. "Yeah, but she wasn't there, eh." Realization bloomed across her features. "But them two fools jammed her the next day. That's why the placa just jammed me about D, Snipes, and you. Fucking rat bitch!" she snarled and kicked over a chair, then spun on Davy. "I ain't never heard nothing about you almost smoking that puta."

"It was near last Christmas. She tried to roll the spot," Davy said. "I never thought, -"

"A junkie bitch rats, and it surprises you?" Sleepy snorted. "You're smart, Viper, but you still got a lot to learn." Her eyes bulged. "Oh shit, eh! Menace is on standby!"

Sleepy waved away his questions as she hurriedly tapped the autodial on her cell. "Hey, nah," she said in it. "It's all cool. Don't trip."

"What the fuck was that?!" Davy demanded as she disconnected.

"The fuck was what?!" Sleepy snarled. "Bitch was the only one there the night that ain't either dead, in jail, or standing in front of you, eh."

"So what? You were just gonna kill her, you loca bitch?!"

The cold face of an angry goddess descended over Sleepy. "No, Viper. You were. Your tío's staring at the needle, and there's only one witness that can put it in his arm. You run away with that witness and start over where the placas can't find her? That works... so long as she ain't the one snitching in the first place. A bullet in her head works, too."

"She's not a rat." Davy said calming down only a little.

A little arrogant contempt found its way into Sleepy's impassive gaze. "You willing to bet Sniper's life on that? All our lives, eh? How much does she know? How bad did she want revenge when she thought you were dead, eh? Maybe she made a call to the placas before she got Green Eyes to drive her off into that shit, just in case. Make sure her payback stuck if she couldn't handle it herself?"

Davy shook his head and looked away. "It wasn't Diablo was it?"

"Wasn't him, what?" Sleepy said, but then nodded. "Oh, your shit? He made that call, but... there was discussion."

"Right. But how often did he not do what you told him to do?"

103

"When he asked? Not often. But then, I'm not often wrong, eh. Your tio, Snipes, he called me, not Diablo"

Davy waved her off. "Oh, I got that. But you were wrong two days ago, just like you're wrong about Lulu now."

"Oh, I was, eh?" the bit snake asked as she uncoiled to strike.

Davy faced her squarely. "Maybe not about green lighting me when Solo called, even though that whole thing still stinks the more I think about it. I did fuck up big."

"So, what then?" she snarled.

Davy nodded. This would work, since if it did not, he and Lulu would probably soon be filling a hole somewhere. "You told him to keep me in the dark. He trusted me; you didn't. If he hadn't, none of that cluster fuck in Ontario would have gone down, and we still might have made it back, but with wheels and soon enough that he wouldn't be lying in the morgue like he is 'cause he had to stick around to lead change. Instead, he listened to you, and we are where we are."

Sleepy relented. "Maybe. Maybe it woulda gone different."

There was something in the way she had said that Davy did not like, and his eyes narrowed. But before he could say anything, she stabbed a finger at him

"Ah! That right there. You're too smart for your own good, sometimes, figuring things out, but not quite figuring them. You fuck shit up at the last second because someone told you a little too much," Sleepy accused. "Stop guessing Viper, and let this one go. It was some complicated shit that didn't work out the way it was supposed to at all. Picking at it will just get people killed who, unlike you, did not get caught doing their dumb shit."

Davy was confused, but he shook it away. "Right, whatever. But this with Lulu, it's jumping to a conclusion, and you said yourself the place is being watched. It would be the stupidest thing -"

Sleepy shrugged. "Not really. So, Moni's a rat. We snatch her up and pop her. That's Bashful's sister, eh. And say what you want, that little chica is damaged. No telling exactly what she'll do." Sleepy came over and wrapped around him; passion in her eyes. "What if she sees us and gets jealous, eh? 'Cause I come with the territory, tú sabes?"

Davy looked at the terribly dangerous creature before him. "That night, Lulu told me that I should have killed Monica. As for the other," he smiled sheepishly, "sucks to say, but much as I'd love to learn everything you could teach me, -"

"Oh no, míjo." Her grip on his body tightened. "It don't work that way. I come with the territory. If you ain't fucking me, then I'm just a bitch telling another bitch what to do, and ain't nobody gonna respect that, tú sabes?"

Davy sighed. It looked like everything was going to work out, and he supposed there were far worse sacrifices he could be forced to make. "But none of that's a good enough reason-"

"No, you're right. It's not, eh," Sleepy replied as warmth began to trickle into her features. "You're learning." She flicked her eyes towards the adjacent room. "C'mon stupid. When I'm done, I don't want to be too far from a bed to crash in, eh."

"Uh, okay," Davy said as she took him by the hand.

He paused her as they reached the door. "You called Menace off before I'd said anything."

Her bewitching smile widened, and her eyes sparkle mischievously. "Just figured that out, eh? Now shut the fuck up. Your older homegirl's got a few more things to teach you, and you better be paying attention, esé. The rest of this shit can all wait 'till you wake up."

Davy missed that last vicious glint in her eye as she turned into the darkness.

Chapter 45

Til you wake up, turned out to be dusk, two days later. Davy woke to find Sleepy long gone and the house silent. His body was rested, but his head still felt thick. A long hot shower improved his state somewhat, and so did two spoonful's of instant coffee in a Pepsi. Halfway dressed, he flopped down on the ratty couch outside the bedroom and noticed his phone's message light was on. He woke the device up and swiped open his phone app, and then sighed. There were twenty-seven texts from Lulu, two missed calls from a number that he did not recognize – so likely Sleepy using burners – but neither had a message. Then he noticed the Auto-Tune app in the corner. The color had changed.

Davy was by no means a master hacker, but he did know how to download an app that watched for malware. The one he was currently using had changed color, bringing him fully awake. A few more taps revealed that his phone had been remotely turned into an eavesdropping device a day and half ago. He let out a small breath of relief that all anyone would have heard on it would have been his snores.

He took a sip of his coffee-soda and set the trace program to work – the data was still going somewhere, and digital footprints were not that hard to find. Possible suspects ran though his mind. At best, it would be Sleepy, but then that made little sense – she was paranoid, but that would be too much. Maybe Risky and Jeanie investigating him? Or, his eyes widened at the thought, god forbid, Lulu. He assured himself that she was not that tech savvy.

When the trace gave a result, he did spit out his drink, though he tried to set the can down. It was a private security firm with a blocked IP address. An instant later, his phone rang. The caller ID was blocked. Davy mouthed a curse, and took the call.

"Hello?"

"Hello," came an authoritative voice. "This is LAPD Homicide Detective Sanderson. To whom am I speaking?"

Davy took a breath. "The same person you've been listening to for the last day and a half. I always thought you guys were supposed to be like super-placas, or do you just get off listening to teenagers snore?"

There was a dark chuckle on the other end of the line. "I'm going to give you the chance to start this conversation over. Step outside. A unit will be by to pick you up in a few minutes, Viper."

Instinct took over. "Sorry, but you're speaking to David Rodrigo. I don't know anyone called Viper, and I have nothing to say to you."

And with that, Davy hung up, then smashed his phone beyond repair or data retrieval. It had been a private security firm, not the LAPD, so they did not have a warrant. So, without an original source once they had a warrant, he knew that any data that they had pulled off his phone so far was unusable in court... he hoped. God only knew what Lulu had put in those twenty-seven texts; probably something incriminating, but it was too late to check as he flushed the bits of phone down the toilet. A few seconds after that, he was out the back door and over the fence into the alley at a dead run.

Chapter 46

Twenty-five minutes later, Davy burst into the lobby of the Starlight Theater. He was breathless and staggering from the four-mile run. He gulped air, and then noticed that the theater was empty – strange for this time of day.

"Lulu!" he shouted hoarsely.

He had to shout several more times before the door to his office opened and she emerged. Davy began to run to her, but stopped short as a tall white man in a suit followed her out. The man rested a hand on her shoulder, and stopped her.

"Davy, -" she began, but the man interrupted by pushing her aside.

"Mr. Rodrigo," he said with a confident swagger as he left Lulu behind the concessions counter and stepped into the open of the lobby. He appeared very comfortable in his charcoal-grey suit, tie and loafers.

"Detective Sanderson," Davy replied. Lulu's expression was unreadable, but she looked as though she had been crying not long before.

"Really, Mr. Rodrigo, you needn't have run all the way here." The detective motioned towards the doors as a patrol unit slowed and parked directly outside. "As I said, they would have been more than happy to give you a lift."

Davy nodded wanly. Why go kicking down doors when they could just get him to run right to them with a simple phone call? He knew that he had to be smarter.

"Like I told you before, Detective, I don't have anything to say to you."

"Standing on your right to remain silent?" Det. Sanderson asked with a trace of a smile.

"That's right."

Sanderson shook his head sadly as a uniformed officer entered the theater. "Well, you're not under arrest, so you don't have that right, son."

Davy did not miss a beat, though he doubted it would be this simple. "If I'm not under arrest, then I'm free to leave. C'mon, Lulu, let's go."

"Well, I'm afraid you're not free to leave, either, son," Det. Sanderson said as he beckoned the officer forward. "You see, you're a material witness in an ongoing investigation, so you'll be getting that second chance I told you about earlier when we spoke."

Davy flinched as the officer passed him and collected Lulu. "Wha?"

Sanderson came over and drew Davy aside, putting a large hand on his shoulder. "Don't worry. We won't be detaining Ms. Sandoval for long, and I certainly doubt CPS will be much interested in doing more than keeping her overnight for observation, and counseling. Seventeen is a little old for a placement. "I doubt they'll even contact you."

Davy opened his mouth, but the Detective turned him so that they stood facing each other. "And don't worry. Officer Davis, here, is a certified CPS advocate," he said, indicating the heavyset black female patrol officer who had entered the theater without Davy noticing. She looked middle-aged and in no way suited to be any child's advocate.

Davy looked back to find the Detective smiling.

"You see, son? Everything's above board."

"Right," Davy said, glancing around the otherwise empty theater. This was not going to end well, he knew. "So, to what do you think I'm a material witness?"

Detective Sanderson laughed. "My, that's some proper English. Where'd you learn that little trick? Nah, never mind. It'll make you more credible on the witness stand when you testify, though."

"Right," Davy replied. "It's too bad I don't know anything."

The detective nodded with mock admiration. "Do you know where you were yesterday afternoon?"

"No," Davy said honestly. "I was asleep all yesterday."

Sanderson nodded again, and the next thing Davy knew, he was staring up from the floor and seeing stars. Pain registered in his cheek from where he had been hit, but before his vision fully returned, something heavy smashed into him, flipping him over onto his face as he felt his arms nearly jerked out of their sockets then the pinch of handcuffs locking his wrists together behind his back. A move to rise was met with a hard knee in his back. All he could see were the Detective's loafers.

"Obstruction, resisting arrest, assault on a peace officer, beat within an inch of your life in a broom closet in Central, and then fucked by an angry black man?" Sanderson said. "Yes, we can go that route, too, if you want to keep on pissing me off. The lump of shit my neighbor's dog left on my lawn this morning is more important than you. Comprendo? You little fucking turd?"

After a moment, Sanderson ordered Davy be brought to a sitting position. The officer still held him by the scruff of the neck, and Davy heard the clack of her collapsible baton being whipped to lock at full extension.

"Now, let's try again, shall we? Where were you yesterday afternoon?"

"I told you," Davy said with an aching jaw. "Asleep."

Detective Sanderson booted him in the stomach, and Davy collapsed with a groan, but was quickly jerked back upright.

"Asleep, where?" Sanderson demanded.

It took a moment for Davy to get his wind back. "Tony Escobedo's house and you know that."

"No," Det. Sanderson said, kneeling to fill Davy's face. "I know that your phone was there, you lying little shit. But that doesn't mean you were there. And it sure as hell doesn't mean that bitch, Miranda Amendola was there with you, does it?"

Davy gritted his teeth. "Miranda was there when I went to sleep two days ago, and the bed was still warm when I woke up this morning. That's all I —"

"Bullshit!" Sanderson roared and backhanded him hard enough to send Davy into a bouncing roll. "Keep playing these games," he menaced with a knee on Davy's chest – he snatched Davy's nose and twisted until he made the boy cry out. He paused, and then twisted violently until the snap was audible. He stood before any blood got on his trousers and stared at Davy in disbelief. "Have you dumb gang-banging mother fuckers really gotten this arrogant? What you and that Amendola bitch did yesterday in broad daylight? And you don't think I'll just put a round in your head and drop you in a hole?"

Davy sneezed blood all over himself and grunted as he was sat up again. The officer had a vice-like grip on the back of his neck, her nails digging into his flesh. "I don't know what you're talking about," he got out, then winced as her nails drew blood. "I was crashed out. I don't know anything about anything...Miranda... did. That's it."

Sanderson nodded to the officer to release her grip. "No, it's not. See, son, your precious little Sleepy is telling a very different story, and so's your friend, Jesse Valdez a.k.a. Menace. Tony Escobedo would probably be telling us a different story, too, but well, I think you know what part of Ontario his body was dumped in."

"What?" Davy blurted, trying to sort through the madness of the past week, but only grasping air.

"They both say you were the shooter," Sanderson continued. "Officer, do you have a GSR kit in your cruiser?"

She nodded.

"Why don't you go grab it?" Sanderson suggested, and she left quickly.

The detective smiled. "Alright, son. Now, we both know that test is going to come back positive, and when it does, we'll go through all the formalities, but that needle will be as good as in your arm." He knelt and placed a hand on Davy's shoulder. "Now, we've got a few minutes before she gets back. Before it's all over. It's just you and me, and now's the time for you to say something to save your life."

Davy let out a long breath, and his words were clear and certain. "I don't know what you are talking about. I didn't kill anyone -"

"Son-" his grip tightened painfully, "-You're not helping yourself. Not when you lie to me. Now, you seem like a smart kid-" he paused to lock eyes with Davy.

"Who the fuck is dead? Davy blurted. "The mayor?! What the hell is this?!"

Sanderson smiled to himself; sure that he had turned the corner with the boy. "No, son. A witness in a safe house in Rialto. A witness in a capital murder case concerning the death of a federal informant who had been executed by contract killers on orders from the Mexican Mafia." At least, that was the bullshit the FBI had fed him, so why not repeat it?

Davy blinked. "I do not know anything about that," he said sincerely.

Sanderson relented after a moment. "You know, I believe that you think you don't, son. And you may very well just be being set up here." The Detective leaned in closer. "And it might not just be you that's getting left with someone else's bag of shit to hold."

"Detective, I don't, -"

"I know, I know," Sanderson said sympathetically. "But maybe your way out of this is more than just a way out for you. It could be a way out for your uncle, too."

And then the pieces began to fit for Davy, or at least some of them. Sleepy and/or Menace had killed Monica, obviously. Menace was her creature, that he already knew as well, but both of them rolling? Doubtful. Still, something much larger had to be connecting it all, but what?

"I can see that it's coming together for you son," Sanderson prompted. "Asleep for a day and a half? Sounds like the bitch drugged you and left you alone with GSR from that little adventure in Pacoima – you're a Loco, you were there, and I don't much care when you little shit birds kill each other. But, you have no alibi – for anything. Bad for you. Worse for you, Miranda's GSR test came back negative, and like I told you, she's got quite a story."

Davy slumped, not sure what direction, if any, led out of this mess. "Right," he said, playing for time more than anything else. The Detective glanced past Davy and shook his head. Davy looked back to see the officer who had silently entered with a small box nod and head back outside.

"So, Monica got killed?"

"Yes. Monica Sandoval was shot to death in the bedroom of a safe house, and so were two uniformed LAPD officers," Det. Sanderson replied. "Do you see now, how if you choose to be helpful, there's quite a bit of latitude in how we return the favor?"

Davy nodded, but he knew none of this really added up. Two placas dead in what looked to the rest of the world like an EME hit, and all he had gotten as a named suspect were a few bumps and threats? No, this asshole was just feeling around in the dark. Then Davy saw something move in the shadows of the hallway off the lobby and did everything he could not to smile.

"So, what do you want? I wasn't lying; I really don't know anything about what Sleepy was up to today, or yesterday. And, I haven't seen Menace in–"

"I know. And that's okay. Just tell me what you do know," Sanderson said. It was always so easy to get these little bastards to flip.

"I know the cuffs are kind of tight," Davy suggested.

Sanderson considered him for a moment, but then nodded. "You understand that emotions can run a little high when it comes to cop-killers?" he said as he unhooked Davy.

"Right, right," Davy said as he rubbed some feeling back into his wrists and hands. "Well, I know a lot of things. Where would you like me to start?"

"Good, and I like your attitude, son. A joint OCT-LAPD investigation collapses, and a lot of people want answers. Let's start with what you know about Armando Fagin, aka Diablo's, relationship with Comadari."

"You mean the EME's number two in L.A?" Davy said as he wondered what was taking Rico so long. Also, what was OCT? It sounded like the Feds.

"Exactly, have you met him?" Sanderson asked eagerly. Had he finally found the light at the end of this sewage tunnel? It even briefly occurred to him to actually try to help the little maggot in front of him, though he dismissed that idea quickly enough.

"Well...No! Don't shoot!" Davy shouted, hoping maybe that would get Rico's dumb ass to pull the damned trigger.

Sanderson whirled, drawing his personal gun, but it was too late as a shot from Rico's Desert Eagle .50 cal caught the Detective squarely in the chest, launching the man into a tumbling sprawl. Sanderson was not moving.

Rico, pale and trembling, stepped from the shadows. "D… did I."

"No, shoot the fucking door! He had a vest on, or there'd be parts of him everywhere," Davy snapped. "Run, and ditch the gun. Go, you slow-ass vato!"

"I–"

"Now!"

Rico fired again, blowing out a good chunk of the front door's Plexiglass with his small cannon. The officer outside broke off her dash. She proned out, and took cover.

"Help! Help!" Davy shouted as he made urgent shooing motions towards Rico, and then ran for the remains of the front door. "Help!" he continued to shout, hoping not to get shot by the placa outside for his trouble. *Why not?* "Officer down!"

An arm jerked Davy over in front of the paneling outside beneath the ticket window as he passed. "How many?" the officer snarled.

"I think, just one. I was, -"

"Shut up and stay here!" she barked, then advanced in a crouch into the theater with her weapon drawn.

Davy was off like a bolt of lighting the moment she was out of sight.

Chapter 47

For the first few blocks, Davy ran in no other direction than 'away'. There was blood all down the front of his shirt, and he was shaking with wide eyed adrenaline as he ducked into a random alley. He crouched, panting, as he heard the high-pitched wail of an approaching siren. A dog barked loudly and he nearly filled his shorts. He flattened himself against the brick wall behind a dumpster. Davy took a few more breaths and swallowed, trying to settle himself. Whatever Sleepy had given him was not out of his system; lingering around just enough to make his thoughts feel dangerously slow.

Davy blew out a breath, and then was running again, now towards the barking dog. This was still the varrio, and everyone hated the placas. He needed clothes and to get cleaned up. Even if Sleepy and Menace had been caught and rolled, which he still doubted, there was one place he might be able to hide out. He could only hope that Rico also had some secret corner to disappear into as well. The world had started spinning out of control four days ago, and now they were all the way to killing placas and government witnesses? It was time to get off this ride.

At the end of the alley was a high wooden fence and the source of the barking. Davy hoisted himself up to peer over. He found a good-sized pit bull chained up in the back yard of a small one-story house in a row of adjoining house. Its lights were off. All the dog was doing was alerting the world to his owner's absence.

The dog's chain looked long enough to let him roam the back yard and come within a foot of the fences. A plan formed for Davy, and he returned to the dumpsters. After a bit of rooting, he found his buried treasure — a Hefty bag full of restaurant trash. Along with the bag, Davy drug a wooden pallet over to the fence and propped it up as a ladder. When he reappeared atop the fence, the barking dog rushed over in defense of his territory.

Davy hoisted the bag, and the dog's barking slowed. His stubby hindquarters began to wag. After a few rounds of, *Who's a good boy?*, to associate himself with the tempting smells, Davy tore open the bag and dumped the contents in a corner of the yard. An instant later, the dog had its nose buried in the refuse and Davy was over the fence making his way to the rear sliding glass door.

The dog looked over briefly, wearing an empty soda cup for a hat and licking chow mein noodles off the top of his snout, but then decided that Davy was not more interesting than his new bounty. The sliding door was latched, but Davy made quick work of it with his pocket knife. He paused to listen as he entered the house, and then relaxed in its silence.

His first stop was the kitchen and its refrigerator. He made short work of a pack of cold cuts and a Budweiser. A search of the pantry revealed a stash of Twinkies, Snickers, and Ding Dongs, and from that, he was finally able to put his grumbling stomach to rest.

His next stop was the master bedroom. Whoever lived here –a nice-looking Paisa family by the pictures on the wall– had a good supply of work clothes that were only a little too big. After picking what he needed to appear presentable, he dumped his dirty clothes in the hamper and hit the shower. He was careful not to make much mess in hopes that the break-in would go unnoticed. His stained clothes vanishing into a stranger's wash would do, and he did still have a call to make.

The shower helped a great deal, as did the OJ he opted for instead of more beer as he dialed a number he hoped he remembered correctly. The call did not pick up until the sixth ring.

"Solicitation is especially unwelcome, and at the dinner hour, I've a mind to report your number to the Better Business Bureau," Ms. Cohen stated sharply, and then the line went dead.

Davy shrugged. It could have been worse, at least she was home, and so he dialed again. This time, it took until the eighth ring, and when the call connected, there was only silence on the other end of the line.

"Ms. Cohen? This is David Rodrigo, and I apologize for the late hour."

"Well, I should hope so. This is hardly a fit hour for a social call," she interrupted. "Raul Sanchez is some relative of yours I presume? I sincerely hope you had not thought that I would recognize the name."

"No." He paused, forcing back the bad habits of using words like *um*. "It's a little complicated."

"I would expect, so. As I said it is quite late, and after such a length of time–" she tsked, "-state your business, or I shall end this call presently."

Davy took a breath. "My uncle Tomás was detained by the police several days ago, and earlier today, there was an incident at the Starlight."

"Oh my, how unseemly," Ms. Cohen interrupted. "How unusual that the police have not yet notified me of any disturbance on my property. Was there damage?"

"Nothing too serious, just the doors, and whatever mess the LAPD makes now that it's a crime scene."

"Crime scene?! Oh my, how upsetting and disgraceful. Oh, I must call my agents at once."

"Ms. Cohen, I… was hoping to speak with you in person."

"To what end?" she replied, clearly eager to end the conversation.

"I was present at the incident. And, I think it would be best to give a report to you, and whoever you, -"

"Whomever, child. Did you learn nothing in your time with me?"

"Whomever. I apologize, but, whomever other agents you see fit... to utilize." Davy winced. He had forgotten just how difficult Ms. Cohen's version of 'proper English' was to use.

There was silence on the line, then. "Were you involved?"

Davy chose his words carefully. "I was a witness, yes."

"Mmm, so in up to your eyebrows, then?"

Davy cleared his throat. "Yes."

"Are the police seeking you?"

"Probably, but just for questioning."

"Very well. Be warned, I shall not harbor a fugitive, however, I rather prefer to be fully informed of matters concerning my estate, and since the police have not seen fit to appraise me properly, and you have, I shall give preference to you. Present yourself immediately."

And the line went dead.

Chapter 48

Roughly an hour and a ditched stolen car later, Davy arrived on foot at the gates of the Cohen estate in Glenwood Oaks. Night had fallen, and in the silence of those secluded avenues, the boy felt as though he had crossed some unknown and vast gulf that at least temporarily separated him from the madness that had become his life. He looked up at the soft whir of a camera mounts motor as it focused its cyclopean gaze upon him. Without any further warning, the great ivy covered iron gates swung outward. For just a moment, he hesitated, briefly daunted by the prospect of placing himself into the clutches of what powers lay within the walled manor. Davy shook his childish thoughts away.

Beyond lay a rich, old, white woman, not the devil. His trek to the front doors, even after three years was a familiar one. Though it was dark, the grounds appeared well kept up, and the portico was swept and clean. Davy rapped on the door with the wrought iron knocker in the lion's mouth twice. A few seconds later, a dim light shone through the front windows of the foyer. One of the large doors opened without a creak. Its gap was quickly filled with a sandyhaired man in his twenties who wore a servant's livery. The man looked put out.

"David Rodrigo?" he asked.

"I am, himself, -" Davy began, but the man rolled his eyes.

"Whatever, dude," he said. "Save it for Ms. C. Bad enough that old bat wakes me up with a bell – yeah, a bell, bro – and has me dress up in this get up at damn near midnight," the man eyed Davy. "Huh, you don't exactly looked dressed for her Majesty to *receive you*."

"Right," Davy replied, dismissing the urge to kick this valley-boy douche bag in the nuts. Then something else occurred to him. "Is… Selene home?"

"Huh? Who?" The man scratched himself.

"Ms. Cohen's niece?"

"Oh, nah, bro. Up in Seattle, I think," he said and snorted up some mucus then cast about for a place to spit it. Finding none, he swallowed it. "College, or some shit. I guess that's why me and Rach and the rest are hired here now. We get to play dress up for the Lady of the manor. Whoopee !" he laughed. "I swear, I should get an Emmy for all this bullshit. Hey, were you part of an old cast? What were you, the ethnic houseboy? That would just be too funny."

"Right. Where's Ms. Cohen?"

"Pfft. Whatever, dude," the man scoffed. "She's in the parlor down the east wing's hallway off to the left. Third door. Go give the old bat a good rodgering," he said with a terrible British accent.

Chapter 49

Davy paused at the parlor door to collect himself, and then knocked twice. There was a pause, and then the instruction to enter. Davy only made it two steps into the room before he stopped. There, sitting in a high-backed chair, which her back did not touch, was Ms. Cohen and her arresting gaze. Her hair was pulled into a tight bun, and she was dressed to receive. She shifted her attention to a cup of tea, and Davy found that he could move again. She took a delicate sip, paused, and set her cup on a plate, then rose gracefully to face Davy. Her poise and presence seemed to drop the room's temperature several degrees. Perhaps to the ass in the foyer, it was all just so much silly costuming and nonsense. That man could not appreciate this remnant of an age of dignity that clung on still, despite the world's attempts to cast it aside in favor or all things brighter, louder, and plastic.

"I had such hopes for you, young David, "she sighed." And now you return to us in such a state of disrepair as to be almost unrecognizable. Are those tattoos? Very unseemly," she said with detached sadness. "Give me your account."

"I'm sorry."

"Mmm, is that an apology for, or description of your condition?"

"Neither," Davy said, recognizing what Ms. Cohen counted as playful banter. "Only for the late hour."

Ms. Cohen nodded. "I must say, you do understand some things better than most. If not the why, then at least that they must be maintained. Let us now be direct; your condition begs explanation, as does your claim of urgency."

Davy cleared his throat, and she glared, "My uncle, your employee, Tomás Rodrigo, has been arrested on suspicion of murder."

"And this purported crime occurred on my property?" Ms. Cohen touched her breastbone with her finger tips as she gasped lightly.

"No," Davy assured quickly. "It was several years ago, and not near the Starlight. The dead child molester in question was also a Federal informant, so-"

Ms. Cohen waved him off and sat. "I've no need for the gruesome details. "Come and sit." She let out a small laugh and poured a second cup of tea. Davy hated tea, but he sipped with a fixed smile of appreciation. After a few moments, Ms. Cohen set her cup down as well. "I must say it is rather shocking to discover a killer in my employ. Though, of more concern is that your presence protends even more dire news?"

"My Uncle Tomás is not a killer," Davy said flatly.

"That statement speaks volumes," Ms. Cohen said with a trace of smile.

"As does yours," Davy replied, not really understanding what volumes she was talking about.

Her eyes glistened with amusement. "Such a bright young man. Yes—" she considered him for a long moment, "-perhaps your uncle is worthy of support, again. Despite his unavoidable deficiencies, I have always found your uncle to be a man of great character, and so let us press on to other matters."

117

Davy nodded with a little surprise, sensing there was something he was missing, but went on to summarize the events of Monica's death and the detective's shooting.

Ms. Cohen frowned as Davy concluded. "I suspect there are a great many details being wisely omitted for my benefit, though, I must admit these circumstances do warrant your presence as you have attended. However, the hour is late, and there is no more to be done this night. Repair to the foyer. I shall send the girl to see you to a suitable guest room. You will be meeting with my attorneys tomorrow, before lunch. You will apprise them of whatever details they feel are necessary, of course. They shall advise me on the most prudent course, afterwards."

She stood, and Davy stood with her. "Thank you, Ms. Cohen…"

"Is there something else?" There was hesitance in her voice.

Davy smiled awkwardly. "I…don't think that I ever thanked you, or really appreciated the things you were teaching me back then. If I ever thought badly of you, then I apologize."

"An odd thing for a man to say." A softness graced the elderly woman's features. "Quite sentimental, but not…unappreciated. I never felt my work with you was quite finished, and so now, perhaps again. Rest well, and we shall see what the new day portends."

Davy retreated politely and shut the door behind him. As he stood in the poorly lit hallway, his problems no longer seemed so insurmountable.

He wondered briefly why he had ever been afraid of Ms. Cohen. The world was simply an ugly and violent place; it was only that she had chosen to resist it with dignity, and had the strength to hold her course.

Davy was grateful he found the foyer empty. He walked over to the display case and smiled at seeing the pewter figurine of the bird on the verge of flight from years ago. He briefly hoped that his stay would last through lunch tomorrow so that he would have a chance to ask about Selene. And then he laughed. Where had his worries gone? Coming to see Ms. Cohen had forced him to be calm and control himself.

As he thought about his situation, new found a new clarity. With Monica dead, the case against Tomás should fall apart, and as Lulu's legal guardian, at worst, she would have to spend a few weeks at a CPS house before they were all back together again. Sanderson had obviously been lying about Sleepy. She and Menace were either dead, or in the wind. If it had been anything else, Sanderson would not have been wasting his time on that ridiculous interrogation at the Starlight. He must have just been there for Lulu, and like a moron, Davy had run smack into him by chance. Anything else, and Davy would have been dragged out of bed long before he woke up, and tossed into some subterranean holding cell. Now, Sanderson was either dead, or in the hospital, and with any luck, Rico had vanished as well, completely unseen.

Davy made a soft snort and shook his head. It looked like his time with the Locos was over whether he liked it, or not. Not quite the end he had expected, but an end none the less. Could it really all be so simple? And if Ms. Cohen gave him and Tomás a little help to push past the last of the details…Yes, the morning would be a good one.

"Excuse me? "Rachel said.

Davy turned abruptly, jerked from his thoughts. The woman before him wore a rumpled black and white maid's uniform, and slippers. A very skimpy maid's uniform, Davy could not help noticing. Her face lacked makeup, and her shoulder length blonde hair was pulled back with a scrunchy.

Davy guessed that she was somewhere in her early twenties. She had a trim, if otherwise unremarkable, figure, and a pleasant disposition for the late hour.

"You're Rachel?" Davy guessed from the doorman's 'Rach'.

She brightened slightly at the sound of her name. "Yes, I am," and then with an *oops* smile, added, "I'm a little surprised Ms. C remembered. I'm usually just, *'girl'*. Like an extra on a set. Girl-4 played by Rachel Vinson. But that far down, no one's still reading the credits, ya know?"

"I guess," Davy replied. "I don't think I ever really thought about it."

Rachel shrugged her shoulders happily enough. "Old dreams. The guest rooms are upstairs. Have you ever been here before?"

"A few years ago."

"Oh, okay, so you like, know where everything is, right?"

Davy nodded. "Breakfast is still at 7:15 sharp?"

Mmm-hmm, Rachel nodded. "And tea at 10:45. You know how to play it out. I swear, that woman is so paranoid, but... I guess I understand."

"Some things don't change," Davy said eager for a bed, and not for another disgruntled employee. "Right, and I'm sorry that I woke everyone up. That other guy-"

Rachel waved him off. "I was up. All we have here is DSL dialup, so I can't go online 'till after 11," again she shrugged, "and I can use the break. And don't worry about Jimmy. He sucks."

Davy laughed. "I got that."

Rachel paused and twisted her lips. "Hey, you think you're going to be here for a while?"

"I don't really know, probably not more than a day or two, why?"

Rachel looked away and shook her head. "Look, I had some, like, troubles? Before I got this job. Ms. Cohen fixed them, but...it's kind of hard to explain, but that's how I got this job. I'm sort of stuck, now, but it's not so bad, really," she squished her face, not wanting to say more, but then adding, "Just...be careful what you agree to." Rachel shrugged again. "I'll show you where your room is."

Chapter 50

Dawn found Davy sitting in a chair and staring out at the horizon listlessly, still dressed in the rumpled, oversized clothes that were now all the more so for his attempts at having slept in them. Everything seemed just ever so slightly off, but he could not put his finger on why, and his mind had refused to abandon the search. A sharp rap on the door brought him out of his hollow reverie. It must be the drugs, he decided.

Davy was a little startled when he opened it. Instead of Rachel or Jimmy, he found a dour-looking man with short-cropped blonde hair wearing a blue suit and polished burgundy wingtips. His icy blue eyes tightened and left Davy with the distinct feeling that he had been weighed and measured.

"If I may, Mr. Rodrigo?" the man asked with polite authority.

Davy nodded and his shoulders drooped a little as he let the man in. He had hoped to at least get some breakfast before his next interrogation.

"You're Ms. Cohen's attorney?" he asked and sat in a chair opposite a small couch with a low table in between.

The man took a seat on the couch and shook his head. "No. My name's Proctor."

Davy blinked. Why did that name sound familiar?

"I'm an agent of one of her attorneys," he continued. "You may, however, consider this conversation as confidential."

Davy made a wan smile. "I may 'consider' it? But that doesn't mean that it is, does it?"

Proctor made a tight smile that lacked amusement and faded quickly. "We are going to speak plainly, Mr. Rodrigo, because I don't care how good their surveillance is, no one is able to listen to what is being said in this room."

At that, Davy sat up, much more awake.

"Ms. Cohen has taken an interest in you. It is my job to ascertain whether that interest will conflict with any of her more significant priorities." Proctor leaned forward with a predatory glint that was more a natural aspect of his personality than any effort at intimidation. "Save us some time, and don't bullshit me, kid. I already know most of your answers, or what they should be, anyway. I'm concerned with risk management, not morality. Are we clear?"

Davy nodded, and Proctor settled back as Davy began his story, his fairly truthful story. Proctor seemed faintly amused over the shootout in Pacoima, and was only concerned with the proper disposal of the weapons and phones. He had no concern over what Sanderson had revealed during his interrogation of Davy at the Starlight. When they came to the subject of Tomás, while dismissive of the crime, Proctor was concerned with whether Davy knew where the gun was.

"Sleepy said," Davy paused to remember her name. "I mean–"

"I know Miranda, kid," Proctor interrupted. "She took care of it?"

Davy hesitated. "Yeah, but–"

Proctor chuckled softly. "Good enough."

120

Now Davy remembered where he had heard the name. It was time for some counter-intelligence. "But the placas said they got her and she rolled. And how do you even-"

"Know her?" Proctor said, still chucking. "Don't worry about it. But the *placas,*" he laughed, "don't have her. Miri knows how to vanish. But be careful, kid, your *street* is showing. Placas." He laughed and shook his head.

Davy let out a breath as the waters he was swimming in felt very deep all of a sudden. "So, if she stays gone, and no one saw who shot Sanderson, and-"

"And you keep your yap shut? Yes, all your troubles should fall apart on their own. The police will want to interview you, of course, but you'll have counsel with you, and you'll be staying here for the time being. Isn't it wonderful how her little ploy just gives you that option? This is the best course, and Ms. Cohen will agree."

Davy nodded along. He still did not understand it, other than he was likely very close to being a lot more screwed than he had ever thought. One problem at a time, he decided. But – little ploy? What the hell was that?

"And what about Lulu?" Davy asked.

"Oh, I'll have someone look into it," Proctor replied off-handedly as he rose. "Shouldn't take too long."

Davy wanted to ask more, but detaining this man he now recalled that Sleepy had said she was afraid of did not seem the best if ideas. It also began to dawn on him that his tío had not been laundering money for Diablo, or at least that was not where it had started. Davy had just walked himself into the center of the spider's web. Here was what connected everything. What Rachel had said came back to him about how all her problems had been fixed, but now she was sort of stuck. Was that how his tío had ended up out at the Starlight? Was Davy the problem Ms. Cohen had solved for Tomás; giving him a job and place to raise a small child in return for being pulled into her web? And here Davy was doing the exact same thing, but the more he thought about it, it did not seem like her deals were that bad. And it was not like he had any other choices in the matter. Still, as he glanced over at the clock and saw that it was nearly seven, he did not feel hungry at all.

Chapter 51

Ms. Cohen was absent from breakfast, and Jimmy was nowhere to be found, which left Davy in Rachel's not unpleasant company, though she seemed distracted and on edge. When Davy asked, she said it was nothing and then kept the spaces between her bites full of idle chatter. As predicted, the LAPD was very interested in speaking with Davy, and just after lunch, he found himself waiting in the foyer as his counsel, Larry Markowitz, received final instructions from Ms. Cohen before they set out for the Hall of Justice, downtown. Davy had been provided with a change of clothes, and while Rachel was nowhere to be seen, Jimmy was listening at the top of the stairs, doing a passable job of concealing himself in the shadows.

Davy glanced about the silent and pristine main floor. He held no illusions that whatever Ms. Cohen's interest in him was that it had anything to do with sentimentality. Yet still, he was not that worried.

The year under her tutelage after Selene had left, while cold and difficult, had changed him for the better. In fact, those lessons were likely the only reason he was still alive after all that had happened. He looked around the foyer – the price for having his current problems solved would probably depend on how much he actually needed solved, and what utility he could offer. Jimmy was a twerp not fit to be more than a lackey. Rachel must also have her deficiencies that kept in the station of *maid*. But his uncle had done well enough.

Davy chuckled at the thought. Maybe he would end up managing a movie theatre somewhere. He shrugged and laughed a little, then thought that since he would be near County with a powerful attorney, he could visit his tío. Then his amusement faded. What if it had not been just because of Lulu that his uncle and *Miranda* – that was her name now – had killed Hector Ortiz?

They might both be in a lot more trouble than he had thought, and it was likely that Miranda was running from a lot more than the police. One thing at a time he reminded himself, and shoved a smile in place as Mr. Moskowitz appeared at the far end of the foyer.

Chapter 52

"Good afternoon, Charles. Denise," Larry Moskowitz said as he entered the large conference room with Davy. It was located on the sixteenth floor of the Hall of Justice, and had floor-to-ceiling window pane on two sides. "Quite a little party you're throwing here. Why don't you introduce us to all these good people?" It was not really a question, and Mr. Moskowitz did not pause from sitting while she answered. A paralegal guided Davy to a seat as well.

L.A.'s current top cop, Chief Charles Summer did not look amused, nor did it appear that the weathered, balding man had ever been amused by anything in a very long life.

"Leo, you know ADA Saroway. She has a few members of her staff with her," he made a slight nod towards the three dark-suited men standing behind the DA where she sat at the oak lacquered table that dominated the room. "Captain John Andrews of LAPD Metro-"

"You mean S.M.A.S.H.?" Moskowitz interrupted.

"Now, Leo, you know as well as I do, there is no such thing as a unit called-"

"Save it, Chuck. This joker's not a traffic cop who's here for educational purposes," Moskowitz said with a laugh, and Chief Summer grew even more sour if that was possible.

Captain Andrews gave a light snort of contempt, and then smiled wickedly at Davy before fixing his gaze on Mr. Moskowitz. "You know, this little myth you defense attorneys persist in clinging to – that there's some secret paramilitary unit operating within the LAPD – it just makes you all look more sniveling and pathetic than we all know you are. Really, Moskowitz, you should know better."

Moskowitz was unfazed. "Sorry, kitten, but my dance card's full today. But, I'm sure you can find someone willing to pop the ugly girl's cherry in the back of the coatroom if you hang around long enough."

A quiet man at the far end of the table angled his head fractionally towards the Chief, and Summer took back control of the conversation. "Snipe at my officers in the courtroom if you want, Leo. This is wasting enough of my time," Summer growled. "The rest here, you know, or don't need to know."

"And the pair at the end? Man and Woman in black?"

"Oh, that's Mr. Cole," he said of the whispy, spectacled man with a thinning top.

"*Mister* Cole?" Moskowitz asked.

The man smiled. "There's no need to be obtuse, I shouldn't think. It's SSA Cole, OCT Division," he said and then set his gaze on Davy. "That's Organized Crime and Trafficking, young man." The FBI agent appeared quite at ease, as though in the company of lessers. "And this is SSA Brodstreet."

The middle aged woman sat politely and tapped a few icons on her pad.

"What's the FBI doing here, Chuck?" Moskowitz demanded.

"Observing," SSA Cole replied for the Chief.

"Outstanding," Moskowitz said with a snort. "So, who's going to be doing this?"

ADA Saroway cleared her throat. "I will be," she said, tapping an icon on her data pad to start it recording. "This is Assistant District Attorney Denise Saroway, conducting initial interview with P.O.I. David Donovan Rodrigo, on or about 2:27 PM, August 12th, 2014. Mr. Rodrigo's attorney of record, Larry Moskowitz is present. Mr. Rodrigo, please state your full name."

"David Donovan Rodrigo."

"How is your health?"

Davy paused. "Um. Fine."

ADA Saroway's gaze flicked up with momentary annoyance and then proceeded with a battery of intensive, but fairly typical questions. There was not a single one of them that Davy did not answer with *I don't recall*, or *on the advice of counsel, I decline to answer*. The interview went on for more than an hour before ADA Saroway concluded the colossal waste of everyone's time.

As Davy and his lawyers were leaving, SSA Cole asked off-handedly, "Tell me, young man, when was the last time you heard from Armando Fagin?"

"Hey, what is this?" Moskowitz demanded as Davy stopped to think.

"Isn't he dead?" Davy said, it had taken a moment to recognize Diablo's name.

"So, not in the past few days?" SSA Cole replied, still with a carefree smile.

"No," Moskowitz broke in. "We're done here. Mr. Rodrigo has been more than cooperative with you people. This is over. Anything further can be directed to my office, or the moon, or up your asses, but any more attempts at direct interrogation of my client will be deemed harassment, and responded to as such!"

SSA Cole gave no appearance of hearing the man. "You should let us know when that changes. But you won't, and they'll kill you both. It was nice meeting you, young man. A pity."

Mr. Moskowitz hustled Davy from the room, still shouting at the FBI agent and the Chief.

Chapter 53

Mr. Moskowitz mistook Davy's silence for nervous concern as they walked down the marble hallways towards the elevators. "Don't worry, kid, you did just fine in there. Fuck that Fed – they're all like that. Think just because they're Feds that the rules don't apply to them. If they'd had anything on you in the first place, well, we wouldn't have been in that room, or talking to those people. You see–"

"Can you get me in to see my uncle?" Davy asked abruptly. He knew very well why he was there; a pretext for that FBI agent to say exactly what he had. "I mean, we're here, and you're you?"

Moskowitz paused. "Ahem, sure, son. Oh, of course. County's right here, and I really should have thought of that myself. It might take a little time, though, so maybe, -"

"I'm sure you have some people here who owe you a few favors," Davy replied. 'Kid' and 'son' had worn through Davy's patience more quickly than any racial or genital based insults ever had. "I want to see him, today. You understand?"

Moskowitz let out a tight sigh. "That's not really what I, -"

"This does not have to take all day," Davy said, digging in. "Now, andalé pues," Davy finished in that flat white accent that gavas always thought was so funny.

Moskowitz chuckled "Why not? You've earned it. I'll see what I can do. Just stay here with Jason, and don't talk to anyone. You never know who–"

Davy helped up his hand. "This is the Hall of Justice. I assume everyone is a cop or a snitch. There are no good and bad, just us and them. Rules only protect people that can pay for them."

Moskowitz chuckled and nodded. "You're smarter than you look, kid."

David shrugged, well concealing the urge to spit in the man's face. Instead he simply said, "It isn't hard."

Moskowitz chuckled again. "Alright. This shouldn't take more than twenty minutes or so. Jason will get you something out of the machines if you want."

"Thanks," Davy said as Moskowitz headed across the bridge to the lockup units in the County Central. His paralegal, Jason, just gave Davy a look and sat down.

Chapter 54

Thirty minutes later, Davy was nodding polite thanks to the deputy who had ushered him into an empty visiting room with its banks of phones and Plexi-glass window that prevented contact. The deputy remained posted at the door, and Davy slid into a hard-plastic chair. He took a few deep breaths to collect and slow his racing thoughts, trying to sort out just what he could ask over a recorded phone.

A few minutes later, Tomás was let in wearing County blues in waist chains. Only one hand was cuffed to the chains. The other was in a sling. The older Rodrigo burst out with a laugh and a smile as he sat and picked up the phone in an ungainly fashion.

"They said it was you, but I thought they were bullshitting me again. How'd you get in here?"

Davy shook his head. "Are you alright? What happened to your arm? The placas did that?"

"Nah," Tomás replied. "I hurt it before they picked me up."

There were a few moments of awkward silence. Those words four days ago still lingered, though they seemed part of another lifetime – another life, Davy realized. He only hoped his tío would see it the same way.

"Davy, -" Tomás began.

"We can talk more later, tío," he said, though it was more of a question. Tomás nodded. They had just been words, and could be forgotten, eventually. "Right. Shit's been crazy since you got popped."

"Since? I didn't think it could get any more way out, míjo. I been hearing these crazy stories 'bout some loco vato they call Viper."

"I know," Davy interrupted, "but there aren't any more Loco vatos. It's all good now, though, so don't trip on it at all. Lulu's good, too."

Tomás shut his eyes tightly, and hung his head. "It was supposed to go so different but then, once it was rolling, and then got rolling off the tracks, míjo, there was just no stopping it."

Davy held up a finger and filed that away. "Right. Everything's all good. Let's talk about you. I know what you're in for. What they say you did, anyway. And there's some good news, sort of."

"You know it's not true, verdad?" Tomás said over the recorded phone.

"Of course," Davy replied. "Monica's dead."

"Davy," Tomás warned, "you can't say things like that. Just because she's telling lies."

"No, tío. I mean she's actually dead," Davy interrupted. "The placas think Miranda popped her *and* the two placas they had sittin' on her."

Tomás leaned back on his stool and blinked in surprise. "Stupid loca vata." He sobered quickly. "Did they snatch her up?"

"No, Miri's in the wind," Davy said off-handedly. Question one.

Tomás' smile of relief vanished as quickly as it had appeared. "What did you just call her?"

"Miri for Miranda? It's common, isn't it?"

"Sí, míjo, but she doesn't like it," Tomás said. "What's going on? And how did you get in here?"

Davy considered the confirming information, ignoring all his tío's questions. "A lawyer hasn't been here to see you yet?" Question two.

"No, it's only been a few days."

Davy sighed, having gotten his answer. Also one he expected. Whatever Tomás' role had been before, he was now being left to flop in the wind, and that would not end well for him. He smiled to himself – Ms. Cohen had offered to change that, to help, but of course there would be terms. He briefly wondered if this was all part of a grand design, or was the old woman simply quick to capitalize on the moments as they came? He supposed that it did not really matter, but as Rachel had said, he had to be careful to what he agreed.

"Míjo?!" Tomás snapped, breaking Davy from his thoughts.

Davy smiled and waved away the concern. "It doesn't matter. They'll drop all this in a couple of days. No lying witness, probably no weapon – no nothing. They don't have a case. You'll be out, soon. We'll get Lulu from CPS, and everything will get straightened out. Trust me."

"Trust you?" Tomás cast about in frustration. "I do trust you, but míjo, you don't know about my past, about … my whole situation. And these placas have it out for me, now. Even if only the gun sticks, if CPS has a hold on Lulu, they're not just going to hand her back."

Davy found himself rubbing his temples. "I know about all of it, tío. And I mean all of it. CPS is … a detail. None of the rest of that shit matters, or won't. And the Locos are done." He looked off and blew out a breath, acknowledging that fact since all that was left of them were a few kids running around in the street now that all the leadership was gone.

"Míjo, what did you do?" Tomás demanded.

"Nothing, tío. Everything just fell apart all at once, and I got somewhere. Now…all things equal, so long as I'm careful, we should be able to just walk away."

"What do you mean? *If you're careful?* And *you got somewhere?* Where would that be? And where did you get those clothes?"

Davy sighed. "We'll talk about it later. I... I have to go. Don't worry, you'll be out soon," he said as he stood.

"Davy!" Tomás shouted into the receiver, fairly certain with whom his little nephew was dealing. "No!"

"We'll talk later." Davy said through the glass.

"Goddamit, míjo, listen to me!"

"We'll talk later. I love you, tío," Davy said, and then left without looking back. Tomás was still shouting, but it did not matter. Davy knew that there would be no *just walking away* from these people; just like his tío did, but what good would arguing with him about it do now that the die had been cast? From here on out, it was all about leverage and bargaining. On the ride back to the Cohen estate, Davy felt like he was taking a knife to a gun fight, but it was what it was.

Chapter 55

Davy arrived at a little past five, and more lights were on in the main house than he would have expected. Jimmy, sullen as ever, met Davy and Mr. Moskowitz at the doors. The lawyer muttered something as the doors shut behind them and Jimmy produced a beeping device the size of a garage door opener with a thick ring attached to the top of it.

"If ya' please, sir?" Jimmy said with his terrible imitation of a British accent.

"That toy isn't worth the powder to blow it up. You're in my way," Moskowitz said, and then shoved Jimmy aside as he proceeded into the hall beyond the foyer, continuing as he went, to matter over the number of people all being in the house at the same time. He passed three men in the dark suits near the first turn of the branching hallway. Two paid him no mind, but the third silently fell in step behind him, and they disappeared from the view.

Davy was more accommodating. "What is that thing?" he asked as Jimmy swept over him.

"It checks for bugs, "Jimmy said, then made an ugly laugh after he finished his wanding. "Surprised it didn't go off – you bein' a cockroach and all, dude."

That was one too many. Davy shot a hard right at Jimmy's nose, but his thoughts of how Jimmy would look with raccoon eyes were interrupted as the sullen doorman flicked his wrist up to block, deflecting the blow, and then striking Davy in his throat with his palm. Jimmy followed up with two quick punches to Davy's midsection.

Davy found himself staring up at Jimmy from the floor. Jimmy gave him a snort. "Your Kung Fu sucks, dude," he said, and left without waiting for a reply.

Davy picked himself up coughing and rubbing at his throat. He had been more stunned than injured, and briefly stared hatefully in the direction Jimmy had gone. Davy let it go for the moment as a hot breath hissed out between his gritted teeth. As he brushed himself off, he saw Proctor standing at the far end of the foyer now wearing a dark grey suit and a trace of a smile.

"Good help is so hard to find," Proctor said as Davy approached, having gained a measure of Davy's fighting skill.

Davy nodded, his pride still stinging.

"Still. Jimmy does have his uses."

"Right," Davy said. "I wanted to see Ms. Cohen before dinner. If that's possible?"

Proctor appeared to give the request some thought, and then shook his head with a disappointing smile. "I am afraid not. In fact, she's probably indisposed for a while."

Davy signed and nodded, not really surprised. He glanced around and changed the subject. "I was here a few years ago."

Proctor nodded. "I recall."

"You do? Right, and that's just it. I don't remember even seeing anyone else except for Selene and Ms. Cohen. There certainly wasn't … all of this."

Proctor smiled and patted Davy on the shoulder. "Let's take a walk, Davy. Or do you prefer David?"

"Either's fine," he said with a shrug as they began down the hallway's west branch which led away from Ms. Cohen and most of the other lit rooms.

"Good, good. You know, back then, I think she had something different in mind for you than she does now. You were just a part of training Selene. She tends to borrow heavily from classic literature in creating her creatures. That way, no matter how hard someone looks, all they'll ever be able to prove is that she's just a crazy old lady. Maybe she is... or not," Proctor replied. "But all this? What, *all this*?"

Davy blinked and started briefly. Yes, he was in over his head indeed. "I don't know. I was just looking for the last place the *placas*-" he began, seeing how the street-stupid stereotype would fare against this threat.

"Police," Proctor corrected.

"Right. That the police would ever think to look. Then... I don't know, be gone by the morning."

"Gone where?" Proctor said as he considered Davy carefully. "And, you didn't answer my question."

"Just gone. On a bus and gone – the way everything went down at the Starlight, running wouldn't be," Davy measured out his words, "unreasonable for a street kid to do. Besides, if I stayed gone long enough, anything I may have known wouldn't be useful to anyone.

Proctor nodded. "So, if you were pressed to cooperate six months from now, you could do so without actually cooperating. Not the best plan, but not the worst either under the circumstances. It is a little surprising that you were ready to run out on your friends and family, though," he said, well knowing the boy was lying, and trying to play games.

"Why?" Davy said. "It's one less reason for the police to squeeze them for anything more than where I've gone. If I'm not here, they can't be used for leverage."

"Interesting perspective," Proctor said as they walked into one of the attached atrium. To hell with what the old lady wanted, this kid needed to go. The one type of person Proctor hated more than any other was a smart one who thought he was smarter than he actually was. Risk management. "And now? With all of this," he chuckled, "how do you see the situation?"

Davy glanced around, very aware of how quiet this area of the house was. The glass around the atrium was triple paned, most views were completely obscure by the indoor gardens, and the smooth tiled floor was something easily cleaned. His hand reflexively touched his pants pocket, but he covered the gesture by brushing away some imagined dirt. He doubted that his pocket knife would have done him much good anyway, even if it had not been still sitting on the dresser in his room. Alone in a quiet place with a very dangerous man who was waiting for answers – Davy was now paying close attention.

"I think I'm a small piece in a bigger puzzle." He tried not to be too obvious in his search for exits from the atrium.

"How so?" Proctor asked, turning his attention like a panther scenting prey in a forest.

"The police have leverage on my uncle. At first, it was just those charges, but they'll fall apart. Now they have Lulu, but they don't have me," Davy replied. "You do."

Proctor made a noncommittal shrug, a little amazed at how this dumb kid was shortening his life span with his every word. "And why do you think any of that would matter to anyone here?"

Davy took a moment "Because you would have either kicked me out, or killed me by now, otherwise."

Proctor leaned back with tears of laughter. "You kids, always so dramatic. Kill you? Why would anyone possibly want to do that?" Now it was getting fun.

Davy knew better than to actually hand the man a reason. He knew that this was not going well. "I don't know," he demurred to stall and think of something else. "It has just been a crazy week, you know?"

"Yes, kid, I do. I do know," Proctor said. Suddenly serious and showing teeth.

Davy cleared his throat and tried to force a smile, but under the man's gaze, the muscles of Davy's face would not cooperate. His tío had tried to warn him, but there had not been, nor was there now, any other choice. "You said Ms. Cohen had something different in mind for me now? What exactly? I... appreciate the help you're giving my tío."

Proctor flinched, seeming of two minds as the instructions had been given warred with the impulse that was plain in his eyes. Davy felt his own body relax, preparing to flee at the man's first twitch. He knew the operation his tío had been managing at the Starlight was now a hopeless shambles, and that it was really anyone's guess as to who connected to it knew that it might be incriminating to this little syndicate operation that Davy had stumbled into with all the grace of a drunken yak in a minefield. The safe bet would be for them to clean house. Ironically, Rico shooting that detective, and the certain shit storm that had ensued was probably all that had given Davy even this small reprieve. As he stood in the atrium, it was inescapably clear that he had run straight to the worst possible place. Soon, there would be a jail house accident, and a shot up corpse dumped in an alley of Davy's neighborhood – not even Det. Sanderson would bat an eye at that. Then what that FBI agent had said came back to him, and the boy had an idea.

Proctor still had not said anything, and had begun to consider Davy as a reptile might consider a particularly obnoxious insect. Just as the man was on the verge of motion, Davy spoke up. "Just how much did Miri and Diablo steal from you guys?"

Proctor checked himself, shivering in restraint. "More than you or Tommy-boy could ever come up with."

"I'm not so sure."

"I am." The kid knew nothing, and Proctor's restraint vanished. His eyes stopped seeing another person, and only a lump of flesh to be diced up. The silenced weapon was almost clear of his jacket, and his hand touched his flensing knife.

It was not exactly a plan – more impulse – when Davy spit in Proctor's face. It was enough however, to make the seasoned killer flinch and give Davy the opening to smack the half-drawn gun from the man's hand. Careless of the threat any *street-rat* could pose, Proctor had let himself get too close.

The gun went flying and Davy dove after it, catching the pistol just as it clattered against the tiles. He slammed awkwardly into a stone planter, felt that the weapon's safety was off, and pulled the trigger as he leveled the weapon. But the gun did not fire. After a few failed pulls, he was left staring stupidly up at Proctor.

"Biometrics, kid," Proctor said, wiping the wetness from his face with a handkerchief. At least the little bastard was going to make it sporting. "The grip reads palm prints. So, hand it over, and I'll make this quick."

Davy scrambled up and ran for the doors, but the locks clicked just as he reached them.

"Alright, have it your way," Proctor said, waving the oversized flensing knife and smiling. "This won't be quick."

"Wait! What about Armando?" Davy cried as he picked a direction and bolted.

"He's dead. You're going to be seeing him soon, don't worry."

"No, he's not." Davy dashed right, then dove through a stand of shrubs as Proctor rushed after him.

"I told you yesterday not to bullshit me. Now, you're just pissing me off."

"No, listen!" Davy dove back through the bushes, hopped over a bench, and then stumbled through a small pool of water. "He's not! Miranda's the one who ID'd the body! She stuck around long enough to make sure the loose ends were tied up, and then split!"

Proctor crashed through the bushes and came to a looming halt at the far edge of the pool. "That's thin' kid – too thin'" he snarled, and was moving again, trying to put aside instructions that were getting harder to ignore. His boss wanted the boy for his wits, and he was supposed to give the little bastard a chance to prove that he had them. If he did not let this go on a little longer, it would be hard for him to explain, and he knew all too well just how many people there were in Ms. Cohen's employ who were no different than him. Hell, he had trained half of them, and it would be one of those that eventually got him. None of them would be quick about it either.

"No! The Fed that was there today even said so! Said you were gonna kill me, but knew I wouldn't cooperate even to save my own life!"

Proctor stopped just as he was about to step into the water. "You should have led with that, instead of all that street-rat crap. What did this Fed say, exactly? And how does any of it actually help you?"

"He wanted to know if I had talked to Diablo in the last couple of days, and was surprised when I said that I hadn't." Davy stopped, seeing Proctor's snarl return. Davy circled away as Proctor started stalking around the pool. "Listen! He's still out there!"

"I am, kid," he said, still stalking.

"The Feds know me and my tío are a dead end. Miranda's gone, but wouldn't roll even if they caught her. Lulu didn't know shit, and I'm sure they've figured that out by now. They wouldn't still be there sniffing around me if they weren't sure Diablo was still out there, and that I could lead them too him."

Proctor paused. "But you can't. Not any more than you could lead us to him. Or can you?"

"I can't, but I know who can," Davy said, seeing that he was nearly cornered. "And I can get him to do it, which you sure as hell can't."

Proctor laughed darkly. "Oh, you'd be surprised at what I can get people to do."

"You don't even know who I'm talking about!"

Proctor snorted. "Of course I know about Armando's little brother, Elvis Fagin – your pal, Rico. You're going to have to do better than that."

"Right. But you'll never find him without me. And you know that you fish with lures, not with baseball bats!"

Proctor stopped and glared down at his wet loafer with distaste. He grunted and put his flensing blade away, then stared at Davy for a long hard moment. At last, he relented and the tension left his features. "I'm still not convinced about you," he sighed, "but she thinks you're more than a jumped-up street punk, or could be, anyway. Myself, I think you're weak clay, and will break."

Proctor reached into his pocket and pressed something. The room's doors unlocked.

"Get up to your room and clean yourself up. I'm sure you can find something to eat in the kitchens," he paused to squint as if searching for something, but then gave up with a snort of futility, "we'll see what the morning brings."

Davy quickly made his way through the newly trampled path in the shrubbery and out the door while keeping a wary eye on the man who was currently occupied with fishing his gun out of the small pond. Davy's heart was still racing as he shut the door behind him. It took every bit of his self-control to keep from running down the hallway. As he passed the turn to the foyer, he noticed that Jimmy was eyeing him with distaste from a chair where he was slouched by the doors.

Down the far hall, Davy saw Rachel and a few other girls coming and going from the kitchens laden with various serving dishes. Dinner was obviously in progress, but Davy had no appetite; not that he was invited anyway. He felt like a fool for having thought he had any control over the situation. On returning to his room, he shut the door and locked it. He had no delusion that it would keep anyone out, but the lock's click might give him a few seconds of warning. A quick look at the windows revealed they were triple paned and did not open. He laughed hollowly as he traced a finger along the cold painted iron framing. At least he was back to being a prisoner in a gilded cage, and not moments away from becoming plant food.

Chapter 56

Somewhere around midnight, the doorknob of Davy's room rattled, and the boy snapped awake. Though he was under the covers, he was fully dressed, and now had his knife in hand. He slid from under the covers in a stealthy crouch to the far side of the bed. There was a shadow of feet lingering in the light beneath the door, and then something was set down near them. Davy crept silently forward, not responding to the soft knock.

He positioned himself by a chair which he had placed near the door, and prepared to kick it into whomever was using their key on the door lock. Davy's stomach growled and he briefly regretted not having eaten earlier. He put the thought from his mind as he took a breath and determined not to go down without a fight.

The door crept open, but the tension left Davy as Rachel's soft face peaked inside. "David?" she whispered. "Are you sleeping?"

Davy glanced around the chair and almost laughed. The other shadow was not some bag of torture devices. It was a covered tray of food. He stood and sighed. "No, I'm not asleep. I don't think anyone in this place sleeps."

Rachel eeped and jumped backwards, stumbling against the door and landing squarely on her bottom. She spilled the tray all over her maid's dress. Davy flicked the light on and was quickly over to help her up.

"Sorry, I...couldn't sleep. I didn't mean to scare you."

"It's okay," she said with a smile and brushed past him. "I just didn't see you earlier, and... I thought you might be hungry, too."

"Right," Davy said, eyeing the mess in the hall, and then Rachel as she twisted to examine the stains on the back of her dress. "And I'm sorry about your dress."

Rachel laughed playfully as she undid the button at the back of her collar and opened the zipper in back. "That's okay. It's not like it was going to stay on much longer, anyway."

The dress dropped to the floor and she stood there, wearing only her lace panties, three inch black heels, and a smile. There was no subtlety to her as she stepped clear of the dress and crossed the few steps to Davy, pushing the door shut. He had yet to move and only remembered to swallow when she placed a gentle hand on his chest.

"Miss Cohen sends her apologies for your rough treatment," Rachel said as she snuggled against him and guided his hands to the more squeezable parts of her anatomy.

"And – you're the apology?" Davy stuttered as his teenaged body began fully responding to her.

"Mmm-hmm," Rachel nodded, and began kissing his neck. "She's very angry with Proctor." She shuddered involuntarily at saying the name and Davy wrapped his arms around her. She gazed up at him with her big, doe eyes, "He's not a nice man. Not to me; not at all."

"I'm sorry," Davy began as she dropped to her knees and slid down his body.

133

"It's okay," she said again as she unzipped his pants and took him in her mouth. She wrapped her arms around his thighs as she plunged down and pressed him back into the wall, all the while gazing up at him lovingly.

Davy stumbled and gasped, finding a chair and collapsing into it with Rachel well attached and working hard on him. As he settled, she began to plunge her head up and down with more force, taking him deep down her throat while her tongue jutted out to lick what parts of him lay just beyond the suction of her plump lips and soft cheeks. Davy was gripping the arm rests of the chair when she reached up to take his hands, guiding them to the side and back of her head. She hummed softly as she wrapped her arms back around his thighs and pulled his pants all the way down in the process. She gave him a pleading look, urging him to control the pace.

The boy was a little hesitant at first. With Lulu, there had always been the sense that if he was not careful, she would break, or fold. With the homegirls, it was more like friendly service, and his experience in Chinatown had been so bizarre that he had just let it happen. With Sleepy there had been no doubt that he had no control of any of it. Rachel, though, was something new and entirely different. She was gratefully yielding to him at every eager turn. Davy tried to hold back, but the woman knew what she was doing far too well for him to manage much restraint. He was quickly gripping her hair tightly as he shuddered while she increased the suction.

Davy rolled his head back as his heavy breathing began to slow after she had finished her work. He looked down to see her patiently waiting with a soft smile, her head pillowed against his inner thigh.

"Wow," he said, and she giggled at the compliment. "Was that... Is that it?" He was still trying to wrap his thoughts around what had just happened.

Rachel shrugged, but did not rise. "If that's all you want. You've got me for the night, so... whatever you like." Her soft smile did not fade in the starlight.

"Oh, right, so you're-"

"Mmm-hmm," she replied cutely, brightening her smile and batting her eyelashes. Then, with a mischievous glint, she pressed her face close to his thigh, butterflying her lashes against his most sensitive areas.

Davy jerked. "Oh, shit," he gasped, and she giggled. "That was alright."

"I am pretty talented," Rachel said rising up to her knees and leaning against him. "Would you like me to show you just how talented I am?"

She twisted her shoulders back and forth, and Davy found himself hardening between her breasts.

"Oh, yeah," he said, and she stood with an eager smile, taking him by the hand and leading him to the bed. She paused to shimmy out of her panties, and then helped Davy get out of the rest of his clothes.

After that, the rest of the night moved both quickly and slowly in a blur of carnal ecstasy for Davy. At some point, exhaustion overwhelmed him. He was fully spent from Rachel, and from a day that had flung him about like a small boat in a ragging maelstrom. He gave no thought to any escape, and sank gratefully into the bosom of oblivion.

Chapter 57

When Davy finally woke, the sun was up, and all that remained of Rachel was rumpled and discarded sheets along with a few stands of her hair in some of the most unexpected of places. Davy sighed and took a little time to stare blankly at the ceiling before making his way to the bathroom. As he stared wearily at his reflection, he could only shake his head. Had the boy known what operant conditioning was, he would have easily recognized what was being done to him. Since he did not, he only saw a face that he was not sure he recognized, and his thoughts pounded around, rebelling at settling on any one of the outrageous events of the past few days. The world he had known had come unpinned to the point where he was not certain what to believe anymore.

The sound of the midmorning bell for tea shook him from his thoughts. He did not even think to wonder at why there was a bell in his room. Still something inside him made him grit his teeth. Staring into a mirror would not help him, and so curiosity, more than anything else, drug him away from the mirror to seek out what 'morning tea' really was in this house where nothing was as he had thought it was.

On his way down the staircase, it hardly surprised Davy that there were no sounds coming from down any of the hallways, and even the ever-sullen Jimmy was absent from his post in the foyers. A faint clinking came from the parlor some distance down in the east wing.

After a few turns down corridors that again looked like they had been vacant for years, there was a growing suspicion in Davy's mind that the past twenty-four hours may have just been a dream. Inside the open parlor, Rachel stood bright and shining like the sun in a sharp, clean maid's uniform and pouring tea for Ms. Cohen. She bobbed a small curtsy as Davy entered. There was no sign of intimate recognition in her eyes, and so Davy had an even harder time believing that the woman now serving Ms. Cohen tea was the house prostitute. The older lady gave Davy a polite smile, and they exchanged pleasantries as Davy sat in a straight-backed chair on the other side of a small tea table.

"You look rather drawn, young man," Ms. Cohen, observed. "Did you not sleep well?"

Davy cleared his throat softly. "The past few days have been taxing. A lot has changed."

"Has it?" Ms. Cohen replied, and then took a sip of tea. "Or are you simply beginning to see the world you have always lived in more clearly? I suspect it is the latter."

Davy looked down with a distant smile. "You're probably right," he said, and she made a noise of agreement. Davy cleared his throat again. "Proctor said you had something else in mind for me than when I was here before. Just before he tried to kill me, that is."

She gave him a brief frown and shooed Rachel from the room. "To start, we will be breaking you of that tedious habit of throat clearing – very unseemly, and quite

135

unbecoming. However–" she paused to listen, then nodded, "-as for Proctor, he is a good man, if overzealous at times, and a bit blunt. Though, I was under the impression that you had already accepted our apology on that count?"

Davy held in a soft laugh. So, it had not been a dream after all. "I did...have."

"Very good. Now, explain the situation as you see it."

"My uncle was running a money laundering operation for you. He and Miranda killed a Federal informant for personal reasons, which only came to light in the aftermath of hers and Armando Fagin's smokescreen of a gang war that was meant to cover their robbing you. I haven't figured out why Miranda stuck around so long after identifying the body that clearly wasn't Armando's, or why she at least temporarily put me in change of what was left of the Locos, or tried to get us tied in with those Asians, or bothered with killing Monica and the two police officers, if she was just going to run away and disappear. Whatever she and Armando had planned either did not completely work, or they're not finished with their plan. I'm inclined to think the latter."

Ms. Cohen nodded with a trace of a smirk as she sipped her tea. "Very good, and all valid points. I should say that her reasons for being involved in the incident some years ago were not entirely personal, and neither were your uncle's. While I can make more educated guesses at her current motivation and goals than you are able to, they remain guesses. Which brings us to you."

Davy looked at her directly. "And nothing I know can change that."

Ms. Cohen arched a brow. "That's not true, and we both quite know that. If you are suddenly finding reticence, I might remind you that yours and your uncle's situations remain precarious. Persons of interest and suspects in the eyes of the police."

Davy snorted at the most thinly veiled threat he had ever heard. He had chosen a confident course, and had no choice but to stick to it. "My tío warned me about working for you."

"Did he?"

Davy nodded. "Don't get me wrong, I'll point out Rico for you since your smartest move is to watch him from a distance – wait until his brother tries to get in touch with him, which will probably be some time from now, and it will probably be through me if I'm with him."

"You know that we would find him with or without your aid."

"Right, but this way takes less resources, and is easier for everyone; more polite, more civilized."

Ms. Cohen made throaty chuckle. "And so, for this accommodation, I should then simply let you and your uncle walk away and back to whatever lives you both may find?"

"Why not?" Davy replied. "With Monica dead, there's no case against him. The police have to let him go, but they'll be watching for a while. They didn't turn him, and now they have even less leverage, that is unless you give them more by setting him to tasks. The help you've given me isn't unreasonable if it ends now – your lawyers have learned everything they could from the police by representing me when they did. I may get questioned again, but I'm not a suspect in anything. The more involvement you have with my family, the more suspicious it looks; the more they'll stay looking. All of which you don't want, and especially since the person you're looking for is the one they aren't yet sure they're looking for in the shooting of a Homicide Detective." Davy felt rather proud of himself for coming up with most of that just off the cuff, though Ms. Cohen's fixed trace of an amused smile told him that this was all still far from over.

"Well said, young man," she replied at case. "Yes, I do indeed have something rather different in mind for you. Something which I believe that, in time, you shall come to quite appreciate as well."

Davy let out a soft sigh and stopped himself from asking the question that had likely ensnared his tío, Jimmy, Rachel, and who knew how many others: "*And what would that be, Ms. Cohen?*" He was not about to ask her to give him an answer he would have to take to his grave.

"Right. If you let me go, it shortens the police's active interest in what connection there might be here by weeks. The Locos, a gang that largely doesn't exist anymore, will take the rap for any accounting discrepancies at the Starlight... everyone who was actually invoked is either gone or dead, and so is the money."

Ms. Cohen's smile stiffened. "And if the authorities should choose to pursue your uncle over these *discrepancies*? I think."

"Monica was the only other one who was around, and she's dead. Me, Lulu, and Rico were just kids who didn't know anything, and you know that. Miranda and Armando are gone with the money, and I'm already giving you your best option to find them," Davy said with growing confidence. This really might work. "So, here and now, your best play is to let everyone who can, just walk away. And believe me, if my tío has to do a few years over some tax fraud, or whatever, to walk away? He will."

Ms. Cohen considered him for a moment as a crane might consider an oddly colored beetle. But at last she glanced down, and took a sip of her tea.

Chapter 58

Later that day, Davy stood calmly in front of the plasticked-over front doors of the Starlight. The police tape was still up, and the remnants of the CSU's efforts lay scattered about inside. It had been a long walk back from Glenwood Oaks, but he had been buoyed by a sense of hope for the future. Here now, he stared into the vacant shell of what had been his past with finality. Ms. Cohen had allowed him to occupy the premises for the next thirty days. To clean it up, order his and all its former denizens affairs, and then depart for whatever new life lay ahead. As Davy tore away the tape and entered the musty lobby, he picked up the faint smell of gunpowder, and that hope began to ebb.

This was the tomb of the life he had known, and he could not help but feel like a ghost as he made his way to the basement to turn the power back on.

Two days later, a dozen full garbage bags had found their way into the dumpsters in the alley. Someone named Jay Garcia had called, claiming that he was with the Public Defender's office, but that he was not Tomás Rodrigo's attorney, and so anything that Davy told him would not be in confidence.

Davy had been fairly certain that was not how attorney-client privilege worked anyway, and when after that warning the man had started asking questions, Davy had hung up. Likely it had been some crime beat reporter, but even if it had been some PD's assistant, everyone unfortunate enough to be represented by them had good reason to call them Public Pretenders.

A quick check of the L.A. County Superior Court's website revealed Tomás' arraignment date, time, and courtroom. It was set for ten working days after his arrest, which Davy took to be a good sign since that was the legal limit. The DA was still fishing for a case. So long as they did not catch anything in the next five days, everything would be fine. A search of the LACPS website and server proved less successful. After an hour of key taps and clicks and two actual phone calls, Davy had gotten no more than the fact that Louisa Sandoval was in the custody of CPS and would be moved to a placement facility within 72 hours of her initial processing. Further information would only be available by court order.

Tomás' car had been impounded for some reason, and Davy dismissed boosting a ride since he was likely under surveillance by at least one law enforcement agency. That left him with the Huffy bike that had been moldering in the basement for the past few years. Finding oil for the rusted gears had been a small chore, and then after his first few wobbly pumps, Davy discovered that it was possible to forget how to ride a bike. He relearned quickly as he set off and wove his way down to Walgreen's and picked up a burner phone along with some microwavable dinner. He doubted that Proctor and his goons would wait forever, so he needed to start making some progress in tracking Rico down.

After Walgreen's, Davy ditched the bike he was still having trouble riding with confidence in traffic, and walked the few blocks that remained to the subway stop. L.A.'s subway service was one of those strange phenomenon that, though it was a sprawling behemoth, few people beyond the city's middle income and poor seemed aware existed. L.A., in fact, did not run entirely on busses, nor close to it.

That night, Davy had no particular destination in mind, and so found himself at Union Station an hour later. The commuter rush had ebbed, but the massive colonnades were far from empty. Davy knew that mixing in with the crowds would only help so much since there was cameras everywhere, and no two Mexicans looked alike as far as facial recognition software was concerned. Still, Davy was a city kid, and felt safer in a crowd.

He strolled past the anachronistic public phone banks and turned into a restroom that had long since given up any pretense. Two bums slept near the door. They smelled of stale urine, alcohol, and bum. Inside the bathroom, it smelled little different, except the aroma of weed was stronger. Around the corner, two junkies were fixing on the counter of a row of sinks, a male prostitute was washing up as his trick made a hasty exit – he wore a nice suit and had a wedding ring – and about a third of the sixty or so stalls were occupied, though very few of the occupants were actually using the bathroom.

Davy sighed, selected an empty stall, and locked it behind him. He propped a foot up on the seat of the backless toilet and leaned against the stall wall. Inside, he was a little surprised to find there was a part of him that still marveled at how quickly his entire life had just unraveled. He flipped open the burner and dialed Rico's phone. It went straight to voice mail. Davy nodded and disconnected. At least Rico had that much sense. Two more calls to alternate numbers netted the same result, and Davy began to mutter a few curses. Rico would choose now to show some smarts and get rid of all his phones that weren't burners. Tracking him down on foot would be a chore, and in all likelihood, Rico was nowhere in the varrio. So, the plan was, steal a car, and then head... Where?

Davy weighed his options. Rico had no family besides Diablo, and would not have been still hanging around the Starlight if he knew where his older brother was. If Rico had had the sense to dump the phones, then he should also have had the sense not to head for any crash pads or motels near the varrio. White Fence was out since, even though it would be a good place for a Loco to hide from the placas, Rico was too well known. And, Davy knew he would not stay somewhere by himself for long; even hiding out, Rico was the type who needed to be around people he knew.

Davy's eyes narrowed in thought briefly, and then he shrugged and dialed Risky. Why not? And, at the very least, he might not have to tackle searching L.A. on foot, or in a stolen car. His funds were not inexhaustible, but the placas had not found most of the emergency stash spots in the Starlight. The call picked up on the second ring.

"Risky?"

There was a grunt.

"Hey, check it out" Davy began, but was interrupted with an impatient grunt, and then the phone switched hands.

"Who this is? What you want?" Jeanie snapped.

"It's Viper."

"Stupid wetback. You forget own name?"

And he was back to this. "Still pleasant as ever. Is Rico around?"

"Who?"

"The only other wetback you know," Davy snarled.

There was giggling on the other end, and then a muffled exchange in Vietnamese. The phone was uncovered, and there was a long pause Davy refused to dignify with a response.

"Maybe," Jeanie replied with a petulant air.

"Put him on," Davy said, though he doubted it would be that simple.

"What you want him for?"

"That's not your problem" Davy replied. "Shit's complicated. Is he there?"

"He...not here."

"Bullshit! Tell him that a lot worse than me is looking for him, and if he wants to ever see his brother again, he'll call me back in the next five minutes," Davy snapped, then disconnected. He waited silently, watching the time display on the outside of the people. A lot depended on what Rico had told them. There were a lot of ways to interpret what had happened at the Starlight and that Davy had gone and vanished off the face of gangland-earth for five days. Were they also asking themselves how much Rico might be worth? Did Davy have any goodwill left with these Asians? Did they think he was working with the police? All these and a hundred other questions flashed through his mind as two-hundred and ninety-nine seconds ticked by until the phone buzzed.

Davy flipped it open and hit the green button. "Rico?"

There was silence, and then muffled shouting in Vietnamese.

The phone was uncovered. "Rico?" Davy said again, but knew it would not be.

"Wait," Jeanie snapped, then continued yelling at someone without bothering to cover the phone.

A long minute later came – "Wasssaaaap!" – and then distant complaints as the phone was taken away.

"Stupid wetback all fuck up," Jeanie muttered, then barked more complaints. The tinny music vanished from the background, and Rico's loaded protests could vaguely be heard.

It could be worse, Davy thought. "Right. Where's he at? I'll take him off your hands, and I got cash for a ride, too. What's up?"

"No so fast. Who want him worse than you? Why? What he do beside shoot cop?"

Davy had to think fast. What he told her could not be too far from the truth, or too close, either. "He didn't do anything. The placas aren't looking for him, yet, but the more people he tells, the sooner that will change."

"What fuck you mean?! More people he tell? He only say to us!" Jeanie interrupted hotly.

"There's no dumb-bitches there? No one overheard? You're positive? How long's that gonna last? How long until someone starts wondering a little too loudly what this Loco is doing kicking it with you when all the rest are getting jacked and jammed over two shootings and two dead placas?!" Davy snapped in an angry whisper. "The homie is hot, and I'm trying to take him off your hands, so quit being a little bitch and tell me where the fuck you're at!"

The call disconnected, and Davy cursed loudly enough that the couple in the neighboring stall banged on the partition. As he ran a hand through his hair, the phone vibrated. No call, just a text message – an address Davy guessed was somewhere in Little Saigon.

Chapter 59

Somewhere in North Hollywood, Davy abandoned the Metro-Link and boosted a car – the old '06 Elantra with its chipped grey paint was as far from flashy as he could manage. There was an Angels cap underneath the passenger's seat, and so Davy felt less bad about stealing the vehicle. Loathe as he was to put it on, he needed something to shield his face from any overactive traffic cams. He laid the seat all the way back, and then headed south.

By ten o'clock, Davy was somewhere in Little Saigon, not really lost, but not quite where he was supposed to be. He parked and slipped into an alley, and after throwing the Angel's ball cap in the dumpster, he memorized the location then made short work of the lock and ignition of a Honda Civic at the far end of the alley. Beads and tassels hung from its rearview mirror, as did a picture of a smiling fat man – *Asians were so weird*, he thought. The vehicle smelled vaguely of curry, or what he assumed was curry, never having actually tasted it. Twenty minutes later, he was parking the Civic a block away from a building with a pink and purple neon sign that blared into the night.

If he could have read the characters, he would have known it was a bar called the Sage Lotus before he got a few feet from the front window where the name was scrawled in red-block English letters.

The Sage Lotus was not the only business hailing passerby's with neon light; some of the others even had a little English mixed into their displays, but it was the only one whose lights inside were off. Down the street, Davy could see the hookers just coming out on their corners, and the other traffic on the sidewalk and streets was light. It was early night, and those out were mostly on their way to somewhere else. Though Davy stood out physically, it was still the same crowd as he was used to, and so he moved along mostly unnoticed.

"You late," Jeanie snapped from the deeper shadows of the alley besides the Sage Lotus.

Davy just shook his head. "And you're a little brat. Where's your brother?"

She tsked with, a look of contempt that only young Asian girls and uppity cats could manage. "Thought you want other beaner?"

Beaner, so a step up from *wetback*, Davy supposed, but he really did not feel like playing. "You're loud," he informed Jeanie calmly.

Jeanie's jaw dropped though her lips stayed shut, and her eyes bulged as her face balled with shock and rage. Davy made a soft snort of surprise at having accidentally stumbled over something that would shut the little brat up. After a few seconds, she blinked and regained herself, though it was clear that this was an insult that would not be forgotten. She turned wordlessly and led the way inside.

The Sage Lotus was a mix of bar and cafe, though it was closed at the moment. "Where is everyone?"

Jeanie made no reply other than to shove a chair out of her way and flip open the bar as she picked up her pace towards the back rooms. She led Davy down a hallway where he had to dodge several low-hanging green, pagoda-style lanterns and to a room with a camera visible above the door. She gave the door panel a single angry slap with the flat of her palm, and then roughly barged in. Davy saw Risky look up with some surprise from a bowl of pho ga. His gaze followed his angry little sister as she stomped across the room and slammed the far door behind her. He then aimed his puzzled expression towards Davy.

"I told her she was loud," Davy replied.

Risky blinked, then laughed and nodded.

The door Jeanie had left through was kicked from the far side. Incoherent yelling briefly followed, and then silence. After a few moments of observing the door, Risky looked back to Davy and shrugged. He nodded over at the couch on the opposite side of the room from where he was eating. Rico lay sprawled and unconscious, though he looked happy.

Davy sighed, not liking the prospect of having to drag Rico out to the car. "Just yesca and pisto?"

Risky shrugged and grunted though Davy had expected as much in response.

Davy paused, feeling that he owed Risky more of an explanation for his having to babysit Rico, and a warning that Proctor, or people like him might come looking. He suspected that Risky might have a sense of the situation. Though, given the lengths he had come to in keeping Rico out of sight, another idea occurred to Davy.

"Right. It's all kind of complicated, but."

Risky only grunted, and waved a dismissive hand at Davy.

The boy paused, and then asked, "So, Proctor told you what's up, already?"

The 28-year old Vietnamese was suddenly perfectly still; his expression inscrutable, and then he shrugged and returned to his bowl of noodles. Without looking, he flung keys in Davy's general direction.

Davy barely caught them. "I... I already have a car."

Risky glanced over, mid-slurp, paused, and then resumed his noisy consumption of the pho ga before him.

"Right," Davy said more to himself. Was this some sort of bizarre test? To see if he would do as he was told, being watched at every step? The or else was blaringly implied if that was the case, or was it just to let him know just how tightly woven the web was that he was stepping away from? Or was it all some bizarre and complicated trap? It was too much for Davy to figure out in the moment.

As he lugged the still comatose Rico through the front of the empty dining area, Jeanie appeared from the shadows. Davy came to a halt and leaned Rico over a table. She seemed on the horns of the dilemma as she looked off, folded her arms and pouted, and then glared at Davy.

"Isn't that your car down the street?" she snapped.

"Yeah."

"So, not your car parked in front?"

Davy was at a loss. Was it a warning? A prompt? "Right. Mine's out front. The other, it's just wired. You can-"

At the last two words, Jeanie perked up and bolted for the alley door. Davy chuckled a little. She had just wanted a car to play with if the older kids were done with it. He sighed and hefted Rico. Rico groaned, and by the time he was loaded in the front seat of the four door Lincoln Mark VIII parked out front, he was beginning to come out of his stupor. Davy belted him in, but jumped at the screech of tires from down the street. He looked over just in time to see Jeanie go speeding past in the Civic, hooting with glee and blaring the music. In that moment, he did not envy Risky in his caregiving duties. Likely, he said so little because he was exhausted from keeping an eye on the little brat.

Davy put the key in the ignition and let out a small breath of relief when he turned it and the car did not explode. He found the title papers in the glove compartment, and then noticed that the center console was unlatched. He opened it and smirked at the little .22 inside with a 'Hello Kitty' sticker on the grip. The radio was set on XUZM, an all blues and jazz channel, which Davy shut off.

"Hey, homie, I was listening to that, eh," Rico slurred as he rolled in the seat. He briefly struggled with the seatbelt, but the button lock was beyond him in his current state. "What's up, esé?" he laughed happily. "Hey, them damn Chinos got some bomb shit, eh. It got me fucked up, eh."

"No shit," Davy said, his eyes focused on the road ahead when they drove away.

"Yeah, eh." Rico paused to rub the velvet of the door's armrest. "Hey, this is plush, eh. Where'd you boost this?"

"It's... a friend's."

"Huh. That's some good friends, eh." Rico snorted and shook his head. He tried to focus his eyes, but only managed to cross them. "Hey, hey, where you been, eh? That shit was crazy. I think I killed that vato. Hey, and what were you doing there? And where is everybody? All the numbers I got were burnt."

"Sleepy took out two placas and Moni for snitching, then she got ghost. They hemmed me up, then you popped up, and I stalled that stupid placa till you finally got around to blasting him," Davy summarized. "He's not dead, but he didn't see you – at least they don't know that they are specifically looking for you. Most everyone else got snatched up, but the way everything went sideways all at once, even if some of the vatos flip, they wouldn't be able to give shit up that would matter anyway. So, for right now, you and me, we're *everybody, me entiendes?*"

"Tú sabes," Rico said in a sing-songy mimic of Sleepy.

"Fuck that bitch," Davy snarled.

"Wha? I thought you and Sleeps were like, cool," he said and bucked his hips, humping the air. "Hey, and I won't say anything to Lulu, but, you gotta be like more," he searched for words, "low key, eh."

Davy shook his head and let out a breath as he glanced over at the lovable moron. He knew he could not just serve Rico up to Proctor and Ms. Cohen and hope they took his advice on how to keep their bait on a long leash.

"She stole some shit from some people she shouldn't have even fucked with, her and your brother."

"Hey," Rico protested. "Mí hermano es muerto, eh. Don't say no bad shit about him, eh."

Davy snorted. "He's not dead. At least the Feds don't think so, and neither do I."

"The Feds?! Rico blurted. "He's alive? What the fuck, eh? Hey, and where you been, fool? I been worried, eh."

Davy did not have good answers. "In some shit. I told you, everything went sideways."

"Wha?"

"Hey, shut up and listen, homie," Davy snapped. "You and me are in some shit right now. Mirá, Sleeps and Diablo made a mess, and we gotta clean up... some of it."

Rico made a dismissive snort. "Homie, I ain't got no big money, and how is Diablo not dead? Sleepy ID'd his... oh. Hey, but what's up with all this Feds shit?" Rico stopped, his eyes widening. "Hey, homie? We ain't fuckin' with the EME, eh? It's just kill every-vato with them, eh. What, so clean some shit up so we just get popped in the head stead of cut up while we watch? Fuck that, eh. We got a ride, so let's just bounce!"

"It's not the EME. It's—I don't really know who the hell they actually are, but they aren't small, and don't play when it comes to getting what they want," Davy replied. "And they're about money. Mirá, they think that getting a hold of you is gonna bring Diablo to the surface."

"Fuck that, eh! Fuck them, and fuck you! I ain't—"

Davy's hand had been resting on the open console, and in one smooth motion had the pistol out and pressed into Rico's forehead as his other hand jerked the wheel and he ground the car to halt.

"I said, shut up and listen, you stupid vato!" Davy roared, and Rico stopped fighting—a mix of angry, afraid, and loaded. "They're ready to clean house! You, me, my tío, Lulu, and anyone else they think might know anything about their little money laundering thing at that damned theater!"

"Huh? Money laundering?"

"Seriously? You don't understand, 'shut the fuck up', even with a gun pointed at your head? Now, listen, homie, I didn't have to tell you any of this, but I'm not just here selling you out to try and save my own ass," Davy said, though, he knew he sort of was. He did lower the gun. "I'm too hot right now for them to just off me. CPS has Lulu, and no one knows where she is. Tío's in jail where they can get him, no pedo. Moni's dead though, so the case on my tío's a wrap. He'll be out, Lulu'll be back, and then... we can all bounce."

"Monica? What's she—"

"A dead rat, and she's a wrap. Not important."

"Hey, well...Where are we going now, eh?"

Davy let out a breath and stared at the roof of the car for a moment as he scrubbed his free hand through his hair. "I...I don't know, exactly. But I know where we're not going. Now just trust me, you stupid asshole. Right now, get out and head down that alley. I got wheels on the other end. Then you're gonna help me switch the plates.

Chapter 60

Three hours later, Davy and Rico were holed up in a fleabag motel in West Covina. Rico was trying to shower himself awake by alternating the water between hot and cold. Davy was lying on the stained blanket of one of the beds, idly flipping through channels as he snacked on a can of peanuts from the minibar that he had no intention of paying for. The little .22 lay on the bed and near to his hand. *Little brat*, he thought. Somehow, he doubted that she was part of whatever game Proctor had set up. He was sick of getting maneuvered, and for a moment, felt like he was back in Ms. Cohen's parlor getting trounced again at a game of chess. He had never once come close to beating the old woman, but then, he hoped that there was a first time for everything. Then, the burner phone in his pocket buzzed. He did not recognize the number, but that did not surprise him. Plan or no, the pieces were moving again.

"David?"

"Right," Davy replied, muting the TV. "Who is this?" He tossed the remote down and picked up the gun as he slid into the space between the beds and leaned himself back against the nightstand. It would be some cover at least.

"David, this is Mr. Moskowitz," he replied. "You met with me the other day, you recall?"

"Right."

"Do you, um, do you have the package?"

Davy drew back from the phone. Seriously? "Yeah, it's all good."

There was a pause on the line. "Well, there is some concern that you have not made… delivery, yet."

"What is this, a bad spy movie? How far does Proctor have his head up his ass? Why would I bring him to you?" Davy chuckled ironically. "Or am I really not on board after all? Answer quickly."

There was a long pause. I'm not... privy to all the details or any arrangements you may have made with any other parties. I was instructed to contact you regarding the anticipated delivery."

"You know, for a lawyer, you don't lie very well."

"Cut the shit, kid!" Proctor broke in. "She has a soft spot for you, and that is the only reason you are still breathing. You didn't want to be on board, remember? Everyone gets to walk away? So that means you are going to dump your little friend off with us, and then go very far away. Far enough that it's not worth me wasting my frequent flyer miles to send someone to find you. That's your deal; his ass for yours, I warned you about bullshitting me."

"Two days," Davy interrupted angrily. "You get him in two days, after my tío's arraignment and they cut him loose. No back alley bullshit. He'll be on the front steps of the downtown courthouse."

"He'll be where I say, when I say, you little-"

"No, he won't. I just told you where and when! Don't call again," Davy said and terminated the call. He snapped the phone closed and lifted his head to shout at Rico over the running water, but blew out a breath as he saw Rico standing in his jeans with a towel in his hands and a nervous expression on his face.

Their eyes met, each trying to read the other, until Davy broke the silence. "Get your shit," he commanded, then snapped the burner in half, dropped it on the floor, and stomped it to plastic bits. Only when Davy tucked the .22 into his pocket did Rico nod and get moving. Davy shook his head as Rico ducked back into the bathroom. They had two more days now, but Davy still had the sinking feeling that he was just being maneuvered around the board.

$$$$$

Two days and three motels later, Davy and Rico found themselves on the third floor of the Hall of Justice and outside courtroom S-22. They were mixed in with a small crowd of families waiting for their loved ones' or most-hated ones' arrangements and bail hearings. As 11:00 neared, the crowd had begun to thin, and Davy was getting sick of Rico's nervous glances. The day before, they had spent several hours at one of the few remaining Internet Café's trying to locate Lulu and not having any success. As a result their current plan was not much of one. Really it was not much more than an escape route. Davy had noticed a man and woman bracketing him and Rico all day, each on a separate end of the hallway. Neither had spoken to anyone all morning nor gotten up to use the facilities or get a snack. Davy had the feeling that they were specifically *not watching* him, only waiting for him to move into their field of vision. They were likely Proctor's, or maybe Feds; far too disciplined for LAPD. If the placas were watching, it would be while sitting in a chair eating something and glancing at a monitor with a feed from the camera above the courtroom doors.

In some ways, Davy felt that all the eyes worked to his advantage, as did the metal detectors; no palm print encoded pistols, flensing knives, or anyone who did not want their picture taken. Now, if they could just get this little formality of a hearing over with, they could get on with the tricky part of the day. With luck, Tomás would just be released from court; a wait down in Central's Receiving & Release would complicate things. Davy was still trying to think of all the angles as the clock approached 11 and he and Rico headed into the courtroom.

The two managed to get seats one row back from Tomás with no one in front of them. His Public Defender turned with a reassuring smile, glad that the boys could make it since the defense side of the gallery was fairly sparse. Not so for the prosecution; their side's benches were nearly all full. There were too many to all be the off-duty officers that typically filled the prosecution's galleries. The PD assured Davy that this was just a formality; why it was left until last on the morning docket; an ADA waiting until the last moment in hopes of discovering some new evidence. He was certain that if they had anything by now, he would have heard something from their offices, and that the case would not have been dumped on to a new ADA.

Davy was doing his best to listen, but his thoughts were set on his real problem. Then something the PD said caught his attention.

"Just look how nervous that bitchy little ADA is. She just came off a loss, and now a dismissal? You can bet her panties are all in a wad."

Davy looked over at the pudgy woman with a bad haircut. She was wearing too much makeup, and her designer-knock off pants-suit was tacky even by varrio standards. He did not like what he saw in her face. She was nervous, true. But it was not any fear of looking foolish or quick failure. No, that was the slight jitter that came before setting to work on a tricky alarm system or any other task where there was a big reward and no room for error. Whatever else she was doing, she was not here to throw in the towel.

Davy broke into the PD's chatter. "You need to pay attention. Something's up."

The PD shook his head with a smile as the court was called to order.

"Nah, five minutes," he mouthed, and then stood for the judge and the introductions.

Following the plea of not guilty, the PD launched into a motion for dismissal based on lack of evidence. As he did, the woman who had been sitting on the far bench outside cleared her throat and slid over to sit next to Davy. He was more than a little startled, not having even noticed her follow him in, much less position herself a few feet from him. She smiled and slipped a cell phone into his jacket packet, then slid back and turned her attention to the proceedings.

Davy sighed. *The games are starting early*, he thought sourly.

"...There has to be more than stating a random charge to make a *prima facia* showing, your honor. Especially in what is potentially a capital murder case, and ADA Arnett has failed utterly in this regard. The district attorney's office should be embarrassed," the PD concluded.

"Counsel, your motion and argument are duly noted," the judge replied, and then turned to the ADA. "Ms. Arnett unless you have more than what your offices have submitted so far," he gestured to a small stack of documents before him, "I am reluctantly going to have to grant defense counsel's motion."

"There is, your honor," ADA Arnett replied, and Davy's head snapped up to focus on her. We have sworn deposition of Ms. Sandoval."

"No," the PD broke in. "Your honor, Ms. Sandoval is dead. Tragic as that may be, anything she said short of a dying declaration, which we already know she did not make—my investigators are through-is hearsay and in "...admissible..." your honor. The DA can't say, oh, we have this inadmissible statement, but keep the defendant in custody while we search for actual evidence. Your honor, keeping a defendant in custody for the purposes of gathering evidence is illegal, unconstitutional, and-"

"That will do, counsel," the judge declared sharply. "Ms. Arnett?"

"More tragic are the brutal murders of the LAPD officers who gave their lives trying to protect Monica Sandoval–"

"Are you alleging a connection between those murders and the defendant?" The judge asked hopefully.

"No, Your Honor," ADA Arnett replied, "Or I should say, not at this time, Your Honor."

"Ms. Arnett? It is into the lunch hour, and my patience is wearing thin. Either present something, or I will grant the defense's motion."

"Of course, Your Honor. As I was about to clarify before I was so rudely interrupted by defense counsel," she shot a look of contempt at the PD, "I was not referring to Monica Sandoval, but rather, her younger sister, Luisa, who, for her safety has been placed into Federal Protective Custody, given the terrible circumstances surrounding the death of one witness in this case already..."

Davy did not hear the rest. The case was bound over as he sat there in stunned silence. Every one of his plans had just completely come apart.

As recess was called, he glanced over to note that the woman was already gone, and there was no sign of her partner even if he had been in the courtroom earlier. He knew he had been boxed in; maneuvered perfectly, and so he knew he would make the only choice left to him. Part of him wanted to laugh, but most of him did not.

The moment they were out of the courtroom, Rico was tugging at him. "Lulu's gone rat?! What the fuck, homie?! She knows everything!"

Davy grabbed a hold of his arm and dragged him down the hallway, out of sight of the staring pair of uniformed LAPD officers. "Keep your voice down. If she gave up everything, we'd both be under arrest right now."

"But, I don't get it, eh? Why would she?"

"I don't care," Davy snarled as they hurriedly made their way to the elevators. "And it doesn't matter."

"Wait, wait homie. What are you gonna do?" Rico complained as the doors shut behind him.

"What I didn't want to. What my tío, and everyone else told me not to do. Now, shut up. I have to make this call before we get outside."

"Call? Where'd you get a phone? We left 'em–"

"Shut up," Davy said as the elevator opened onto the main concourse on the first floor. They went to find a quiet area with reception, and then went to the autodial. There was only the one number. It all seemed a bit much, but then, Ms. Cohen seemed to love her theatrics. The call picked up on the second ring.

"Hello, young man," she answered.

"Ma'am," Davy replied.

"Is this a courtesy call, or are you in need of my assistance?"

Davy gritted his teeth and checked his habit of clearing his throat.

"Your assistance, ma'am."

"You may have all that is mine to offer, should it be necessary. You understand my terms? Simple reciprocity?"

All that was his to offer, should she find it necessary. In none of his exploits, had Davy ever found himself so really and truly screwed. Davy chose to ignore how Rico was staring at him like a lost puppy.

"I do," he said at last.

"Always such a clever boy. I knew you would see reason soon enough."

"And... your dog?"

Back on his leash, and serving as I direct. As always,"

"Right."

"Recall that we dress for dinner, and inform your companion."

The call was terminated before Davy said anything. As he stood there, surprisingly, he felt lighter. The game was lost, but at least it was over.

"Vipes? Who was that" And-"

"That," he paused as it settled in, "was our new employer. Get your shovel, Rico. The only way out of this hole is to dig all the way to China."

"I don't get it, eh. Ain't those the fools you said been tryin' to pop us? The ones that wanna use me as bait?"

Davy patted him on the shoulder. "Yeah, but we're out of options, unless you want to grow a tail like Lulu and Moni."

"Fuck you, esé. That ain't cool to say. Ever, puto," Rico fumed. "But, you got a plan, yeah, eh?"

Davy almost laughed a little. "Right, oh, and my bad, Elvis."

"Hey, don't call me that shit, eh. I hate my stupid nombre. Eh, what about my brother, eh?" Rico asked as they headed out towards the front steps.

"No matter what, he'll stay lost for a while. Him and Miranda won't be popping their heads out of whatever hole they found to hide in anytime soon, which is good for us," Davy explained. "These people, they ran us through a maze, maneuvered us and got what they wanted, so now the bullshit can stop for a while. You're bait, and I'm in and doing what I'm told. For now. More than anything, we have some time and what we need to get my tío out. It's not the best deal, but it's not the worst for us either." Davy paused him as they reached the top of the steps, "And all bullshit aside, they have a pretty slick operation."

A grey BMW sedan pulled up to the curb near the bottom of the steps, and the passenger side door opened. Rico looked over at Davy and nodded. "I guess it could be worse, eh."

Epilogue

Six months later, Lulu had recanted her testimony and vanished. Tomás had spent four months in County after pleading out to possession of an unlicensed firearm. On his release, he almost immediately moved to Chicago and said goodbye to no one. Davy and Rico had also vanished from Los Angeles; their personas scrubbed from the system. Both had been relocated to Seattle with new identities and set to co-manage the Whale Watcher, a coffee house that struggled to compete with several nearby Starbucks. The Whale Watcher also had a boutique shop 'Ana's Everything,' which sold Inuit and Asian art. Attached to its lease was a large warehouse down by the docks. Of Diablo and Sleepy, there had been no sign, but somehow, Davy doubted that really mattered to Ms. Cohen. She had her new agents in an enterprise far more extensive than the simple money laundering operation that had been run through the Starlight. Davy had a loyal lieutenant, and then a few months later, he was given a third member for his young crew. The little brat was not happy about being relocated, and made her displeasure known regularly, and loudly. Risky had dropped her off with a nod and a single grunt, but the expression on his face left no doubt that just like Davy, he had been put into a terrible situation, and then left with this as his only way out. It was a lot for a look and a grunt, but then, the lost always had a way of understanding each other.

THE END

About the Author

Alex Valentine, author of <u>Lost Angels</u>, and its forthcoming sequel, <u>Handmaiden of the Nameless</u>, was born in Oak Ridge, Tennessee (go Vols), and moved to San Diego when he was a teenager. He was a varsity wrestler at Torrey Pines High School, and went on to study engineering at Harvey Mudd College. His life was then rudely interrupted by his incarceration at the age of nineteen.

In the decade and a half since, he has earned a college degree, practices Buddhism, and has come to grips with what brought him to prison; accepting the responsibility for his choices. Along with writing, he now spends a good deal of his time involved with efforts to improve the prison environment where the Courts have assigned him to spend the rest of his life.

  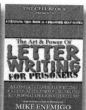  

BOOK SUMMARIES

THE BEST RESOURCE DIRECTORY FOR PRISONERS, $19.99 & $7.00 S/H (* OR 4.5 BOOKS OF STAMPS): This book has over 1,450 resources for prisoners! Includes: Pen-Pal Companies! Non-Nude Photo Sellers! Free Books and Other Publications! Legal Assistance! Prisoner Advocates! Prisoner Assistants! Correspondence Education! Money-Making Opportunities! Resources for Prison Writers, Poets, Artists, and much, much more! Anything you can think of doing from your prison cell, this book contains the resources to do it!

THE ART & POWER OF LETTER WRITING FOR PRISONERS, $9.99 & $4.00 S/H (* OR 2 BOOKS OF STAMPS): When locked inside a prison cell, being able to write well is the most powerful skill you can have! Learn how to increase your power by writing high-quality personal and formal letters! Includes letter templates, pen-pal website strategies, punctuation guide and more!

A GUIDE TO RELAPSE PREVENTION FOR PRISONERS, $15.00 & $5.00 S//H (* OR 3.5 BOOKS OF STAMPS): This book provides the information and guidance that can make a real difference in the preparation of a comprehensive relapse prevention plan. Discover how to meet the parole board's expectation using these proven and practical principles. Included is a blank template and sample relapse prevention plan to assist in your preparation.

CONSPIRACY THEORY, $15.00 & $5.00 S/H (* OR 3.5 BOOKS OF STAMPS): Kokain is an upcoming rapper trying to make a name for himself in the Sacramento, CA underground scene, and Nicki is his girlfriend . One night, in October, Nicki's brother, along with her brother's best friend, go to rob a house of its $100,000 marijuana crop. It goes wrong; shots are fired and a man is killed . Later, as investigators begin closing in on Nicki's brother and his friend, they, along with the help of a few others, create a way to make Kokain take the fall .... The conspiracy begins.

THEE ENEMY OF THE STATE (SPECIAL EDITION), $9.99 & $4.00 S/H (* OR 2.5 BOOKS OF STAMPS): Experience the inspirational journey of a kid who was introduced to the art of rapping in 1993, struggled between his dream of becoming a professional rapper and the reality of the streets, and was finally offered a recording deal in 1999, only to be arrested minutes later and eventually sentenced to life in prison for murder... However, despite his harsh reality, he dedicated himself to hip-hop once again, and with resilience and determination, he sets out to prove he may just be one of the dopest rhyme writers/spitters ever .... At this point, it becomes deeper than rap .... Welcome to a preview of the greatest story you never heard.

LOST ANGELS: $15.00 & $5.00 (OR 3.5 BOOKS OF STAMPS): David Rodrigo was a child who belonged to no world; rejected for his mixed heritage by most of his family and raised by an outcast uncle in the mean streets of East L.A. Chance cast him into a far darker and more devious pit of intrigue that stretched from the barest gutters to the halls of power in the great city. Now, to survive the clash of lethal forces arrayed about him, and to protect those he loves, he has only two allies; his quick wits, and the flashing blade that earned young David the street name, Viper.

LOYALTY AND BETRAYAL, $12.00 & $4.00 S/H (* OR 3 BOOKS OF STAMPS): Chunky was an associate of and soldier for the notorious Mexican Mafia -- La Eme. That is, of course, until he was betrayed by those he was most loyal to. Then he vowed to become their worst enemy. And though they've attempted to kill him numerous times, he still to this day is running around making a mockery of their organization .... This is the story of how it all began.

MONEY IZ THE MOTIVE, $12.00 & $4.00 S/H (OR 3 BOOKS OF STAMPS): Like most kids growing up in the hood, Kano has a dream of going from rags to riches. But when his plan to get fast money by robbing the local "mom and pop" shop goes wrong, he quickly finds himself sentenced to serious prison time. Follow Kano as he is schooled to the ways of the game by some of the most respected OGs who ever did it; then is set free and given the resources to put his schooling into action and build the ultimate hood empire...

UNDERWORLD ZILLA, $15.00 & $5.00 S/H (OR 3.5 BOOKS OF STAMPS): When Talton leaves the West Coast to set up shop in Florida he meets the female version of himself: A drug dealing murderess with psychological issues. A whirlwind of sex, money and murder inevitably ensues and Talton finds himself on the run from the law with nowhere to turn to. When his team from home finds out he's in trouble, they get on a plane heading south...

TO LIVE & DIE IN L.A., $15.00 & $5.00 S/H (*OR 3.5 BOOKS OF STAMPS): It's the summer of 2003. A routine carjacking turns into the come-up of a lifetime when a young cholo from East L.A. accidently intercepts a large heroin shipment. Soon, a number of outlaw groups, including the notorious Mexican Mafia, is hot on his trail. A bloody free-for-all ensues as the deadly cast of characters fight to come out on top. In the end, only one can win. For the rest, it will be game over....

MONEY IZ THE MOTIVE 2, $12.00 & $4.00 S/H (OR 3 BOOKS OF STAMPS): After the murder of a narcotics agent, Kano is forced to shut down his D&C crew and leave Dayton, OH. With no one left to turn to, he calls Candy's West Coast Cuban connection who agrees to relocate him and a few of his goons to the "City of Kings" -- Sacramento, CA, aka Mackramento, Killafornia! Once there, Kano is offered a new set of money-making opportunities and he takes his operation to a whole new level. It doesn't take long, however, for Kano to learn the game is grimy no matter where you go, as he soon experiences a fury of jealousy, hate, deception and greed. In a game where loyalty is scarce and one never truly knows who is friend and who is foe, Kano is faced with the ultimate life or death decisions. Of course, one should expect nothing less when...Money iz the Motive!

MOB$TAR MONEY $12.00 & $4.00 S/H (OR 3 BOOKS OF STAMPS): After Trey's mother is sent to prison for 75 years to life, he and his little brother are moved from their home in Sacramento, California, to his grandmother's house in Stockton, California where he is forced to find his way in life and become a man on his own in the city's grimy streets. One day, on his way home from the local corner store, Trey has a rough encounter with the neighborhood bully. Luckily, that's when Tyson, a member of the MOBTAR, a local "get money" gang comes to his aid. The two kids quickly become friends, and it doesn't take long before Trey is embraced into the notorious MOB$TAR money gang, which opens the door to an adventure full of sex, money, murder and mayhem that will change his life forever... You will never guess how this story ends!

BLOCK MONEY, $12.00 & $4.00 S/H (or 3 BOOKS OF STAMPS): Beast, a young thug from the grimy streets of central Stockton, California lives The Block; breathes The Block; and has committed himself to bleed The Block for all it's worth until his very last breath. Then, one day, he meets Nadia; a stripper at the local club who piques his curiosity with her beauty, quick-witted intellect and rider qualities. The problem? She has a man -- Esco -- a local kingpin with money and power. It doesn't take long, however, before a devious plot is hatched to pull off a heist worth an indeterminable amount of money. Following the acts of treachery, deception and betrayal are twists and turns and a bloody war that will leave you speechless!

THE MILLIONAIRE PRISONER, $19.99 & $7.00 S/H (OR 4.5 BOOKS OF STAMPS): Why wait until you get out of prison to achieve your dreams? Here's a blueprint that you can use to become successful! The Millionaire Prisoner is your complete reference to overcoming any obstacle in prison. You won't be able to put it down! With this book you will discover the secrets to: Making money from your cell! Obtain FREE money for correspondence courses! Become an expert on any topic! Develop the habits of the rich! Network with celebrities! Set up your own website! Market your products, ideas and services! Successfully use prison pen pal websites! All of this and much, much more! This book has enabled thousands of prisoners to succeed and it will show you the way also!

HOW TO HUSTLE AND WIN: SEX, MONEY, MURDER, $15.00 & $5.00 S/H (OR 3.5 BOOKS OF STAMPS): How To Hu$tle and Win: Sex, Money, Murder edition is the grittiest, underground self-help manual for the 21st century street entrepreneur in print. Never has there been such a book written for today's gangsters, goons and go-getters. This self-help handbook is an absolute must-have for anyone who is actively connected to the streets.

* All stamps MUST be NEW Forever Books of stamps!

Made in the USA
Middletown, DE
12 January 2020